Midnight DREAMS

Midnight DREAMS

KAYLA PERRIN

ARABESQUE®

If you purchased this book without a cover you should be aware
that this book is stolen property. It was reported as "unsold and
destroyed" to the publisher, and neither the author nor the
publisher has received any payment for this "stripped book."

MIDNIGHT DREAMS

An Arabesque novel published by Kimani Press/November 2007

ISBN-13: 978-0-373-83025-1
ISBN-10:   0-373-83025-4

First published by BET Publications, LLC in 1999

Copyright © 1999 by Kayla Perrin

All rights reserved. The reproduction, transmission or utilization
of this work in whole or in part in any form by any electronic, mechanical
or other means, now known or hereafter invented, including xerography,
photocopying and recording, or in any information storage or retrieval
system, is forbidden without written permission. For permission please
contact Kimani Press, Editorial Office, 233 Broadway, New York, NY
10279 U.S.A.

This is a work of fiction. Names, characters, places and incidents are
either the product of the author's imagination or are used fictitiously,
and any resemblance to actual persons, living or dead, business
establishments, events or locales is entirely coincidental.

® and TM are trademarks. Trademarks indicated with ® are registered in
the United States Patent and Trademark Office, the Canadian Trade Marks
Office and/or other countries.

www.kimanipress.com

Printed in U.S.A.

This book is dedicated
In loving memory
to my dear aunt,
Roan Marcia Perrin.
(1956–1998)

You left this earth
much too soon,
but your legacy of love,
laughter, and courage
lives on.

Prologue

THE SCREAM ESCAPED HER throat the moment she heard the shuffling of feet in the darkened room. *Stupid!* she scolded herself as she closed the bathroom door behind her, immediately realizing that she should have kept her mouth shut. If the intruder wasn't deaf—and she was sure he wasn't—then her scream had alerted him to the fact that she was in the back of the salon. How long would it take him to discover she was locked in the washroom?

God help her, she had to get out. It was her only chance. No way would she stay here and become a statistic. If she'd been thinking straight initially, she would have dashed for the back door, but she'd been so frightened that she'd darted into the washroom instead.

Forcing herself to draw in a slow breath, she glanced down. No light shone beneath the washroom door, meaning the salon was thankfully still dark. If she could carefully open the door, slip into the room and hug the wall while she tiptoed to the back door, she would be home free.

But what if he heard her and she wasn't quick enough? A shiver of dread raced down her spine. Lord, why hadn't she listened when everyone had suggested she get a gun?

Don't stay here like a coward—get moving! her mind screamed, and she realized it was now or never. Her hand gripped the bathroom's doorknob at the precise moment she heard her name. Her hand stilled. Pressing an ear against the door, she listened. Was that…?

"Jade? Where are you?"

Her shoulders sagged with relief as she let out a breath in a nervous rush. It was Terrell. Opening the bathroom door, she stepped into the darkened salon. Streetlights cast soft rays through the store, providing enough light to see Terrell's tall form and his gleaming onyx eyes.

"Jade." His baritone voice was soft, merely whispering her name, yet sending shivers of delight all over her body. Now she knew the meaning of the expression *bedroom voice.*

"Terrell." She hadn't meant to whisper his name in reply, hadn't meant to sound raspy and seductive, but her voice had betrayed her. "What…what are you doing here?"

"You know why I came."

She swallowed as he took a step closer. She did know. Had known from the moment she heard him call her name. "You shouldn't be here."

"I couldn't stay away. You know that."

Her eyelids fluttered shut as he closed the distance between them and wrapped a strong arm around her waist. She should step away from him, break the physical contact, but God help her, she was paralyzed. "I…I have to go."

"Not yet, Jade. Not until we've talked."

She didn't bother to ask what he wanted to talk about, for she knew. She knew, and a part of her was glad he was here though she shouldn't be. Her eyes popped open. "How did you get in?"

"The front door was open."

"Really?" Where had her mind been? She never forgot to lock it. "Then I should—uh—lock it."

"I already did. I want no interruptions."

She trembled at the intensity of his words, at the intense look in his eyes. She barely managed to say, "Oh. Okay."

His other hand snaked around her body, resting on the small of her back. Jade's breath snagged in her throat. "Jade, don't do it. I never thought I'd beg you, but I am now. Please—"

"Don't," she said quickly, cutting him off. Did she not want him to voice the doubts her own heart had? "We've already discussed this."

"No, we haven't. I didn't know what to say when you told me you were still going to marry Nelson. I didn't know what to think. But I know now. I can't let you marry him."

"You…you can't stop me."

"I won't stop you if you really love him. Do you love him? Tell me you do and I'll walk out of your life forever."

The air between them was thick with tension, and she gulped at it, desperate to fill her lungs. "I…" Her voice trailed off.

"You can't say it, can you?" He tightened his grip on her, crushing her breasts against his chest, the intimate contact thrilling her more than she'd ever been thrilled in her life. "You know why, Jade? You know why you can't tell me that you're in love with Nelson?"

She didn't know what to say, let alone think. Closing her eyes, she dropped her head forward, resting it against Terrell's chest. Wrong move for the alluring smell of his cologne mixed with his own masculine scent suddenly made her think of getting naked with him—and only made her wonder about his question. She loved Nelson, she was sure of it, but every time she was around Terrell, she felt confused.

"Because Nelson doesn't make you feel the way I do, does he?"

"That's not…our relationship…it's based on…more…" On what exactly, she didn't know right now. Not while Terrell was holding her so tightly, like he never wanted to let her go. The feel of his hands caused her body to burn with feelings she shouldn't have for another man.

"Look at me."

She couldn't. She didn't want to see his eyes.

He made her. Placing a finger beneath her chin, he lifted her head upward. Finally their eyes met. His dark eyes were beguiling and offered her more than she was willing to contemplate.

"Kiss me," he whispered, his voice making her feel like she'd been jolted by an electric current.

She shouldn't. Kisses were reserved for Nelson, her fiancé. But her heart defied her mind, and her fingers slowly crept up his arm, finding his wide shoulders. She gripped them tightly, as though they were a lifeline offering to save her from a stormy sea. Was that how she felt about marrying Nelson? That he was a stormy sea, one in which she might get swept away and drown?

Pushing the irksome thought to the back of her mind, Jade ran her fingers over Terrell's shoulders, feeling the corded muscles beneath his thin T-shirt, wishing she could explore his strong body without the barrier of clothes between them. Her fingers paused. This was two times in less than two minutes that she'd thought of getting him naked, and Jade was truly startled. When had she become this…this wanton? But the answer to that question fled her mind as heat emanated from his body to hers. And suddenly she wanted to be lost in that heat—simply enjoying the feel of his body pressed to hers. She wondered how wrong it would be. One night of passion before she committed to Nelson for the rest of her life…

Her heart pounded furiously as his face neared hers, as his warm breath gently fanned her face. She was paralyzed, unable to move, unable to speak. How could something so wrong feel so good?

Slowly his fingers ran up and down her back, flirting with the exposed skin. The dress she wore crossed at the back, leaving gaping areas uncovered from her waist to her neck. *This is dangerous,* she told herself as his hands fiddled with the straps, slipping beneath, caressing her heated skin. And all the while he edged his face nearer hers, ever so slowly—she thought she'd go insane if he didn't just kiss her senseless and get it over with.

His nose touched her face, intimately skimming her forehead, her eyelids, one cheek, then and her own nose. Jade was lost, and as he softly kissed the tip of her nose, she parted her lips on a sigh. Her nails dug into his shoulders now as a need unlike anything she'd ever experienced consumed her.

"Oh, yes, Terrell. Yes." Who was this woman who had taken over her body, her thoughts, her desires?

"Jade…"

His lips covered hers. They weren't tentative and shy but hungry and desperate. It was as if he were trying to prove a point with the kiss, to make her forget Nelson and her engagement to him. Or maybe he was giving her a piece of him she would never forget.

He broke the kiss moments later and the sounds of their heavy breathing filled the warm, night air. She felt dazed. It was hard to keep a level head near Terrell; he exuded a raw sexuality that was impossible to ignore.

She wanted more. Arching on her toes, she leaned into him,

but he released his hold on her and stepped back. Confused, she stared at him. "Don't…don't you want me?"

He dragged a hand over his face, emitted a groan, then spoke. "Yes, I want you, Jade, but I don't just want a piece of you."

He was asking the impossible. She was drawn to him, wanted him in a way that made her crazy with longing, but how could she cancel her wedding? It was next weekend. Nine days away. All the invitations had been sent out, the church and reception hall booked. She even had family coming from England for the event.

Maybe, if she'd met Terrell before…

As if he couldn't stay away from her, he stepped toward her again. "I can make you happy, Jade. Happier than Nelson ever can." When she said nothing, he went on. "I know I can't offer you the financial freedom Nelson can. I'm thirty-two and still establishing myself, but I'm going to be successful one day. Give me a chance, Jade. I love you."

He loved her. The words caused a sharp pain to grip her heart.

"Tell me how you feel, Jade. Tell me what I already know is true."

"But we…Nelson and I…I've already made him a partner. I—I can't…"

"Do you honestly want to become Mrs. Crumm?" He gave her a look that said he couldn't believe she was even considering it. "If that name isn't a clue to get going while the going's good…"

Jade bristled at the sound of *Mrs. Crumm*. She didn't care for the name, either, but she wasn't marrying the name, she was marrying the man. "This isn't about names. I'm a nineties woman. I—I don't have to take his name."

"That's right. You're a nineties woman. You can call off the wedding."

"Terrell, I've already explained. Th-this isn't right."

"What's not right is Nelson. He's not the right man for you. If he is, there's no way you should have kissed me the way you just did."

He was right. "But I… The salon—"

"You're going to become Mrs. Nelson Crumm because of this salon?" Even in the darkness, she could see the disbelief in his eyes. "Partnerships can be broken."

"Not this one." Jade was surprised at the strength she'd summoned. Before she lost it, she went on. "Terrell, I'm sorry. It's too late."

Frustrated he turned, and Jade felt all the pain he must be feeling as all her veins seemed to criss-cross and knot. But she couldn't give Terrell what he wanted. Nelson loved her. Maybe he lacked the passion Terrell had, but he loved her and it would be unfair to break his heart. She was a woman of her word and she planned to stay true to Nelson.

But still it hurt to see Terrell so hurt. Slowly she approached him, placed a hand on his arm. He shrugged it off. "I'm sorry," she said softly. "I can't do what you ask. You have to understand."

"I don't."

She sighed. "Please, don't…let's not end our friendship this way."

He faced her then. Were those tears she saw glistening in his eyes, or was it just the way the outside lights shone on them that made it look that way? "Friendship?" he asked, as though she'd offered him a consolation prize. "I can't be your friend, Jade."

The words crushed her. But deep down, she knew it was true. For her and Terrell, it was all or nothing. "We…we can try."

Slowly he shook his head. "No, Jade. I can't."

"Then what are you saying? That this is it?"

He didn't answer right away and Jade wondered if her legs would sustain her. "If you insist on marrying the wrong man, Jade," he finally said, "then I can't be part of your life. A part of me will never accept your marriage. A part of me will always want you. For your sake and mine, it'll be best that we stay away from each other from now on."

"But—"

Without notice he moved to her, sweeping her into his arms, and for a moment, Jade wished they could stay this way forever, that the rest of the world would simply disappear.

"Don't let me go," he whispered into her hair. "If you tell me you'll leave Nelson, I won't go."

She closed her eyes as the onset of tears threatened to choke her. "I…I have to marry him."

He released her just as abruptly. The look of desolation on his face was one Jade knew she would remember forever.

"I'm sorry," she said, knowing the apology was not enough. It would never be enough.

With that, he turned. Jade merely stared at his back as he retreated, not knowing what to say, what to do. He unlocked the front door, pushed it open, then paused before stepping into the night air. He cast one last look at her over his shoulder and said, "I'm sorry, too."

Then he disappeared into the night, and Jade knew she would never see him again.

Chapter 1

Six years later...

IF JADE ALEXANDER HAD ANY guts, she would dump the mug of steaming hot coffee in the jerk's lap, then quit before her boss had a chance to fire her. Nobody—regular customer or not—put a hand on her butt and got away with it. As a waitress, she was used to a degree of sexism, to men losing their manners around an attractive woman. Maybe it was the fantasy of a smiling woman serving them food and drinks with no complaints that made them lose all reason, but that still didn't make it right. There were limits to the abuse she would take, and Mr. Madden had just crossed the line.

Glaring at him, she opened her mouth to tell him what he could do with his hand. But the words didn't come. The truth was, Jade couldn't afford any guts, much less a roof over her head. She desperately needed this lousy job and the tips she made more than anything else right now. So what if the men who frequented The Red Piano were inconsiderate morons? She'd dealt with them for a year. She could deal with them for another.

No pain, no gain, as the saying went.

And she'd certainly had her share of pain. If you looked up the word in the dictionary, you'd find a stunned picture of Jade. This past year had been the worst of her life, such an emotional and physical struggle, that she'd more than once contemplated packing it in and moving back to New Orleans to live with her parents. But while she was lacking in guts, she certainly wasn't lacking in pride. There was no way she would ever admit to being a failure. She wasn't a victim, she was a survivor. It was all in how you looked at it.

Even if her jerk of an ex-husband had taken her to the cleaners.

"Huh, Jade? What do you think?"

Placing the mug of coffee on the table, she stepped away from him, casting a long look at his offending hand, hoping he'd gotten the picture. "I'm sorry, what did you say?"

"I asked," he began slowly, "if we could get together sometime. You know, outside of this restaurant. I love seeing you here, but it's not enough, know what I mean? Maybe we can get together for some drinks, a little dancing. Or something." He winked.

Jade could only imagine what he meant by *or something*. And she certainly wasn't interested. "Mr. Madden…"

"Please, call me Milton."

"Milton, I—"

Reaching out, he took her hand. Jade lost her thought.

Originally she was going to be nice, let him down gently. Now she knew he'd get the picture only if she told it to him straight.

Pulling her hand from his, she said, "Mr. Madden, I am as interested in spending time with you as I am in dating a slug."

His widened eyes and slackened jaw said he was too stunned to speak, but Jade didn't care. She turned quickly, marching to the kitchen. If her manager got on her case, so be it. Milton Madden could find another woman to harass. She'd had enough.

Once in the kitchen, Jade leaned against a tiled wall and closed her eyes. The assorted smells of different foods washed over her, combining in a not-so-appetizing way that made her want to gag. God, she hated this job.

"Hey, hon. What's the matter?"

Opening her eyes, Jade saw Gerald's concerned face. Gerald was a fellow server, and one of the best things about working here. "Oh, Gerald. Thank God you're here. I need you to take a table for me."

"That bad?"

She nodded. "It's Mister Touchy-Feely Milton Madden."

"Uh-oh. And I guess his hands went a-touchin' and a-feelin' today."

"I don't know where that man learned his manners," Jade said, marveling at Milton's nerve. "I have to wonder if he has a mother."

"Well, don't you worry, hon. I'll take the table."

"Thanks, Gerald. I served him a cup of coffee, but I didn't ring it in yet."

"No problem," Gerald said with a wave of his hand. Winking, he added, "This should be fun."

Chuckling, he left the kitchen and went to the dining room. Jade smiled. Gerald would see to it that Milton got a taste of his own medicine—though Milton certainly wouldn't like it. Gerald was gay.

Relieved to have gotten over that hurdle, Jade grabbed a large tray, filled it with the hot plates of food for her customers, and returned to the dining room floor. The Red Piano was full this evening, and the collective sound of voices and music was so loud it was hard to think. Two days after Christmas, and New York City went on without missing a beat. Outside, people crowded the streets as if it weren't the holiday season. Manhattan truly was the city that never slept.

No doubt, some tourists had already arrived for the world's biggest party—New Year's Eve in Times Square. Funny, Jade thought, that most New Yorkers she knew had never even been to the grand event—herself included. While she'd been born and bred in Louisiana, she'd been in Manhattan for twelve years and considered herself a New Yorker through and through. She'd even been able to lose her Southern accent.

She brought six plates of chicken teriyaki and rice to a table with six women, wondering as she said "Enjoy your meals" why they'd all ordered the same thing. People were definitely interesting; though Jade had already known that. Working in a restaurant confirmed that fact every day. And it was amazing the things she witnessed, like engagements, heated family arguments, two people who were so obviously having a secret affair that they may as well have had a neon sign above their heads that said CHEATERS.

When Jade turned from the party of six, she saw the hostess seating yet another couple in her section. She groaned. It was only a little after 7 p.m., and she was already so exhausted she didn't know how she'd make it through the rest of the evening. Having taken a few days off and visited her family in New

Orleans, it was harder than she'd expected to get back into the groove of working at this restaurant.

Especially when she was aware that in four days, it would be a new year. A new millennium. And she was far short of reaching her New Year's goal.

Fourteen months ago, the year 2000 had seemed like a realistic goal to reopen her salon. She'd been down but not out when she'd lost her successful business, and was convinced that a year or so's hard work would earn her enough money to lease a new shop. She'd even dreamed of christening her salon with a New Year's celebration, then open for business two days later. Yeah, Jade had had a lot of dreams, but the truth was, she was approaching the New Year with barely enough money to survive, let alone enough to start another business.

On days like this, she hated her ex-husband. She'd been raised a Christian and believed in forgiveness, but every time she thought about Nelson's betrayal, forgiveness was just too hard to manage. She'd trusted Nelson Crumm, had believed in him, and he'd failed her. He'd more than failed her. He'd taken away the life she'd worked so hard for. Once she had been the successful owner of Dreamstyles, a hair salon in midtown Manhattan for women of color. Her salon had catered to several different types, from students to artists to professionals, and she was proud of the success she'd achieved. It wasn't uncommon for businesswomen to stop in her salon over lunch for a cut, a wash, or even a color if they had a two-hour break. She opened early and closed late, allowing for people who needed to come in at different hours to get different jobs done. Sometimes she would be at her salon until close to midnight, finishing a weave or braids or whatever time-consuming job needed to be done to have her clients looking their best. She didn't mind, however, because she loved her job.

And while she'd initially feared the long hours she put in at the salon would affect her marriage negatively, Nelson hadn't seemed to mind her hours, mostly because he worked as an in-house Vice President of Finance for an advertising firm as well as a freelance accountant. In other words, he worked crazy hours as well. He was nothing if not dedicated to his career, as Jade was to hers, and she thought he'd make the perfect business partner as well as the perfect marriage partner.

Jade had never been more stunned than when she'd learned Nelson had been stealing money from her salon. Having met him when she'd already owned her salon and when he'd already worked ten years for a Manhattan advertising firm, she had easily trusted him with her salon's books once they were engaged. However, five years into the marriage, she'd discovered the painful truth that Nelson led a double life. He loved to gamble, and when he'd run out of his own money to throw away on stupid illusions of striking it rich, he'd stolen hers.

Jade had thought everything was fine until her checks started bouncing. Unable to fathom what was going on, she'd confronted her bank manager, who had told her that her account had been depleted. Stunned, Jade had confronted her husband. Nelson angrily denied any knowledge of a problem, saying the bank must have made a mistake. But three weeks later, after a lot of tension and no answers, he packed his bags and left. His note said that he was leaving her for someone who trusted him. At first Jade had been so devastated with the knowledge that she'd pushed Nelson away, until the bank records showed the whopping amount of money he'd withdrawn. Then she'd gotten angry, but a lot of good that did. In the end, with no assets, Jade was forced to sell the salon, and even the money from the sale was used to pay her overwhelming debts. She'd barely had two pennies to rub together after that.

Shaking her head, Jade forced the disturbing memories from her mind. She didn't want to think about the depth of her husband's betrayal. Thinking about it wouldn't change the facts. With a new year approaching, she had to concentrate on moving ahead and forgetting the past.

That thought in mind, she walked to the table that housed her new customers, forcing herself into "cheerful waitress" mode. The couple sat on the same side of the booth, their linked hands resting atop the table, the sides of their faces pressed together as they giggled at some private joke. Jade stopped midstride as she saw the loving couple, a pang of sadness gripping her. She didn't miss Nelson, but she did miss the memory of what they'd had in their early years.

But even the memory was false. Nelson had never been the man he'd claimed.

"Good evening," Jade said, forcing a smile on her lips as she moved forward to stand at the edge of the table.

The giggling couple looked up. "Good eve—" the woman began, but abruptly stopped. Recognition flashed in her eyes as she looked at Jade. "Hey!" she exclaimed. "Jade?"

Jade's own eyes narrowed as she regarded the other woman. Her hair was longer than she remembered, but the pretty face and bright brown eyes were certainly the same. "Cassandra!"

"Jade!" The other woman jumped out of the booth and wrapped her in a bear hug. "Oh, my God! I can't believe it!"

"Neither can I." Jade pulled back and looked at her old friend, her brain still processing the fact that it was really her. "I thought you were in Los Angeles."

Cassandra nodded. "I was, but I'm back. Hey, you've got

to meet Kenny." She gestured to the attractive, well-dressed, dark-skinned man sitting in the booth. "Jade, meet Kenny. Kenny, meet Jade."

"How you doin'?" Kenny asked, shaking her hand.

"I'm good, thanks." To Cassandra she whispered, "Mmm. He's cute."

"I know. And we're engaged!" She flashed a big, sparkling diamond for Jade's inspection.

"My Lord," Jade said, taking Cassandra's hand in hers. "Congratulations. I hope you're both very happy together."

"Thanks," Cassandra and Kenny said in unison.

Cassandra returned to her seat—actually, to Kenny's lap—throwing an arm around his neck. Kenny placed an arm around her waist. They were a beautiful couple and definitely seemed happy together, Jade thought with a smile. But then the thought hit her, she couldn't help it. Was Kenny really who he said he was? Were his feelings for Cassandra sincere? Nelson had claimed to love her, and look what he'd done.

Kenny isn't Nelson, she told herself sternly. She didn't have a right to think the worst of him; she'd barely met him. Though thinking anything decent about members of the opposite sex was a real challenge these days.

"So, girl, what are you doing here?"

Jade paused. The last time she'd seen Cassandra was three years ago when she'd quit as her receptionist with plans to move to Hollywood to pursue an acting career. Though sorry to see her go, Jade had wished her well. That was two years before she'd lost the salon, so Cassandra didn't know what had happened.

"I'm... I work here," Jade finally said. What had happened wasn't her fault—she'd trusted her husband—yet she was embarrassed by the drastic turn her life had taken.

"Why?" Cassandra asked, clearly stunned. "Aren't you busy with the salon?"

"I wish I was." Jade sighed. "Cassandra, I lost Dreamstyles."

"What?"

Jade nodded. "And it's a long story, so don't ask."

"I'm sorry to hear that."

"Me, too. I lost everything."

Cassandra's eyebrows bunched together. "What do you mean, *everything?*"

"Everything. The salon. My home." Her dreams. Her future.

"But you still have Nelson, right? You two are still together."

"Nelson who?"

"Oh," Cassandra said, then made a face. "Let me guess. Don't ask."

"Now isn't a good time. Maybe later."

"God, that's gotta be rough." Cassandra glanced over a shoulder at Kenny, as if for assurance that their marriage would work. He nuzzled his nose against hers. She smiled, then turned back to Jade. "I'm sorry."

"Don't be. I think it all worked out for the best."

"Still, it can't be easy."

"No. It's not." She changed the subject. "What can I get you two to drink?"

Kenny said, "We'd love a bottle of champagne."

"You're celebrating."

He nodded, then smiled as he held Cassandra a little closer.

He didn't need to say anything else. It was clear that for a guy like Kenny, love itself was a cause for celebration.

She'd never had that kind of love with Nelson, though she'd desperately craved it. In the beginning he'd been charming and romantic, but the honeymoon phase had quickly died. Nelson never held her at night unless he wanted to make love. She'd had to ask for good-bye kisses and for hugs. When she'd sat back and thought about it one day, she'd realized that she had to ask for even the smallest show of affection, so finally she'd stopped asking. She'd come to accept that Nelson just wasn't the sweep-you-off-your-feet romantic type.

Jade brought Cassandra and Kenny a bottle of champagne then gave them some privacy. It was nice to see Cassandra, who had years earlier gone through man after man, finally happy.

"Jade, can I see you for a minute?"

Jade turned from the computer terminal to see Pierre Lamont, the owner and manager of The Red Piano, standing behind her. His eyes held a hint of anger. "Sure," she finally replied.

"In my office, please."

Jade swallowed as she followed her manager through the kitchen doors and into the small office at the back of the kitchen. Pierre wasn't prone to calling staff into his office to congratulate them on jobs well done. Her stomach suddenly a ball of nerves, Jade couldn't help wonderful what she'd done wrong.

"Have a seat," Pierre said.

She didn't like his tone. Cautiously sitting on the edge of a well-worn chair, she asked, "What's this about?"

"I had a chat with Milton not too long ago, Jade. He was very upset."

"Oh," Jade said matter-of-factly, feeling a modicum of relief. "I don't know what he said to you, but I'm the one who should be upset, Pierre. Not him."

"He said he's heard better language coming from a trucker than what you subjected him to tonight."

"That's a lie!" Jade replied, indignant.

Pierre raised an eyebrow. "Then what did you say?"

She hated the fact that her manager hadn't even given her the benefit of the doubt, but that's the kind of man he was, and one of her reasons for wishing she didn't have to work here. "Did he tell you that he put his hand on my butt?"

"No."

"Well, he did. Then he asked me out. I turned him down."

"That's all you said?"

"I should have said a lot more than that. I don't enjoy being fondled by my customers."

Pierre shrugged. "I'm sure he didn't mean anything by it."

Jade stared at him in stunned silence. Finally she found her voice. "Didn't mean anything by it? Pierre, he has to know what he did was wrong, He's lucky I'm not charging him with sexual harassment."

"Sexual harassment?" Pierre chuckled. "I forgot, every man has to be careful what he says and does. Otherwise, women will cry 'sexual harassment' whenever it's convenient."

"*Excuse* me?" Jade shot out of her chair.

"Lighten up," Pierre said. "You're going to have to if you want to continue working in this business. Sometimes you just have to forget the small stuff. Men unfortunately will be men. But I don't want to have valued customers feeling unwelcome in my restaurant. Understand?"

Only too well. Jade should have known. Though Pierre had never come on to her, he had a weak spot for the blond bartenders. "I understand."

"Good. That's all."

Jade left Pierre's office feeling angrier than ever. Angry at Nelson for putting her in this situation. She'd first worked at another restaurant after she'd lost the salon and had had the same problem—men who felt it was their right to tastelessly flirt with their waitress. She'd finally gotten a job at The Red Piano, a Manhattan restaurant that had a reputation as being one of the busiest in the Upper East Side, and despite the problems she'd stayed here because she made pretty good money. Now she wondered if she'd have to find another job.

That thought made her stomach lurch. She didn't want another waitressing job. She wanted her salon back.

Trying to forget the ugly incident with Milton and Pierre, she brought out hot food, got bills for customers, poured coffee. It was the same boring thing she did day after day. The only thing that gave her strength to continue was the dream she didn't want to give up.

She walked to Cassandra's table to see if they needed anything. She found the two in a lip-lock.

"Ahem." Jade cleared her throat.

The two flew apart, and giggling, Cassandra looked up. "Sorry. Must be the champagne."

"No doubt. Have you decided on dinner?"

"Actually," Cassandra replied, "we're just going to have the champagne. We already ate."

"No problem. I'll check on you in a bit, then." Jade turned to leave.

"Don't run away so quickly," Cassandra said, smiling. "I have something to ask you."

Jade turned back to the table. "What?"

"Excuse me," Kenny said, patting Cassandra's thigh. She rose, "Nature calls."

She stepped out of the booth to let him pass. "Don't be gone long."

He bent to kiss her softly on the lips. "I'll be back in a flash."

Cassandra watched him leave, her eyes lingering over his body as she dragged her bottom lip between her teeth.

"You two should be locked up for that kind of behavior," Jade couldn't help saying. They certainly gave a new meaning to mushy.

Cassandra whirled to face her. "Sorry. It's just that…I'm finally, truly happy."

"I can see that." A smile touched Jade's lips. "Anyway, you were saying?"

"Oh yeah." Cassandra slipped into the booth. "Have you heard of *UpClose* magazine?"

"Of course I have," Jade replied. *UpClose* was a popular magazine that featured anybody who was a somebody in the world of entertainment.

"Well, *UpClose* magazine is doing a feature article on me that will come out in February."

"You go, girl! That's amazing." If the magazine was going to feature Cassandra, then she must be doing well. "Congrats!"

"Thanks. Anyway, they're doing a color photo spread of me at home and at work, to go with the story. So I was thinking that if you're interested, I can suggest to them that you do my hair for the shoot they do at my home. I always loved how you did my hair."

Jade looked down at Cassandra as if she'd grown horns.

"What?" Cassandra said.

"I…I don't know what to say," Jade finally replied. Doing hair for a magazine like *UpClose* would mean a lot of exposure.

"Say yes," Cassandra told her. "You're one of the few people I trust with my hair."

"Thank you, Cassandra. Really, I appreciate the offer. But I'm sure they already have a stylist."

"True, but it won't hurt to suggest someone I've known and trusted for years, will it?"

Her life had been such a mess in the past year, Jade was afraid to even get her hopes up.

"I'm not making any promises," Cassandra continued, "but I can suggest it."

"What's this all for? The feature story, I mean."

"Oh, of course. I haven't even told you. Well, I'm starring in an Off-Broadway play!"

"You go, girl!" Jade said. "So acting is finally happening for you."

"Yeah. I didn't get anywhere in Los Angeles so I came back to New York…and bingo. I started getting some bit parts, and then I lucked out with the lead in this play that is so true to my life, it could have been written for me. It's called *Through the Wrong Door and Up the Wrong Tree*."

"Wow. What a title."

"It's a great story. Essentially it's about a woman who's looking for love and goes through one bad relationship after another. See what I mean about it being like my life?" Cassandra shook her head ruefully. "Anyway, the play has been getting really wonderful reviews. Someone from *UpClose* came to see the play, loved it, and now they're going to feature me in their magazine."

"That's fantastic."

"Thanks." Cassandra opened her small purse and searched its contents. She withdrew a notepad and a pen. "What's your number?"

Jade recited her number and watched as Cassandra scribbled it down.

Kenny returned then, and slipped into the booth beside Cassandra. He gave his fiancée a quick peck on the lips, and though Jade wasn't surprised, she rolled her eyes to the ceiling.

"Here's my card," Cassandra said after filling Kenny in on her proposal to Jade. "If you don't hear from me in the first week of January, call me."

"All right."

Kenny said, "Baby, who don't you invite her to the party

on Friday night? Since some of the people from the magazine will be there, it will be a great chance for Jade to meet them."

Cassandra's eyes lit up. "Great idea. Thanks, honey."

"No problem, baby."

As their lips met for another brief kiss, Jade wondered if Cassandra would ever think one of Kenny's ideas was anything other than great. She doubted it.

Jade cast a nervous glance at her watch. She hoped Pierre hadn't seen her spending so much time at this table, for it would surely make him even more upset.

Cassandra faced her. "I'm throwing a New Year's Eve party. Are you working that night?"

"Actually, I've got the evening off." She'd taken it off to spend the evening alone, a tribute to the way she'd be spending the new year. But even her roommate had thrown the proverbial kink in that plan, as she, too, had taken that evening off.

"Great! Then you have to come."

"Where is it?"

"At the Marriott Marquis in Times Square. Girl, it's gonna be a great party."

"I don't know."

"Look, you have to come. Not only will this be the party of the century, but as Kenny said, some of the people from *UpClose* will be there. I can introduce you…"

Jade shrugged. It was tempting, even for just a change of pace. Work and more work had been her focus recently. Maybe she needed a break. "My roommate and I actually were planning to just rent a few videos and hang out at home."

"Roommate?" Cassandra asked, raising an eyebrow. "Hmm…"

"My roommate is female," Jade informed Cassandra, ending any illicit thoughts. "And she's my best friend."

"Well, bring her. It's a party so the more the merrier. You can watch movies any other day. How often does the new millennium come around?"

Jade wrinkled her nose. "I'm kinda getting tired of the party scene." Nelson had always drunk the night away at parties, barely remembering she existed. "Besides, every New Year's Eve party I've ever been to has always been for couples."

"Don't even worry about that," Cassandra said, dismissing that thought with the wave of a hand. "I've been planning this party all year, and it was originally going to be a singles event. Now that I'm engaged, I guess I have to invite Kenny." Kenny shrugged, and to Jade's surprise, instead of kissing him, Cassandra gently rubbed his arm. "In other words, some people will have dates, some will be single. It really won't be a big deal."

Easy for her to say. Last New Year's Eve at The Red Piano, Jade had been so overwhelmed with the raw emotions of her recent breakup that she'd barely gotten through the evening. When the clock had struck midnight and all the customers had embraced their loved ones, she'd felt a devastating rush of sadness. Seeing all the couples so happy together had only reinforced the fact that her marriage had failed a few months earlier. And she hadn't been able to get the picture of a happy Nelson and his new pregnant girlfriend out of her mind.

"I'll think about it," Jade promised, pushing away her thoughts, hoping that soon the pain of Nelson's betrayal would be a thing of the past.

"Do more than think about it," Cassandra said sternly, playfully shaking a finger in her direction. "Be there. We're gonna party like it's 1999. And I promise, you won't regret it."

Chapter 2

JADE AWOKE SLOWLY, as if some force had gently pulled her from her slumber. Sunlight spilled through the blinds and onto the bed, promising a bright winter day, but she knew that hadn't awakened her. Light or dark, loud or quiet, Jade could sleep through almost anything.

It was more like a sense that she wasn't alone that had lured her to consciousness.

Quickly her head flew to the left. There she saw Kathy, her roommate, clad in a pink terry cloth robe and socks, sitting on her armchair.

"Good. You're finally awake," Kathy said.

"You've been waiting for me to wake up?"

"Yeah."

Jade glanced at the clock, then groaned. It was 8:27 a.m. "Kathy, do you know what time it is?"

"Eight twenty-seven."

"A.M. As in, the morning. As in, I worked till two a.m. last night."

"I know," Kathy said. "And I'm sorry. I just needed to talk."

"Can't we talk in four hours, when I'll actually be able to process what you're saying?"

"I'm having an emergency," Kathy explained calmly.

"Then call 911."

"Ha-ha. C'mon, Jade. I need your opinion."

Jade resigned herself to the fact that Kathy would not leave until she'd had her say. Sighing, she sat up, dragging a pillow onto her lap. "What is it?"

"It's Tyrone." Pause. "He wants to get serious."

"Serious how?"

"Serious married."

"It must be something in the water," Jade said, remembering Cassandra and Kenny.

"What?"

"Oh, nothing." She yawned, then continued. "I thought you liked Tyrone."

"I do. But marriage?"

"I can see your dilemma. Tall, gorgeous, established African-American male wanting to commit. My advice: run, don't walk, to the altar."

Kathy flashed her a shocked look. "You know I can't do that."

She did, which was exactly why Jade had suggested it. Maybe the early hour had her somewhat cranky and in the mood to play devil's advocate. "Really? Why not?"

"Because I…because Tyrone was just a…a fling. I never meant to get serious with him."

"Yeah, and?"

"And this wasn't supposed to happen."

Jade knew all too well that Kathy had hang-ups with commitment, and truthfully she couldn't blame her. "Look, I'll be the first one to tell you that love often sucks. Been there, done that, got the T-shirt, trying to remove the tattoo. But hey, that's me." She shrugged, then continued. "You, on the other hand, have never been married. You haven't given any man the chance."

"You know why, Jade." Kathy's eyes held hers for a moment before she looked away, then back at her. "As you've said a million times, look at what happened to you. You trusted Nelson, and he turned out to be...well, I don't have to tell you that. And after Sheldon..."

Sheldon, the one guy Kathy had truly fallen for, had broken her heart. Jade suspected her friend wasn't over him.

"Do you love him?"

"Sheldon? God, no. How do you love someone who joined the military to get out of marrying you?"

"Not Sheldon," Jade replied, give her friend a pointed look. "Tyrone. With all this talk of your dilemma, you haven't said whether or not you love him."

Kathy shrugged. "I love spending time with him. And he's got a great body." She smiled. "What can I say?"

"I don't think this is an emergency." Jade lay back, getting comfortable on the pillow. "All you have to do is tell him that you want to think about it. Give him a call and let me get to sleep."

"He's in the next room."

Jade shot up. *"What?"*

"I told him I had to go to the washroom."

"What if he comes looking for you?" Jade's eyes flew to the door. "You have to go back to him!"

"I know. But he wants an answer, so I...I had to come see you. You think I should tell him I need time?"

"I think you should get back to your bedmate. Girl, you're crazy."

Rising, Kathy ran a hand through her short braids. "All right. Oh, one more thing. I've got to work New Year's Eve."

"I thought you had the night off."

"I did, but they all but begged me yesterday. And after Tyrone's surprise announcement, I figured I did not want to spend New Year's Eve with him. I called work minutes ago and told them I'll be in."

"You are crazy." And once again, her plans for Friday night had changed. Though she'd originally wanted to spend the night alone, she'd been looking forward to ringing in the New Year with her best friend and some comedies. Oh well. She could always do the move marathon by herself.

Or she could go to the party Cassandra was throwing.

Kathy said, "I'm sorry."

"It's all right. I'll find something to do."

Terrell Edmonds wanted to kick himself for not taking the day off. To say he had a busy schedule was an understatement, and he was getting busier by the day. In the last few years, his reputation in Manhattan as a photographer had grown considerably, resulting in many more lucrative jobs. But the hours were exhausting, and he knew that, as his mother always told him, he should slow down and take care of himself.

Today of all days, he should have followed his mother's advice. He was up early after a very late night as a favor to a friend and agent who wanted some shots done for one of his new models before the New Year. But this job was proving to be more of a hassle than anything else, and certainly not worth the few extra bucks he would make.

"Put your clothes on," he said simply, his back turned.

"I want you to do some nudes of me," the young woman said behind him. "I trust you."

"Put your clothes on," he repeated.

"What's the big deal?" she asked in a young, naive voice that made it clear she didn't know what kind of sharks might prey on teenagers like her. "I'm sure I don't have anything you haven't seen before. Please? I want some nudes for my portfolio."

"Please don't treat me like an idiot. I wasn't born yesterday; I know what you're trying to do." He hated talking to her with his back turned but he wasn't going to give her any satisfaction by turning around.

"Is it so bad that I like you?" She sounded vulnerable and oh-so inexperienced. When he didn't answer, she continued. "I—I just want to be with you. I'm not asking for a commitment, if that's what you're thinking."

What Terrell was thinking was that he wished he could start this day over. He wasn't into meaningless rolls in the hay, especially not with seventeen-year-olds. But he suspected that the more he chatted with Bonnie, the less willing she'd be to back down. So he said, "I'm going to the bathroom. When I come back, I want you gone."

She whimpered softly. For goodness sake, she was just a child. Didn't she have any idea the kind of trouble she'd get herself into if she threw herself at the wrong man? And what was it about models that made them feel their bodies were the key to getting everything they wanted?

"I'm sorry," she cried. He saw her run past him, slipping her simple black dress over her pale, naked body. She hurriedly put on her coat and boots, then disappeared through the door without a backward glance.

"Man," he mumbled when she was gone. Moving to the door, he locked it. Maybe he should give up freelancing with model and talent agencies. How many times a week did he have women like Bonnie, both young and old, hitting on him? Three? Five?

Too many, Terrell decided. At least when he did professional photo shoots for magazines and shows, the models were professional. They knew he had a job to do and they respected that. Sure, there was the odd time when someone hit on him while doing a job, but he could handle a sexy smile or a piece of paper with a phone number being discreetly slipped into his shirt pocket. What he couldn't handle was some dejected little girl telling tales because he wanted nothing to do with her.

It had happened, once. Hopefully it never would again. Then Terrell had been devastated when an eighteen-year-old he'd rejected had turned on him, telling her agent that he had fondled her. The call, the accusation, and the thirty-six hours that followed had been the worst moments of his life. Eventually, since the girl had had a reputation for causing trouble, she hadn't had much credibility and the agency hadn't pursued the matter. Terrell had been relieved, but always knew that the scenario could have been played out entirely differently. If the agent had believed Darlene Simpson, perhaps nothing Terrell said or did would have saved the career he'd worked so hard to build.

Looking back, he knew he'd handled the situation badly. When, for no apparent reason, Darlene had burst into tears during the photo shoot, like a fool he had offered her comfort. He hadn't even considered the fact that it could have been a ploy to get close to him, but it had been, and the girl had used the opportunity to wrap her body around his. When he'd physically pushed her away, the rejection was probably that much worse than if he'd simply had to tell her he wasn't interested. If he had it to do over again, he would, but at least he had learned a lesson. Now, regardless of the situation, Terrell's policy was strictly hands off.

His head pounding over the incident, Terrell walked from the vestibule to the kitchen in his loft. He needed coffee.

Forget the coffee, he decided. He had an hour and a half before his next appointment was to arrive. He'd take a quick nap instead.

"...three more days before the Y2K bug hits. Are you prepared? Some people are predicting pure chaos...."

Jade flipped the channel, looking for something decent to watch. She'd heard enough of the Y2K bug and didn't believe the hype. Unlike her, Kathy didn't know what to think and was "prepared," with enough bottled water and canned goods in the spare bedroom to open her own grocery. But the way Jade saw it, the only chaos this new year would be caused by man's own stupidity.

Finding nothing on television she wanted to watch, Jade turned the television off. Standing, she walked to the living room window, noting that the sun had retreated and the sky was now gray. Light snowflakes fell over Brooklyn, and Jade found herself wishing she was back in New Orleans. At least there she wouldn't have to deal with the white stuff.

Turning, she leaned against the wall and surveyed the room. The place could use a good cleaning. And she had laundry to do before she went to work this evening.

At least Kathy and her twenty-seven-year-old stud were gone. Jade had met Kathy in her salon seven years ago and the two had developed a quick friendship. The fact that they were friends despite being so completely different gave credence to the phrase "opposites attract." While Jade had been perhaps a little too cautious when it came to dating, Kathy's motto seemed to be "I'm here for a good time, not a long time." In all the years Jade had known her, Kathy had been running from commitments like they were the plague. Oh, she liked men's company—she just wanted it with no strings attached.

Maybe Kathy has the right idea, Jade conceded, dropping down onto the plush sofa and closing her eyes. At least Kathy always had somewhere to go, something to do, someone to hang out with. And she was always happy, so the life of the never-dateless couldn't be that bad.

Jade, on the other hand, worked or stayed at home. Occasionally she and Kathy would go for a bite to eat, but that was rare. She hated to admit it, but outside work, she really had nothing else in her life.

Not true. She had her dream. That dream helped her make it through many a night. It might not keep her warm the way a man would, but still it gave her a sense of hope. No one could take it away from her. Not even Nelson.

But the fact that if she was ever going to make something of her life had meant she had to start from scratch hurt like the devil. After everything she'd achieved, how hard she had worked, it simply didn't seem fair. She knew she was fortunate compared to others, but that knowledge didn't help ease the pain. At age twenty-four and fresh out of cosmetology school, Jade had lucked out with a lottery win. Nothing that would let her be on easy street for the rest of her life, but enough to open a business as she'd always dreamed of doing. Her salon had been small, but over the years she'd built a loyal clientele. That the man she'd loved had taken it all away from her was almost unbearable.

"Get over it," she told herself sternly. It was certainly easier said than done, but the truth was she'd get nowhere if she harbored resentment over Nelson's betrayal. The drive to get even, however, might do her some good. What had Trump's first wife said—that living well was the best revenge? Well, Jade planned to live well. She had once. She would again.

She just didn't care if Nelson ever knew it—which kinda weakened the whole revenge plan the way she was sure Ivana Trump had meant it. But as far as Jade was concerned, her life would be much better if she never saw Nelson's face again.

The ringing phone frightened Jade, but she was thankful for the distraction. Stretching her body across the sofa, she grabbed the receiver from its cradle on the end table. "Hello?"

"Jade?"

"Speaking."

"Good. I'm glad I caught you. This is Cassandra."

"Oh hi, Cassandra. What's up?"

"I just want to let you know that I spoke with the editor-in-chief of *UpClose* magazine about what we discussed. I told him there's this absolutely fabulous stylist who I'd love to have do my hair for the shoot. He said he'll run it by whoever he's got to run it by, then let me know. But it sounded hopeful. In fact, he said he's looking forward to meeting you at the party."

"Cassandra…"

"Uh-uh. Not a word. I'm just trying to help you, Jade. You were always a great help to me. I don't know if I ever said it, but I truly appreciated your letting me take off for all those auditions. You didn't have to do that."

"I know." A smile touched Jade's lips as she remembered outgoing Cassandra at her salon, always making people laugh with her easygoing, charming personality. She'd been an asset at the salon, the type of sister who was beautiful but didn't make other women feel insecure.

"So come to the party. Let me introduce you to the editor, help you stick that foot in the door. I know how much you love doing hair. You're a hair artist—I'm a stage artist. I know how rough it is to do a job just to get by."

"Working at the salon wasn't that bad, was it?" Jade asked, but was sure it hadn't been.

"Oh, no. Of course not. I had a blast working at the salon. The jobs I did in L.A., however… Well, that's another story. I'm not wrong, am I? You're not one of the few artists waiting tables who actually loves that job?"

How did Cassandra know so much? "No, you're right. More than you realize."

"Hey, I'm not just a pretty face."

"Apparently not."

"Watch it, girlfriend." Cassandra chuckled. "So you'll come, then? The party starts at seven—well, I said seven, because you know our people. Tell them seven, they'll be there by ten."

"Ain't that the truth." Though Jade knew exactly what Cassandra was talking about, she herself believed in being punctual. "So I should plan for ten?"

"Yep. Or nine, if you want some of the food."

"Wow. You're going all-out."

"I guess I am. But like I said before, we're gonna party like it's 1999. Now I'll have to send you a ticket—you know what Times Square is like—if you're not there by four, forget about getting through."

"That's right." As Jade had never been to Times Square for New Year's, she hadn't actually experienced the hassle of trying to get through the barricaded streets.

"I can send it via courier, if you like."

"Sure." Jade gave her the address.

"Of course, you can always come early and escape the madness," Cassandra added.

"I'll see. Send the ticket and I'll decide later."

"No problem." Pause. "Just a second, hon," Cassandra said to someone else. Then to Jade she said, "I've gotta run."

"Before you go, do you need me to bring anything?"

"Just yourself. And your toothbrush, if you want to crash here. Which may be a good idea, considering the crowds expected."

"All right, then."

Giggle. "See ya Friday."

"See you."

Jade replaced the receiver and allowed herself a quick smile. Oh, Lord, what if she landed this job? *UpClose* was a major magazine and she'd no doubt make a pretty penny. It wouldn't be enough to start her business again in the new year, but at least a decent amount to put into the bank.

Closing her eyes, Jade let out a nervous breath. She didn't want to get her hopes up. She hadn't gotten the job yet. If and when she did, she would celebrate then.

Chapter 3

"WHAT DO YOU THINK? The black or the taupe?" Jade held up both evening dresses to her body in turn.

Securing an aquamarine stud in her ear that complemented her royal blue skirt, Kathy turned from the bathroom mirror to glance at Jade, who stood in the bathroom doorway. "Mmm… Well, black is so common. But that is one hot dress. The slit should be illegal."

"I wonder how the fashion police ever let you out of the store with it."

"Oh, hush. I'm letting you raid my closet, am I not?"

"Forcing is a more appropriate word."

Kathy rolled her eyes to the ceiling, then returned her gaze to Jade's face. "I am not going to let you go to any New Year's Eve party looking like a frump. What will my friends think when the word gets out?"

"Hey, my suit is not frumpish." Jade looked at the flowing

maroon pantsuit that hung on a hanger atop the bathroom door. She loved that suit.

"Maybe it's good for a corporate dinner, but not for the New Year's Eve party of the millennium." Kathy turned back to her reflection.

"All right," Jade said, giving in. She moaned when she took a look at the come-get-me slit in the black satin dress. "Honestly, Kathy, don't you think this slit is too much?"

"Lord, no," Kathy replied without hesitation, pausing in her application of burgundy lipstick to her mouth. "And for you especially, I think it's perfect. It's about time you lived a little."

"So, which one?" Stepping into the bathroom, Jade held up the glittering taupe dress and glanced over Kathy's shoulder at her image in the mirror. "I was kinda thinking of this one. Or I could do the black with a gold shawl. Believe it or not, I do own a slinky black dress too."

"I've seen your slinky black dress," Kathy said with another roll of the eyes. "Even a nun would feel comfortable in it." Turning from the mirror, she faced Jade head-on. "Forget the shawl." She stood back, taking in the entire view of the dress against Jade's body. "Ooh, this one has a nice slit too. And ample air-conditioning in the back. Perfect."

"It's ten degrees outside. I'm hardly concerned about air-conditioning."

"Honey, in that dress, you don't have to be concerned about anything." She sighed wistfully. "As I said, it's perfect."

Jade threw her gaze from the mirror to Kathy. She could only wonder what direction her friend's thoughts had taken. "Perfect for what?"

"Don't give me that look."

"I know you, Kathy. If you're suggesting I'm on the prowl…"

"Wow, what a concept." Kathy grinned. "You'll be sure to get any man you want in that dress."

"Oh, stop. You know and I know that I'm not out to pick up any man."

"Honey, it's not a crime. And how long has it been? Over a year?"

"Kathy!"

"Exactly. There's nothing wrong with getting a little somethin'-somethin' now and then."

"You should know," Jade mumbled, then smiled sardonically.

"I heard that," Kathy said as she refilled her makeup bag. "And you're right. I do know. That's why you always see me smiling when you're frowning."

Jade opened her mouth to refute that, but knew she couldn't. Though in reality, her frown didn't stem from a lack of sex, but rather from the knowledge that she was far from achieving her New Year's dream.

Frustrated over the process of deciding what to wear, Jade looped the dresses over her arm. "Speaking of sex, what did you tell Tyrone?"

Kathy's hands stilled on the top button of her cream-colored blouse. "I feel so bad, Jade. I told Tyrone that I thought we should slow things down and he was really crushed. I told him I still wanted to see him but he told me he didn't have time for games."

"Ouch. Sounds like you care more about him than you thought."

Kathy slipped into the royal blue blazer that matched her skirt. "Maybe I do. I don't know."

"What's to know?"

"He's a baby!"

"That's not what you said about his body yesterday, now is it?"

A dreamy sound escaped Kathy's lips, and Jade could only imagine the X-rated thoughts that were running through her mind. "No, I sure didn't." She flicked her wrist forward and glanced at her small silver watch. "Oh, I've gotta run. Did you decide what dress you're going to wear?"

"I'll probably just stick with my pantsuit."

"Bo-ring." Kathy shook her head reproachfully. "Well, I'd better get out of here. I can just imagine what the subway will be like."

"Yeah, I know what you mean. The eve of the millennium? It's gonna be worse than a zoo. Have fun tonight."

"I'm sure I will." But her tone couldn't have been more sarcastic. Looking upward, she asked, "Oh, why did I agree to this shift tonight?"

"Poor Tyrone. I bet he's wondering what he did wrong."

That comment drew Kathy's eyes to her instantly. "I'm sure Tyrone will take care of himself. He won't be sitting home alone on my account."

And therein lay her friend's reason for not wanting to commit, Jade told herself. She didn't trust men, and Jade couldn't blame her. In fact, it was pretty much a good rule to live by.

Jade followed Kathy to the door. Kathy said, "Forget the pantsuit. Raid my closet some more if you don't like those two dresses, but do not step out of this place looking like some old maid."

"Yeah, yeah." Jade watched while Kathy slipped into sensible boots and a long wool coat. When she was finished, she opened her arms to Jade for a hug.

Jade stepped into her friend's embrace. "Take care. I'll see you next year, okay?"

Kathy pulled back and smiled wryly. "Cute."

"And true."

"I guess it is. See you next year."

After Kathy left, Jade decided that if she was going to the party, she'd be crazy to stick around and try to head out later that evening. She could just imagine the chaos on the subways then, with everyone heading into Manhattan for one party or another. And while the snow had stopped falling, a couple inches covered the roads which would no doubt make travel a little slower. She may as well leave early, bring an overnight bag and a selection of clothes, and beat the rush.

She packed the black dress, the taupe dress, and her favorite maroon pantsuit. As far as she was concerned, it was elegant—not frumpy. Either way, she'd have something decent to wear tonight.

Jade took one last look around the apartment to make sure she hadn't left anything on or plugged in that shouldn't be. Satisfied that she hadn't, she hugged her torso and smiled. She was actually looking forward to tonight. Maybe it was the feeling that the year 2000 would be her year, but Jade was suddenly in the mood to celebrate.

"Live a little," she could hear Kathy say.

"Why not?" Jade responded aloud.

She grabbed her bags and headed for the door.

"Thanks so much for squeezing me in. I really appreciate it."

"No problem, Dawn," Terrell said. "The proofs will be ready in seven days."

The attractive brunette faced him with a surprised expression. "Seven days? Don't you take any time off?"

"When I can squeeze it into my schedule." He smiled.

"My goodness. Haven't you heard that this is the holiday season?"

"I think I heard that somewhere, but I was too busy to pay attention."

Dawn bristled. "Well, I don't envy you. I hope you at least have plans to ring in the new year with style."

Terrell shrugged. "I've been invited to a few parties, but to tell you the truth, I may just stay home and crash."

"You're *kidding?*"

"Hey, I've got to sleep sometime."

Dawn lifted her leather jacket from the coat tree and slipped into it. "Like I said, I don't envy you. I'm going to party tonight, sleep tomorrow. I hope you do the same."

"We'll see."

"Thanks again." She stepped to the door. "I look forward to seeing the proofs."

"If you don't hear from me in seven days, call me."

"Will do." She opened the door and stepped into the hallway, throwing Terrell a quick smile before she closed the door behind her.

Terrell stood staring at the closed door for a long moment, wondering what to do. Should he party, or sleep? Right now, he was leaning toward sleep.

He glanced at the clock. Seven fifty-four. The editor-in-chief of *UpClose* magazine had invited him to a party at the Marriott in Times Square tonight, but he might as well forget that one. Despite the numerous cabs on the road, it was next to impossible to get one on New Year's Eve. And he certainly didn't feel like driving.

There were other parties in New York and its boroughs that he'd been invited to, but again the dilemma was how to get there from his SoHo loft. Of course, there wasn't a single party he knew of in this part of town.

If he couldn't make it to a party, that left one logical alternative: sleep. For the first time in ages, Terrell was looking forward to a night of blissful slumber.

At Cassandra's urging, Jade wore the long taupe party gown with the killer slit in the back. And she didn't look half bad either, even if she was careful not to bend too far forward for fear of her underwear showing.

Jade was more of a pantsuit kind of girl, preferring the classy and conservative to the bold and flashy. When she'd first slipped into Kathy's sexy dress, she'd felt uncomfortable, not because it wasn't beautiful, but because it hugged her curves like a second skin. She wasn't used to wearing such tight-fitting clothing, and had had second thoughts about wearing it tonight. But when she'd seen Cassandra's sequined number—low cut enough and short enough to make Madonna blush, Jade had decided to throw her concerns to the wind and follow Kathy's advice and live a little.

And now four hours later she was glad she had. The glittering taupe was definitely better than the too-common black, and certainly more suitable for a party than her pantsuit. With simple gold jewelry to accessorize the gown, even Jade had done a double take in the mirror, surprised by how good she looked.

Now she headed down the hallway from the washroom. The music was loud, the atmosphere charged, and Jade was glad she'd decided to go out. Just minutes to midnight, the party was in full swing. The suite Cassandra had rented was lavish and large and filled with all kinds of people. Some of Cassandra's fellow actors, who had also helped fund the party, were dressed in outrageous costumes. From feathers to leather, you name it, it was there. Others were more conservatively dressed in suits and evening gowns; a few men sported tuxes. The party was wild and it was fun and Jade was actually enjoying herself.

"Five minutes, everybody," a man dressed in a bull-fighter outfit yelled. To a casual observer, this would look like a masquerade party. From the man's position on top of a chair, he cupped his hands around his mouth and hollered, "Fill up your champagne glasses now!"

The theme song of the evening, Prince's "1999," went up a notch. Champagne corks popped to overwhelming cheers and the bubbly liquid flowed. Jade edged her way through the crowd, in search of a drink to toast the new year. A woman dressed as an angel passed her one before she even made it to the bar. Smiling her thanks, she accepted the plastic flute filled with champagne and brought the glass to her lips.

"Not yet!" someone beside her yelled. Startled, Jade jerked forward and almost spilled the contents of the glass right down the front of her gorgeous dress. Annoyed, she turned to face the person who'd practically scared her half to death.

A short, stocky, balding man stood beside her with an apologetic smile, and Jade's annoyance fled.

"Oops," he said apologetically. "I didn't mean to scare you. I just figured you should save that for the first toast of the new year."

"You're probably right," she agreed, out of politeness more than anything else. There was enough champagne that she could get a refill, but as midnight was fast approaching, she decided she'd do as the man suggested.

"Three minutes!" the bullfighter yelled. Jade felt anticipation run down her spine. It was almost here. A new millennium.

The short man extended a hand, saying, "I'm Fred. You are…?"

"Jade." They shook hands, and Jade was a little surprised at the strength of his grip.

"Want to go out on the terrace? I don't know about you, but it's getting a little stuffy in here."

"Sure." Jade had recently been out there, watching with fascination the crowd below. There were literally thousands and thousands of people filling the streets of Times Square. She'd never seen the Times Square celebration live before, and it was all simply incredible. The giant-screen TV showed the hosts for the evening, behind whom the excited crowd was visible, arms waving exuberantly, party favors dancing around like they had a life of their own. Near the platform on which the hosts stood, enormous mounds of balloons were ready to be released. The sounds of cheering were deafening. No doubt about it, people were definitely excited about greeting the new millennium.

"Fred!" another short man exclaimed as they stepped out on the terrace. "There you are!"

Fred turned to Jade. "Excuse me for a minute."

"Sure."

Raising his glass in a toast toward the man who had called, Fred crossed the terrace, leaving Jade alone. She didn't mind. A moment alone at midnight suited her fine.

She made her way through the crowd, moving to the balcony's railing, gripping the cool metal with one hand. The digital clock adjacent to the giant-screen TV showed that it was less than a minute until the year 2000. The crowd below was so pumped up, some hugging each other and dancing in groups, Jade could only watch and listen in awe. Where were these people the other 364 days of the year? A smile spread across her face as she remembered something someone had once said to her: New Year's Eve was the one day of the year when New Yorkers were actually friendly and carefree.

Jade glanced from the crowd to the famous glittering ball that made its descent the last minute before the New Year. It was almost near the bottom of the pole. The clock read five seconds. Her heart sped up. It was almost here. Three seconds. Two. One.

Fireworks exploded all around the Square, brilliantly lighting the sky. Confetti seemed to appear from nowhere, raining down on them in a spectacular shower. The balloons soared upward in a grand celebration. And the big screen TV flashed the words in bold letters: HAPPY NEW YEAR!

Jade closed her eyes, drew a deep breath, and felt an unexpected moment of sadness for her aunt who had died of cancer in October. She prayed she was in a better place. Then holding back her tears, she made a wish. "Let this be the year I open my salon again," she whispered. "Let this be the year all my dreams come true." She paused. "Please, God, let this be my year."

She opened her eyes slowly, and for some reason, she turned. Then immediately squeezed her eyes shut again, certain they were playing tricks on her. But when she opened them for a second time, the image remained.

Jade's heart stilled as familiar onyx eyes met and held hers across the balcony. Despite the cold, the energy between them sizzled, and a long forgotten wave of desire rocked her to her core. Terrell Edmonds, looking as cool and sexy as ever, flashed her the most charming of smiles.

Then as though he was here specifically to meet her, he stepped fully onto the terrace and made his approach.

Chapter 4

JADE DOWNED THE CHAMPAGNE she was holding in one gulp. That seemed to kick-start her heart; it resumed beating but went into overdrive. Fleetingly she wondered if such a fast heart rate would put her at risk of dropping dead.

The only risk to her health, she realized with a nervous breath, was the man a few feet away.

Terrell Edmonds. He wasn't a hallucination. It was really him standing there, staring at her, walking toward her.

Oh, God.

As if no time had passed since the last night she'd seen him, she remembered with startling clarity the feel of his hands on her body, the scent of him as he'd held her close, how badly she'd wanted him that night over six years ago. And suddenly her body felt more alive than it had in ages, as though it had just come out of hibernation.

He looked the same but different. He was bald now, and

Jade decided she liked the look. Dressed in a black designer tuxedo with a white satin shirt, he looked sharp…and too darn sexy. The shirt was unbuttoned at the collar, allowing her a glimpse of his smooth, chocolate-colored chest. Why couldn't she tear her eyes away from him?

He was even more beautiful than she remembered. His dark skin was flawless, but the years had added a few laugh lines around his eyes that she could see clearly now because he was smiling.

Smiling at her.

Oh, God.

A squeal erupted from Jade's throat as hands abruptly circled her waist from behind. As she'd been so mesmerized with Terrell, the offending hands startled her so badly that she nearly jumped out of her skin. Whirling around to see who had grabbed her, she saw Cassandra's beaming face.

Throwing her arms around her neck, Cassandra planted a kiss on her cheek. "We made it, hon. Happy New Year!"

"Oh, Cassandra. Thank you." Jade's eyes misted as she embraced Cassandra heartily. What was it about a new year that made her feel so emotional? Maybe the fact that when the clock struck twelve everyone was given a brand new slate, another opportunity to right all the wrongs in their life. Jade intended to make the most of that opportunity this year. "Happy New Year."

"You haven't met Jeff yet," Cassandra said, pulling back to look at her. "He's the editor in chief of *UpClose* magazine. That's him—the redhead." She pointed toward the sliding glass doors. "Anyway, he just arrived, and already he asked if you were here." Cassandra cocked an eyebrow. "Tell me that doesn't sound promising."

Before Jade could reply, she felt Terrell's presence. And for some reason, she felt the way she had always felt around him—inexplicably drawn to his undeniable sex appeal. She couldn't help giving him a once over, lazily dragging her eyes over his tall frame. It was lean yet muscular, powerful and protective.

"Excuse me," he said to Cassandra. "May I borrow Jade for a moment?"

Cassandra looked at Jade, then arching a brow, looked back at Terrell. Her lips curled in a mischievous smile. "She's all yours." To Jade, she said, "I'll see you in a bit."

Suddenly apprehensive, Jade watched Cassandra walk away, not yet ready to meet Terrell's eyes. Had it really been six years and a few months since she'd last seen him? She couldn't think of a single thing to say to him.

"Hello, Jade."

"Terrell."

His eyes moved over her slowly, from her open-toed heels to the tip of her short coif. Despite the chill she had felt in the cold air, she now felt warm beneath his gaze. "You look…wow."

She flashed him a tentative smile. "So do you. Uh, what are you doing here?"

"I came with a friend. What about you?"

"I know Cassandra." Well, she needn't have worried about not knowing what to say to him. "She and some friends are throwing this party."

"She's the receptionist at your salon, right?"

"She…was." Jade wasn't ready to tell Terrell that she no longer had her salon. "But we still keep in touch."

"Mmm-hmm." Again, his eyes seemed to drink in every part of her. Then suddenly they jerked to her face and he asked, "Where's Nelson?"

The question momentarily shocked her. She and Nelson hadn't been together for a little over a year now. And discussing Nelson with Terrell…well, that wasn't exactly something she wanted to do. After all, he'd told her she was marrying the wrong man and she hadn't listened. "Uh…Nelson and I…" She swallowed her pride. "We're divorced."

"Really?" He asked the question as if they were discussing which plant fertilizer worked better than another.

"We split a year ago November." She wasn't ready to tell him that Nelson had stolen money from their salon to support a gambling habit. And she certainly wasn't about to mention the fact the he'd decided to have children—with someone else.

"I'm sorry to hear that."

He seemed sincere enough. At least he had the good grace not to rub her failed marriage in her face, considering everything.

"You've got to be cold in that outfit," he said. "Do you want to head inside?"

"No…I'm fine." She needed the cool air to keep her head clear.

"Then here," Terrell said, taking off his jacket. "Take this."

Looping his arms around her, he placed the jacket across her shoulders. His fingers brushed her skin as he did so, and Jade could swear her flesh tingled. He let his hands linger on her shoulders, even as she took hold of the lapels and pulled the jacket tighter around her. For an awkward moment their gazes met. Held. Then Jade blinked and looked away. Softly she mumbled, "Thanks."

Terrell dropped his hands to his side with an audible slap, then stepped past her to the railing. For a moment, Jade didn't turn. What had she read in his eyes? She didn't want to think about it, not now after so long, because it certainly couldn't be true. Instead, she clutched his jacket tighter and drew in a deep breath…and was rewarded with a whiff of his musky scent. Oh, that scent…

She turned. Terrell stood at the railing's edge, his arms folded over his chest, looking down at the crowd in Times Square. Jade's eyes roamed his broad back, noting the definition of muscles beneath his shirt. She remembered the feel of him that night over six years ago, how she'd wanted to explore his body on a more intimate level. That thought made her face flush with warmth. But the warmth was replaced by cold when she remembered the choice he'd given her: him or Nelson. She'd chosen Nelson and had lived to regret it.

Now at thirty-four, because of Nelson, she was starting her life over. Thinking of Nelson right now made her remember her personal vow; her first priority this year was to get her life back on track careerwise. Anything else, like another relationship with a man, was something she might consider one day down the road, but not now.

Still a part of her couldn't help wondering how her life would have been different if she had chosen Terrell.

Stepping toward him, she met him at the railing. "It's quite a sight, isn't it?"

He nodded.

"Happy New Year!" a heavy-set woman dressed as an elf bellowed, then wrapped her arms around both of them in turn. Despite the fact that Jade had never even spoken to the woman tonight—she hadn't seen her until now—the woman planted a kiss on her cheek. Then she anchored herself on Terrell's arm, tipping on her toes to stretch for his cheek. He bent his knees, allowing her access.

"What a hot young man you have," the woman said when she stepped away from Terrell, fanning herself with a hand to illustrate her point. Then reaching behind her, she produced a twig of mistletoe. She didn't bother to try to hold it above their heads—Terrell was too tall—but she held it between them. "Come on, you two. It's your turn."

Instantly nervous at the prospect of getting that close to him, Jade's eyes darted to Terrell's. The corners of his lips curled upward in a slow smile. Oh, so he was cool with the idea. Jutting out her chin, she decided that if he could seem so cool about it, so could she.

But then the memory of the last time she had kissed him filled her mind and suddenly she didn't know if it would be smart to kiss him again.

"Hey, you guys," the woman said, her words slurring slightly. "What are you waiting for? Don't play bashful. Pucker up!"

Jade, determined to be as cool about this as possible, made the first move. She stepped toward Terrell, placed her palms against his chest for support, then leaned up to meet his mouth.

Beneath her fingers, she could feel his pounding heart. Maybe he wasn't as unaffected by the prospect of kissing her as he seemed to be.

Finally he reacted, wrapping his arms around her back and pulling her against him with more force than Jade expected. Her eyes fluttered shut…and she waited. Just as she popped her eyelids open, wondering what was taking him so long, he lightly brushed his lips over hers.

It was a soft, sweet kiss. Nothing like the one that had rocked her world just over six years ago, but nonetheless it made her wonder what she had missed. It ended almost as quickly as it began.

"Happy New Year," he said.

"Happy New Year to you, too," Jade replied, surprised at how breathless she sounded. She assured herself it was a result of her chest being so firmly pressed against Terrell's.

Forcing herself to look away from him, she saw that the woman was gone. As there was no longer a reason to be wrapped up in his arms, she squirmed a little, and as Terrell released his hold on her, she stepped out of his embrace.

"So…"

"So…"

Jade looked over her shoulder. "I don't want to keep you. Your girlfriend or wife must be wondering where you are."

"I don't have either."

"Oh." She was surprised. How long did a fine brother like Terrell stay unattached? "I'm surprised."

That look again. "Why?"

"I just…I figured you'd be married by now."

"The only woman I wanted broke my heart." He stared at her, his dark eyes challenging her to tell him he was lying.

That was a challenge Jade wasn't about to accept, so she did the next best thing—changed the subject. "Well, I'm getting kinda cold. I'm gonna head inside." She slipped his jacket off and passed it to him.

"Keep it," he said. "Until you warm up."

In other words, he was going to stay with her. It wasn't the worst thing, was it? She shrugged into the jacket. "Okay."

He placed a hand on the small of her back, leading her across the concrete terrace. As she walked, her heels made soft clicking sounds that seemed to match the quick tempo of her heart.

When she stepped back into the hotel suite, the warm air enveloped her. The tail end of Kool and the Gang's "Celebration" blared from speakers all around the room. Seconds later, Barry White's unmistakable voice filled the air, crooning a love song.

"Wanna dance?" Terrell asked.

Jade faced him. "Uh, sure."

He took her hand, weaving through the crowd until he

reached an empty spot near the wall. Spinning around, he faced her, pinning her with an intense expression before slipping his arms beneath his jacket to encircle her waist. Jade drew in a sharp breath as his hands nestled in the groove of her back. Leaning forward, he bent his tall frame and rested his face against hers. They hadn't seen each other in years, yet he was holding her more intimately than Nelson had held her during most of their marriage. And it felt good.

Jade slung one arm around his neck and placed her other hand on his firm, well-sculpted biceps. As Barry's deep voice serenaded them, as Terrell slowly swayed her back and forth, she couldn't help closing her eyes. She wanted to savor this feeling, the right here and right now. Just because what they'd had ended years ago didn't mean they couldn't enjoy tonight.

And it felt so good to be in his arms. Her body molded to his, her curves fitting against his hard muscles. He said nothing to her, just moved with her to the romantic melody.

Too soon, Barry White was drowned out by a funky tune. But still they held each other for an awkward moment, both of them not sure whether the other wanted to continue dancing. Jade was the one to pull away.

Terrell spoke quickly. "You want a drink?"

"No thanks. I've had enough." Maybe the few glasses of champagne explained why she'd all but melted in Terrell's arms.

"I wouldn't mind a beer. Will you wait for me?"

"I've still got your jacket."

He smiled. "Okay. I'll be right back."

Jade watched his sexy stroll as he crossed the room. Heads turned as he passed. He had that kind of presence.

She still couldn't believe Terrell was actually here at this party. If she was the type to believe in signs, she'd have to wonder at his timing; he appeared just after she'd made her New Year's wish. She hadn't wished for a man—that was the last thing she wanted—but what kind of game was fate playing with her emotions by sending her the one man she'd had such a hard time resisting.

Jade scanned the crowd. She wondered who he'd come with. A male? Female? Well, he'd abandoned whoever it was in favor of spending time with her. Though that realization made her want to smile, it really wasn't fair to monopolize his time. Besides, the way tonight was going—and half the blame could be placed squarely on her shoulders—Terrell might get the idea that they could just resume their relationship where they'd left off years ago. Jade couldn't do that. Despite the fact that she was happy to see him, that for some reason she felt alive in his arms, she wasn't ready to contemplate a relationship with him. With anyone. Maybe she would be better off today if she'd chosen Terrell that night, but she hadn't, and she was no longer the person he'd known then.

So far he hadn't asked her about the salon, for which she was grateful. She knew it was silly, but she was too embarrassed to admit to him that her mistake of marrying Nelson had cost her more than her emotional happiness.

As he made his way back to her, he walked past at least a dozen women who sent coy smiles his way, hoping to get his attention. He didn't even notice them. God help her, it seemed he only had eyes for her.

"Are you sure you don't want anything?" he asked when he returned.

"I'm fine." She swayed a little, then grabbed his forearm to balance herself. "I wouldn't mind a chair."

His face instantly registered concern. "Are you okay?"

"My feet are killing me." Jade looked down at Kathy's four-inch, open-toed, black platforms. "I don't usually wear such high heels."

He followed her gaze. "They look great."

"Thanks. The sacrifices women make for beauty."

"Let me find us a seat."

Jade wanted to tell him that she was fine on her own, but he was being so nice she didn't want to offend him. And part of her enjoyed his company. It was hard not to enjoy being around Terrell.

He placed a protective arm around her shoulders and led her through the crowd. He'd always been a gentleman, and clearly time hadn't changed that fact. Across the room were some comfortable sofas and armchairs, but all were either occupied with people or coats.

He took a pile of coats off one of the chairs, making room for her. "Sit."

"But what about those coats?"

His gaze shot to the nearby table. The next instant, he nudged aside a large, empty tray with an elbow, until he'd made sufficient room. He arranged the coats in the empty spot.

"You didn't have to do that."

"I know."

Jade leaned forward, telling herself to undo the straps at her ankles. But she really wanted to escape Terrell's soul-piercing gaze.

"Make sure you soak them when you get home."

"What?"

"Your feet."

"I'm not—" Jade stopped herself when she realized she was about to tell Terrell that she was staying here tonight. He didn't need to know that. "I'm not sure that will help."

"That bad?"

"Oh, I'll survive." She wriggled her toes, thankful she'd decided to polish the nails last week. She slipped the shoes off and sat back. "I feel bad…me sitting, you standing."

"I'll survive." A smile touched his lips, and he crouched beside her.

"Here's your jacket." Jade twisted in her seat until she'd freed herself of the jacket, then handed it to him. "I don't need it anymore."

"Thanks." He placed it on the chair's arm. "So tell me, Jade. What have you been up to?"

"Oh, just work," she hedged. "I don't have time for much else."

"And you're really divorced?"

Jade laughed mirthlessly. "Absolutely."

"I can't believe it. How could Nelson ever let a woman like you go?"

If Terrell was fishing for information, she wasn't about to supply any. Along with her personal vows for the new year, never mentioning Nelson again was right up there.

"I guess that's just life," she finally said. "I didn't plan on getting divorced, but then nobody does, I suppose. Yet fifty percent of us do."

"Yeah, times certainly have changed." He surprised her by taking her hand. Her eyes flew to his. "Look, Jade, I'd like to—"

"Jade!" Cassandra exclaimed, appearing out of nowhere. "There you are."

Jade pulled her hand from Terrell's grasp. "Hey, Cassandra."

"C'mon." Cassandra took her hand. "Get that lazy butt out of that chair. I've got someone I want you to meet."

Jade flashed Terrell an apologetic look as she slipped into her heels and refastened the straps. She had the feeling she'd been saved by the bell. "Hold that thought."

"You bet."

Terrell watched Jade's shapely form disappear into the crowd of partying guests. Cassandra holding her hand and giggling excitedly. Man oh man oh man. Was he ever glad Richard, a fellow photographer, had swung by to pick him up. The decision to come to this party was the best decision he'd made all year.

When Jade was completely out of sight, he rose, wincing at the sound of his knees cracking. Being double jointed he was used to the sound, but he couldn't help wondering if one day his old bones would give out and finally pop from overuse.

He didn't usually feel old. Active in a gym, he was in tip-top physical shape and could outperform some guys twenty years his junior. But he did feel old on nights like tonight, when he remembered he was a thirty-eight-year-old man who had never been married.

Jade. He would have married her if she hadn't married someone else. But unable to have the woman he knew was his soul mate, he hadn't been able to even consider marriage to anyone else. He loved children and wanted a family, but he didn't want it at the expense of marrying the wrong woman.

He wondered what had happened to Jade and Nelson. Had she given up on him? Or had he given up on her? Had she been faithful to him? Had he been faithful to her?

That was a silly question. He didn't have to ask to know that Jade had been faithful to her husband. She'd been faithful to him even before they'd married, some bizarre sense of loyalty prevented her from ending their engagement even though she was fiercely attracted to another man. Sure the two of them had gotten hot and heavy that one time, but that was before she'd had a ring on her finger and besides, nothing had happened. No, their marriage had not ended because of Jade's infidelity.

But none of that mattered. What did matter was that she and Nelson were no longer together. It was hard to believe, but after the countless nights he had lain awake wishing he and Jade had met before Nelson had entered her life, he was finally free to pursue her.

Fate was giving him another chance. One he was more than happy to accept. After all, he'd never stopped loving Jade, never stopped wishing that she'd followed her heart that summer night over six years ago.

How many people got a second chance like this? Not many, he was sure.

This time, he wouldn't blow it.

Chapter 5

"IS THAT TERRELL?" Cassandra asked, casting a furtive glance over her shoulder at the tall, sinfully attractive man who had just stood to his six-foot-plus height.

"Yes." Jade took a quick peek to see if he was watching her. He was. Why did the fact that he was staring at her across the room send shivers of delight dancing up her spine?

"I thought I remembered him coming into the salon. He was a photographer, right?"

"An aspiring one. He's the one who took the pictures for the salon's magazine I published. I'm not sure what he's up to now."

"You didn't ask?"

"I didn't get a chance."

"I guess not." Cassandra smirked. "I saw you two dancing. In fact, you've practically been joined at the hip since he got here."

Jade opened her mouth to clarify just who was joined at

whose hip, then promptly closed it. It was a nonissue. The truth was, though she'd been shocked to see Terrell walk into the party, she was happy to spend some time with him.

"Hey, no need to be embarrassed." Cassandra rubbed Jade's arm. "I'd say that's a helluva way to start the new year."

Jade forced a smile. "Hmm."

"All right. I won't bug you about it anymore." Cassandra slipped a hand around Jade's waist. "C'mon. Let's go meet Jeffrey Pinto."

It seemed like hours before Terrell saw Jade's smiling face again. Cassandra was no longer with her, but Jade stood chatting and laughing with a group of people who could only be actors. Terrell had taken enough head shots to know the type. Overly bubbly, always animated.

He was about to start toward her when a man moved next to her, placing a hand on the small of her back. Apparently startled, she turned to him, then flashed him a radiant smile. Terrell's stomach twisted into a tight knot. This wasn't like him, but he suddenly felt territorial. Who was this guy and why didn't Jade mind the fact that he had his hands all over her?

Terrell didn't notice he had started walking until he was halfway across the room. The tall black man still had his hand on Jade as they chatted and laughed. And chatted and laughed some more.

The moment he was near enough, Terrell placed a hand on her shoulder. Instantly she whirled around. A smile spread across her face when she saw him, and his heart leaped. "Oh, there you are, Terrell. Meet Kenny. Kenny, Terrell."

Terrell nodded at the other man. "What's up?"

"What's up?" Kenny replied.

"Kenny is Cassandra's fiancé."

"Oh." Terrell felt a tad silly for having overreacted. "Well, you shouldn't mind if I borrow Jade, then?"

"She's all yours." Kenny smiled. "I'll see you around, Jade."

Though he knew the other man was engaged, Terrell wasted no time leading her away from him. When she almost tripped over his feet in his haste, Jade flashed him a quizzical expression. "What's wrong?"

"I missed you, that's all."

"Really? I'd swear you're jealous."

He felt like a fool. "I'm sorry. I know I have no claims on you."

"That's right, Terrell. You don't."

"You're angry with me."

She paused, exhaled a slow breath. "No."

"Then will you dance with me?"

"Okay."

Slipping his arms around her waist possessively, he pulled her close. Jade moved within his arms, readjusting her body so that it wasn't pressed snugly against his. Her actions said he was moving too fast, that he was making her uncomfortable, so he relaxed his hold on her to ease the tension.

As they swayed to the music, he rested his chin beside her forehead, then looked down at her short, brown hair with auburn highlights. It was pretty much the same as it had been over six years ago, except her hair had been jet black then. He inhaled, enjoying the sweet smell of whatever conditioner she used mingled with the floral scent of her perfume. He could easily get addicted to the feel of her in his arms. "Hold me."

"I…am."

"Tighter."

She did as told but her voice betrayed her concern. "Terrell, what is it?"

"Shh." He just wanted to feel her, to hold her, to pretend

that she was his. He wanted to block out the jealousy he'd felt at seeing her with another man. Kenny wasn't Nelson. She wasn't married to Nelson anymore.

They danced in silence for a long while. Then Terrell said, "I never forgot you, Jade."

"Terrell…"

"Are you seeing someone?"

"No."

"Good." He suddenly felt the need to tell her what he'd gone through without her. "I always hoped, prayed, you'd come back to me. That you'd realize you loved me, not Nelson."

"Why are you saying this?"

"Because I realized tonight that my prayer was answered. You came back to me."

She stepped away from him and he wondered if he should have been so frank about what was on his mind. Maybe not, but he needed to get it out.

"I…I never meant to hurt you."

"I know."

"But about me coming back to you—"

"Shh." He placed a finger on her lips to silence her. "Let's not talk. Let's just concentrate on right now." He placed his arms around her, resuming the dance where they had left off. He didn't know what Jade had been about to say, and truly, he didn't want to know. He only knew that she felt so right in his arms, like she was meant to be there. Was it possible to feel even more attracted to someone after not seeing them for years? Apparently so.

He wondered if she felt the same way. Or was she merely amusing him by spending time with him?

The slow jam ended, and Jade pulled away. "I'm feeling a bit hot. I'm going outside."

"Can I join you?"

She flashed him a tentative look but finally said, "Okay."

She walked ahead of him, and he watched her shapely form in the incredibly sexy dress she wore. With each glimpse of a leg through that slit as she moved, Terrell found his thoughts growing more and more lurid. Those long, slim legs led to a bottom that was round and full and enticing. She had definitely developed a few more curves than she'd had six years ago.

He liked her this way.

Outside, she sauntered to the balcony's edge and held the railing with both hands. Terrell didn't think when he slipped his arms around hers, intimately touching the front of his body to the back of hers. Maybe it was the fact that he hadn't been with a woman in over a year, but he suddenly wanted to leave the party with Jade and show her a night she'd never forget.

"Feel like leaving?" The question escaped before he could stop it.

"You mean, with you?"

He rested his chin on the top of her head. "Why not?"

Slowly she turned in his arms, facing him. "Terrell, are you asking what I think you're asking?"

"If you'll go home with me?" It *was* what he was asking, wasn't it? He may be crazy, but he'd always regretted the fact that he'd never made her his when she'd been so willing that night. Maybe if he had shown her the full extent of his love for her, she never would have run back to Nelson. "I guess I am."

"I'm surprised."

"Why?"

She paused, then said, "Because when you had the chance years ago, you didn't take it. Not if you couldn't have the whole package. Now you want to rush into bed with me? That seems a little out of character."

He was surprised at her frankness, but she was right. He wasn't a no-strings-attached roll-in-the-hay kind of guy. Yet something about Jade made him lose all reason. "I just want to be with you."

"But you don't even know me anymore. I don't even know myself."

"I know that I want you."

"You think you want me."

He framed her face with both hands and drew her to him. "I *know* that I want you."

"Terrell!" She pushed him away from her. "What's wrong with you?"

"I'm sorry, Jade." Where had that impulse come from? The same place that his overwhelming desire to sweep her into his arms and take her home came from. "I was just trying to—"

"Forget it," she said softly. Wrapping her arms around her torso, she stepped away from him, turned her back to him. "So much time has passed, Terrell. Too much time."

Here he was blowing the one chance he promised himself he wouldn't blow. What had possessed him moments ago? That wasn't like him—propositioning a woman for a one-night stand. Even if that was his style, Jade wasn't an ordinary woman, which meant it was that much more important to prove his feelings were sincere. If and when they established a relationship, there would be plenty of time to take it to the next level. "You're right. Forget I asked."

Silence fell between them. As he regarded her back, not sure what to say, she visibly shivered. Terrell moved to her and ran both hands up and down her arms to give her warmth.

The fact that she didn't shrug him off gave him courage. "Let me say what's really on my mind."

Jade turned to face him. "Go ahead."

"Jade." He paused, let out a quick breath. "You know how much I cared about you back in the day. When I lost you… It made me wish that we'd met before you'd gotten serious with Nelson. I knew you'd made your choice, but still I couldn't help wondering how things might have been different if your fiancé wasn't in the picture. Well, meeting you here tonight, now that you're in fact unattached, it's like a wish coming true. Of course, I would have preferred not waiting so long…" His voice trailed off and he offered her a small smile. "I'd like a chance, Jade. To get to know you again." *To see if we'll be as good together as I always imagined,* he added silently.

Jade, who'd listened patiently, who'd even smiled at him in return, now sighed. On her face, he saw many conflicting emotions, and that worried him. He knew she felt something for him, that she'd reacted to his touch. Yet what he saw on her face was something entirely different than desire.

"Terrell, this has all happened so fast."

"It's been over six years in the making."

"For you, maybe. But when I married, I'd planned to marry for life."

Her words pained him, and he swallowed. "But you're not married anymore."

"I've made my share of mistakes. I know that."

"I didn't mean—"

"I'm sure you didn't, but the truth is I'm not ready for another relationship. Truly I don't know if I ever will be. Work has to be my focus now. Terrell, I hope you understand."

Understand? She didn't even want to give them a chance.

How was he supposed to understand that? "What are you saying?"

She sagged against him, then just as quickly pulled away. "I...I can't think."

"What's to think about? You either want to get to know me again, or you don't."

"It's not that simple."

"Why not?"

"Because..." But the answer died on her lips. "I'm going inside."

"Wait," he said when she started to move past him. "Okay, maybe I've come on too strong. But when I lost you before, I lost your friendship, too. I don't want to lose that this time. At least give me your number. Let me call you."

"Relax, Terrell." She grinned as she affectionately squeezed his forearm. "I'm coming back. I just have to go to the washroom, okay?"

Terrell's shoulders drooped with relief. He felt like a fool. "Of course."

She left him standing on the terrace. Though he was tempted to follow her to the washroom door, he stood where he was and watched her hustle inside. He needed the cold winter air to clear his head. Jade needed a little breathing space; they both did. When had he become so impatient?

Turning, he looked down at the crowd that still lingered in the Square. Several hundred people had left, but many others still lingered, partying in the streets. The ground was a sea of colored confetti.

Terrell rested a hip against the railing. He wasn't that impatient, was he? Six years was a long time to wait for a woman. Long enough, as far as he was concerned. He didn't want to wait another day.

* * *

Much later, Jade lay on a comforter in the bedroom, unable to sleep. Except for two voices she could hear outside the room, the suite was quiet. As well it should be. Daylight had already begun to light the horizon.

She felt like an idiot.

When she'd gone to the bathroom hours earlier, she'd had every intention of returning to Terrell. But instead of making her way back to him on the terrace, she'd escaped to the bedroom instead. She'd suddenly realized that going back to Terrell was a dangerous thing to do. She didn't trust herself around him. Being near him, she felt things she didn't want to feel. If he hadn't taken back his offer to head to his place, she might well have been tempted to leave with him and finally give in to the passion that consumed her.

But a one-night stand with Terrell, the man she'd almost left her fiancé for years ago, would have been a mistake. For Terrell, it would have been much more than just a night of sex, and in the end, giving in to her desire would only cause them both pain. Jade had had enough pain. And though once long ago she'd been tempted to let her desires rule her actions, she was a different person now, a person who had nothing to offer Terrell and knew there was no point even pretending otherwise. After a failed marriage and a scarred heart, she'd pretty much given up on love. Now all she wanted was to do hair, to reopen her salon. Reclaiming that dream required that she give it her complete attention.

Terrell had survived without her for over six years. Though he said he hadn't forgotten her, Jade wasn't naive enough to believe she was the only woman for him. In this day and age, men and women fell in and out of love so often it was almost a joke. Just because he hadn't found someone to settle down with in the years they'd spent apart didn't mean he never would. And Jade would bet he'd had plenty of women over the past years.

Jade rolled onto her side, resting her head in the crook of her arm. It was best that she and Terrell go their separate ways. For both their sakes.

Chapter 6

IT WAS LATE AFTERNOON when Jade stepped into the Brooklyn apartment she shared with Kathy. Immediately her friend, who had clearly been awaiting her arrival on the living room sofa, jumped up to greet her as she entered.

"Well, well, well," Kathy said in a singsong voice, a smile playing on her lips. "If it isn't the prodigal roommate!"

"Morning, Kathy."

"*Morning?* Hon, look outside. It's late afternoon."

"Happy New Year to you, too."

Kathy placed both hands firmly on her hips. "Oh, no, you don't."

"Don't what?" Jade finally took a moment to dump her bags off her shoulder.

"Don't you dare keep the details from me." Kathy's eyes danced with excitement. "Well, it must be a new millennium.

Jade Alexander actually had a one-night stand! Or is this the beginning of a new affair?"

Jade slipped out of her coat. "Sorry to disappoint you, Kathy, but I did *not* have a one-night stand. I stayed at the suite with Cassandra. The party ended way too late to even contemplate going home last night."

Kathy flashed her a look that said she didn't believe a word she said. "And you just *happened* to walk in with an overnight bag?"

Jade kicked off her boots. "No. Cassandra had invited me to come over earlier if I wanted, and after you left for work yesterday, I realized that I'd better head into Manhattan before evening if I ever wanted to make it to Times Square. End of mystery."

Kathy frowned, and Jade knew she finally believed her. "Oh. That's no fun."

"At least I took your advice and went out. And I wore the taupe dress."

"And still spent the night alone…?" Her voice trailing off, she scratched her head as if contemplating the world's most baffling puzzle.

Free of her physical burdens, Jade strolled into the living room. "So how was work last night?"

"My God, it was brutal. Security was running around all night, kicking people out of the hotel lobby. Everyone and their dog kept coming inside to keep warm. It was total chaos." She plopped down on the sofa. "On the positive side, I did get a few phone numbers from some eligible bachelors."

"A woman who knows her priorities." Jade sat across from Kathy on the love seat.

"No doubt. But nothing will come of it. They're all from out of town."

"And what about Tyrone?"

"I haven't heard from him."

"Did you call him?"

"No."

"So it's really over?"

"Jade, it has to be. He's too young for me."

Jade tried to read Kathy's expression, but it gave nothing away. "Well, I'm sorry to hear that. You know me—I'm no advocate of relationships, but you're one person I'd like to see settle down."

"Settling down is overrated."

As Kathy said the words, she picked at fluff on her sweater, a telltale sign to anyone who'd known her for any length of time that she wasn't telling the truth. Kathy had been engaged once, eight years ago, but her fiancé had suddenly changed his mind about marrying her and had moved to a military base in Germany. Kathy had been crushed, and after that, from what Jade had deciphered, she'd totally changed her mind about commitment. Deep down, Jade knew that Kathy wanted what most people wanted—a faithful, loving partner and a normal family life. But having her heart broken, she was too scared to take the risk.

Jade had taken the risk and had failed. She wouldn't take that risk again. Part of the problem, aside from a broken heart, was the knowledge that she couldn't have children. It had always been a bone of contention between her and Nelson, and she was sure it would be with other men. And as crazy as she told herself the thought was, a part of her wondered if Nelson would have hurt her the way he did if she'd given him a child. Maybe his frustration with their situation was what led him to drink and gamble and eventually knock up someone else.

"So how was the party?"

Kathy's voice pulled Jade from the bitter memories. "It was great. A lot of fun."

"And?"

"And nothing. It was a party." Jade folded her hands in her lap.

"You know something, Jade? You are so transparent. I ask you a question you don't like, and what do you do? Fold your hands every time. That means there's something else going on you don't want me to know about."

Jade was about to tell Kathy that she was pretty transparent, too, especially when picking fluff off her clothing with painstaking detail, but decided against it.

"C'mon. Tell me."

"Girlfriend, you live for gossip."

"You know it. So tell me."

Jade sighed. Kathy must have some type of radar; she always knew when there was a story to be told that involved a man.

"All right. But it's no big deal, really. It's just—"

"Tell me!"

The corners of Jade's lips twitched, and for the life of her, she didn't know why. She had no reason to smile. Like a coward, she'd run out on Terrell and had no way of reaching him. Still when she remembered the way he'd held her close when dancing, the way his eyes had lit up each time he looked at her, she wanted to smile. "Remember Terrell?"

"You mean Mr. Oh-So-Fine Terrell Edmonds? The one you were nuts about years ago?"

"I wasn't nuts about him."

"Oh, sure you weren't. You may have married Nelson, but you didn't fool me."

Jade silenced her with an exasperated look. "Do you want to hear the story or not?"

"Sorry. So what happened? Don't tell me you met Terrell again? Oh, my God—he was at the party!"

"Yep."

"Darn, why did I go to work last night? Seeing you two together would have been priceless."

"There was nothing to see." An image of Terrell, standing across the terrace, smiling at her in the first few seconds of the new year, filled her mind. Jade shook her head, trying to toss the image from her brain.

"Yeah, right. Then why the silly smile on your face?"

Man, what was wrong with her? "We had a good time. We talked, we danced a bit."

"Is he married?"

"No." Jade swallowed, remembering his reason for not marrying. "He said the only woman he ever wanted married someone else."

"Get out!" Kathy placed a hand over her mouth to stifle her squeal of delight. "I told you then that man had it for you bad. He's still in love with you."

"Don't be ridiculous. That was more than six years ago, Kathy."

"Love, when you find it, is timeless."

Jade flashed her friend a skeptical look. "And how would you know?"

"I…I'm not stupid. I saw how Terrell used to look at you."

"Yeah, well, that was a long time ago. We've both changed."

"How does he look now?"

"Just as fine as before. He's bald now, though. I like it."

"Mmm. And when do I get to see him again?"

Jade fiddled with the throw cushion beside her. "I—I don't know."

Kathy's smile faded. "Oh, no. What does that mean?"

"It means that last night was…last night. It was nice, but that's all. I don't have time for a relationship. I don't want another one. Reopening my salon has to be my number-one priority."

"In other words, you didn't give him your number." When Jade was silent, Kathy said, "Oh, man. What's wrong with you?"

Her friend's words made Jade see red. "Nothing is wrong with me. I don't want to be like you, seeking the warmth of a man's body to mend my broken heart." At Kathy's stricken look, Jade covered her face with the throw cushion, then tossed it on her lap. "I'm sorry. I didn't mean that the way it sounded."

"Sure you did. And that's okay." Kathy stood. "I get the point. What you do with your life is your business. Just like what I do with my life is mine."

"Kathy," Jade said, rising to meet her. But Kathy was already walking out of the living room. Seconds later, her bedroom door slammed shut.

Stupid, stupid, stupid! Jade chastised herself. Then she grabbed the throw cushion and threw it across the room.

The dream was always the same.

He was standing at the front of the packed church, his eyes flitting over the crowd, waiting. After several seconds, the back doors opened and she entered, wearing a spectacular wedding gown. No music played as she walked down the aisle toward him, her face expressionless. But when she was a mere few feet away from him, almost within his grasp, Nelson appeared at the back of the church. Suddenly she turned from him and started walking toward Nelson. The guests turned, too, and the back instantly became the front. He tried yelling, but nobody seemed to hear him. Jade didn't even turn. She simply walked into Nelson's arms and embraced him, much to the delight of the guests. The next instant, he was outside on the church's steps, yanking on the locked door.

A phone rang. He didn't remember sticking his cell phone in his tuxedo pocket.

Terrell bolted upright, realizing that the ringing phone was actually beside his bed. Without thinking he rolled over and snatched the receiver. "Hello?"

"Mr. Edmonds, did I wake you?"

"Who is this?"

"Mr. Edmonds, this is Tony Carracciolo."

Terrell's brain cleared and he recognized the Italian accent before the man finished identifying himself. "Hello, Mr. Carracciolo. How are you?"

"Is this a bad time? I can call you later."

A quick glance told him it was just after 1:00 p.m. He'd slept that long? "No. No, that's okay."

"Good. I won't keep you long. I suppose you know why I'm calling."

"Yes, I do." Mr. Carracciolo, the man behind Carracciolo Designs in Milan, had recently offered him a position as his house photographer. An assistant had first called him with the offer, telling him to take as much time as he needed to consider it. However, two days later, Mr. Carracciolo himself had phoned in an effort to influence his decision.

"And have you given my offer any consideration?"

"I need a bit more time," Terrell replied, swinging his legs over the side of the bed. The cool air chilled his skin. Before last night, he'd been seriously considering the job. It would provide a change of pace, one he'd felt his life needed. Since he didn't have any commitments here—namely a woman— he wouldn't mind the move. Now having met Jade again had Terrell rethinking Milan.

"I am prepared to increase the remuneration."

The designer had already made a very generous offer. "I'm tempted, Mr. Carracciolo, really tempted, but I can't make a decision yet. There's been a…new development here. Something I have to take care of before I decide."

"I want you on my team. You know that. Whatever you want, just ask."

"I appreciate the offer—I really do. But right now, all I really need is time. Can you wait a month?" He'd had two weeks so far. "I'll give you a definite answer by then."

"I will wait, yes, but I do hope that you will decide before then."

"I hope so, too."

"I look forward to your reply. Have a good day, Mr. Edmonds."

"Take care. I'll be in touch."

When the older man hung up, Terrell replaced the receiver. For a moment, he thought himself a fool for putting off Mr. Carracciolo another month. This opportunity was fabulous. How often would he get such a chance? To put it all on hold for Jade, surely that was nuts.

But he had to see what could happen.

Terrell frowned. What a challenge that would be, considering she hadn't given him her number. Man, he *was* nuts, sitting here giving Jade a second thought after she'd made it clear last night that she wanted nothing to do with him. But God help him, he couldn't help thinking about her. She was an enigma, and he couldn't quite figure her out. He hadn't imagined her body softening in his arms, the flash of desire in her dark eyes. Or had he?

Before he'd known it was her, he'd seen her back as she'd stood at the balcony's railing, and had immediately been drawn to her. And it wasn't just because she wore that incredible dress that hugged every inch of her incredible body; he'd sensed something familiar about her. Then when she'd slowly turned and faced him, it was almost as if time had stopped. Their eyes had met, and realization had hit him like a ton of bricks. And just like the last time he had held her in his arms, he'd wanted her. After everything, it didn't make sense, yet he had. He was sure she felt something, too, because in those dark brown eyes of hers he'd seen a spark of interest. Of something.

But if it had been a spark of interest, then why hadn't she given him a way to reach her? She was no longer married, so that wasn't an issue. And she claimed she wasn't involved with anyone currently. So what was the problem?

Terrell thrummed his fingers on the mattress as he contemplated the only logical answer to that question. He didn't like the answer one bit, but how could he ignore it?

The truth was, Jade hadn't given him a way to reach her. She'd had the chance to do so but had run away instead. Without a way to reach her, Terrell had to face the facts. As far as having a future with Jade, the chances were slim to none.

Chapter 7

"EXCUSE ME, MISS."

Jade abruptly stopped at the table where a middle-aged couple sat. The woman was clearly not pleased. Jade asked, "Is something wrong?"

"Yes, there's something wrong," the woman snapped. "I specifically asked that the onions be sautéed. That's the only way I eat my onions."

Jade didn't remember the woman asking anything about onions, but she consulted her notepad to be sure. She was right. The woman had asked for tomatoes and mushrooms, and Swiss cheese instead of cheddar. Still she said, "I'm sorry. I'll get that for you right now."

"By the time you bring out the onions, my dinner will be cold. I'd like a fresh dinner."

Though a feeling of annoyance spread over her, Jade smiled. She had learned to deal with difficult people over the past year that she had been waitressing. "Okay." She picked up the woman's plate, noting that there were considerably fewer fries. "I'll tell the kitchen to put a rush on that for you."

Jade was about to head for the kitchen when she heard the woman whisper, "I hope you don't mind eating without me. Who knows how long this new plate will take to arrive."

Annoyance turned to anger, but Jade did her best not to show it. Some people expected the world for a seven-dollar burger. "Sir, would you like me to get you a fresh plate of pasta as well?"

He shook his head. "Don't worry about me. I'm perfectly fine." As he said the last words, he glared at his date.

A small smile lifted Jade's lips. At least she knew she wasn't overreacting to the woman's requests. "I'll be back in a few minutes, ma'am."

The kitchen was busy when she entered, dishes clattering, skillets sizzling, voices carrying orders. She stopped before the head cook, calling his name.

Mike faced her. "What?"

Jade frowned at his irritated voice. He might be having a bad night, but so was she. Despite her bad mood, she had to present a smiling face to customers, so the least Mike could do was be a little more professional. "Mike, I need another order of this." She passed the plate to him across the metal shelf that housed fresh orders of food. "She claims she wanted sautéed onions with the burger, and now doesn't want her meal to get cold while she waits for them."

"Sheesh. I don't have time for this crap. Tell her to get a life."

"As much as I'd like to, you know I can't. She won't be happy unless she gets a new burger. Can you please just start up a fresh one?"

Mike's lips twisted in a scowl. Angrily he grabbed the plate. "All right. Give me a few minutes. I'll sauté the onions, reheat the patty, throw it on a fresh bun, give her some fresh fries. Will that suit Her Highness?"

"I won't tell her," Jade replied. There was nothing wrong with the beef patty, so that wasn't the issue. "I'll be back in a sec."

She hurried to a computer terminal to ring in new orders of food. *Oh no,* she thought, realizing she'd forgotten to ring in a well-done steak. How long ago had she taken that order? At least five minutes. But the case of the missing sautéed onions had thrown her off course.

She entered the code to put a rush on the steak, hoping Mike wouldn't be totally peeved with her. It was a busy Saturday night as usual, and mistakes were often made.

Seconds later she went back to the kitchen and approached Mike. The old plate of fries sat under a heat lamp, free for any staff member to munch on. When he saw her, he all but hurled the new plate at her. Biting her tongue, she quickly picked it up. "And Mike, sorry to do this, but I need a rush on that steak."

"Yeah, yeah." He went back to the grill and poured oil into a skillet.

Jade was about to ask if he'd heard her, but didn't bother. Mike was often miserable, no doubt because of the stress of working in the kitchen. Still she hoped he gave that steak top priority. She didn't want another angry customer.

Unlike the kitchen staff, she relied on her tips to make a decent living.

Terrell was just about to remove the roll of film from the camera when he heard the doorbell. Hurrying from the darkroom, he rushed down the stairs in his loft. This late in the evening, it was probably Greg, his assistant, bringing by the photos from the lab down the street.

Just as he reached for the lock, the doorbell sounded again. He turned the lock, then swung the door open.

"Hi." Her voice sound raspy and seductive. "You're home."

His mouth slackened when he saw the tall, ebony beauty. "Keisha. Wh-what are you doing here?"

She smiled. "Can I come in?"

Taking a step backward, he held the door open in invitation. She did a sexy strut into the room, her long faux fur coat dancing around her heels. It was then that Terrell saw the bottle of wine she held.

"Uh, what—what's going on?" he asked.

Keisha slipped out of the coat and passed it to him. Terrell held it while she bent to take off her high-heeled boots. Only when she stood did she finally reply. "I wanted to see you. You've been so busy, I decided to take a chance coming over." She planted a soft kiss on his cheek, then whispered, "Happy New Year."

"Happy New Year." For Keisha, he'd been deliberately busy, hoping she would disappear from his life. It wasn't that he didn't like her; she just wanted more from him than he was willing to give. He'd told her repeatedly that he didn't want more than friendship from her, yet she still spoke of "waiting for his love." Terrell had finally realized that the best thing to do was cut her off.

"I missed you."

"Keisha, this isn't the best time. I was just about to develop some pictures."

"You and work. Has anyone ever told you you're a workaholic?"

"My mom. All the time."

Keisha framed his face with one hand, rubbing the pad of

her thumb back and forth across his skin. "You should listen to her. Take some time to enjoy your life. Let's sit."

He didn't want to hurt her. In a way, they were kindred spirits, both having looked for love in a lot of wrong places. For that reason, he let her take his hand and lead him into the living room. She sank into the leather sofa, forcing him down beside her. "Tonight, you're going to relax. I'm going to make sure of it."

"Are you?"

"Yes." She crossed one slim leg over the other, then flung her hair over a shoulder. No doubt for his benefit. "I figured I should start the new year off right and do a good deed."

"You make me feel like an abandoned pet."

Her head fell backward as she laughed. "That, you certainly aren't. Not that I would mind adopting you."

Uncomfortable, Terrell looked away. "Keisha, why—"

"Shh." Placing a finger beneath his chin, she angled his face to meet hers. "Terrell, I know what you've said about not being ready for a relationship." When he opened his mouth to speak, she clamped a hand over his lips. "I—I understand that. And I'm willing to wait for you. But in the meantime, can't we just enjoy each other?" Removing her hand from his mouth, she winked. "I promise I don't bite."

Keisha was extremely beautiful and part of him was tempted to take what she was offering. Maybe one night of passionate sex with someone like her was exactly what he needed to take his mind off Jade.

Taking the bottle of wine from his hands, she stood. "I'll pour the wine."

Terrell watched her go, her spandex-covered hips swaying every step of the way. When she was out of sight, he dragged a hand over his face. Oh, man. For the first time in his thirty-eight years, he wondered if something was wrong with him.

He heard the cupboards open and close as she searched for glasses. Most men would be thrilled to spend time with a woman like Keisha. She was beautiful, sexy, willing. Despite the fact she knew he wasn't interested in a serious relationship, she was still willing to give him her body for his pleasure. Another man would take what she was offering without a second thought.

Why couldn't he?

Maybe, just maybe he could, if he could actually find it in his heart to believe they might have a future. But now more than ever, he knew that wasn't possible. Not when Jade constantly occupied his thoughts.

Jade, a woman who wanted nothing to do with him. Yet here was Keisha, a woman who wanted whatever piece of him she could get.

Her soft footfalls on the hardwood floor snapped him from his thoughts. Rising to his six-foot-two height, Terrell stood before her. As he opened his mouth to speak, she passed him a wineglass filled with the rose-colored liquid and said, "Let's make a toast. To keeping our options open this new year."

Terrell could drink to that. She clinked her glass to his, then took a slow sip. He followed her example, enjoying the dry, rich flavor of the wine.

"Have you eaten?" she asked.

"I had a sandwich."

She flashed him the kind of concerned look his mother gave him when she said she was worried about his health. "A sandwich is hardly enough. I can make you some dinner."

"That's not necessary."

"I know," she said, placing the wineglass on the black lacquer coffee table. "I want to."

Terrell placed his glass beside hers, then faced her. "Keisha, don't."

"Why not? A dinner is hardly a commitment."

Hurting her was not something he wanted to do, but she seemed determined to leave him no other choice. "Keisha, I know you say you don't want to pressure me, but I actually feel very pressured right now. The more you do for me, the more you say you love me, the guiltier I feel."

Suddenly she threw her arms around his neck, surprising the heck out of him. "Please don't tell me to go. Terrell, let me stay. Even if it is just this night."

"Keisha, no. I can't give you what you want. And if I have sex with you and don't love you, you'll eventually hold that against me."

"No, I won't. I just want to be with you."

Her mouth covered his in a desperate kiss, and he didn't pull away. As she sighed into his mouth, he closed his eyes and prayed that he'd feel something, *anything*. If only to get Jade out of his mind.

But as her soft lips moved over his, as she pressed her body to his, Terrell couldn't help imagining that it was Jade's lips on his, Jade's hands around his neck.

Jade who wanted him.

He broke away from Keisha, abruptly ending the kiss. Disappointment marring her beautiful features, she stared up at him expectantly.

His thoughts swirling around like a tornado in his head, he stepped away from her. He never should have let her get that close to him. But at least he knew now what he'd always suspected. He didn't have any feelings for her.

A hand touched his arm. "Terrell, it's okay. We don't have to rush it."

He faced her. "Keisha, you don't get it. I don't want to hurt you, but…you and me… It won't work."

A quick flicker in her brown eyes was the only indication that his words had affected her. "All right. I'll go. But first, let me say something."

"Go ahead."

"Promise me you'll hear me out."

"Okay."

She took a deep breath, exhaled slowly. "I know you don't love me. Maybe you never will. But I think we can be good together. I never would have thought this ten years ago, but maybe I don't need love. I just want a partner. I think you'd make a good one."

"I don't—"

She held up a hand, silencing him. "Hear me out. Would it be so bad—you and me? We wouldn't have to get married. And I wouldn't expect anything other than friendship. But I'm not getting any younger. And…and I'd like to…have children."

Terrell's eyes nearly popped out of his head. *"What?"*

She looked away, then back at him. "It's not so unusual. Women want to have children all the time. I…I just figured since I have no one else… I know other women who've had friends father their children."

"Absolutely not." All along, he'd thought her crazy for still pursuing him, yet she wasn't crazy at all. She was a woman with a mission, an ulterior motive, and probably would have slept with him first, filled him in on her plan later, if she'd had it her way.

Well, as much as Terrell wanted to have children one day, he surely wasn't going to have them with a woman he didn't love.

"You wouldn't have to be part of the child's life," Keisha added, clearly hoping to warm him to the idea. She placed a hand on his forearm and gently squeezed. "Nor mine. C'mon, Terrell. Think about it."

The expression he turned on her said he was sure she'd lost

her mind. "Keisha…" He wanted to tell her she was crazy, but thought better of that. "I want you to go. I can't be the man you want. And the last thing I want to do is bring a child into this world who isn't conceived out of love."

"Dammit, Terrell, I'm not asking for marriage."

"You're asking for more than I can give."

She gave him one last pleading look before she marched toward the door, her head of weaved hair bouncing every step of the way.

Man, what was this world coming to?

He followed her to the door, took her coat from the coat tree and passed it to her. "I'm sorry I can't give you what you want, Keisha." She didn't reply as she hurriedly dressed in her outerwear. "And I think it's best if you don't call me, don't drop by. Not unless you're willing to accept that I can't offer you more than friendship."

Her mouth fell open at that remark. "I don't need another friend, Terrell."

He shrugged, feeling bad for her but not knowing what else to do. "Let me grab your wine."

"You keep it. Toast your loneliness. God only knows how a red-blooded male survives without a woman for so long."

He didn't dignify her comment with a response.

"Good-bye," she said curtly.

"Later." He closed the door behind her.

Not a pretty scene, he thought, taking a moment to exhale his frustration. Again, he wondered why he was so different from other men who would ruthlessly enjoy Keisha's body and not care if they hurt her.

Because he just wasn't that type of man. Didn't want to be. His love for his mother made it impossible for him to disrespect a woman.

But a small part of him had been tempted to take what Keisha was offering. If he could lose himself in mindless sex, he might just be able to forget about Jade.

Jade. There she was, on his mind again. He had to forget her. The way she had forgotten him.

With that thought, Terrell rammed his hands in his jeans pockets and slowly walked toward the stairs. He may as well get back to work.

Her heart pounding, Jade raced to the front of the restaurant. She stopped in front of the host, who stood at the podium skimming a magazine. "George, did you see table fourteen leave?"

"You mean the two guys?"

"Yeah."

"Mmm-hmm. They left about five minutes ago."

A chill raced down Jade's spine. "Did they leave the payment with you?" Sometimes customers left it with a host or another staff member, to make sure it didn't go missing.

George shook his head. "Naw, they didn't give me anything. But you can check with Isabel."

Isabel was the bus person. When she cleared tables, she often picked up money. Jade's panic level went down a notch. "Thanks."

Whirling around on her heel, she saw Isabel at the opposite end of the restaurant. She hurried toward her, her heart still racing. Those two men had been so nice. They wouldn't have stiffed her, would they?

"Isabel." Jade was somewhat breathless when she spoke. "Did you see any money on table fourteen?"

"No, I didn't see anything."

In her late forties, Isabel had been working at The Red

Piano for seven years, ever since she had emigrated from
Puerto Rico. Unlike some of the other bussing staff, Jade
trusted her completely. "Oh, no."

"What's the matter?"

Instantly she had a migraine. "They stiffed me!"

"Why not check with George?"

"I did," Jade replied, squeezing her forehead. "They didn't
leave the money with him."

"I'm so sorry."

Jade groaned. "They both had lobster." And wine. And
desert. Their bill was over seventy dollars. "Damn!"

"Oh, my."

"You're sure, Isabel? You didn't see anything there when
you cleared the table?"

She shook her head. "Not even a tip. I'm so sorry, Jade."

"It's okay." It wasn't, but interrogating Isabel wouldn't
help. "I'll ask the other servers, just in case."

Jade made her way to the kitchen. She would make the
rounds, as if anyone had seen her money, but she wasn't about
to hold her breath.

She knew she'd been stiffed.

Hours later, Jade's feet were killing her. Finally the last of
the tables had left and she was actually leaving early for a
Saturday night—just after 11 P.M.—because Sandra had vol-
unteered to work until closing for her. Thank God, for Jade
didn't know how much more of tonight she could take.

For all her efforts, the walkout had made the evening a total
waste. A few of her colleagues had pitched in to help cover
her loss, but it hadn't been enough to cover the entire bill. Now
she was heading home with less than ten bucks in tips.

As she sat on the bench in the change-room, she lowered

her head, then covered her face with her hands. She fought the tears but they escaped anyway.

How was she going to do this? How was she going to put her life back together? No matter how hard she tried to forget what Nelson had done to her and move on, the constant reminder was always there. He'd stolen money from their salon, then left her to clean up the mess. His new girlfriend was from a wealthy background and had enough money to give Nelson the cash he needed to support his gambling addiction. But Jade had nobody.

Not that she wanted someone to take care of her and solve her problems, but sitting on the bench, with a lousy few bucks in her wallet, she realized how incredibly alone she really was. And she was starting to wonder if she'd ever open another salon. How could she, when she was barely making enough money to live on?

What a horrible way to start the new year. She'd only been stiffed one other time—two teenagers had ordered a couple of burgers and left without paying. The bill had been less than twenty dollars and hadn't ruined her entire night. Tonight's walkout was much worse.

Maybe tonight's negative turn of events was only further proof that she should give up her dream. She couldn't see herself reopening Dreamstyles in the foreseeable future.

No, she decided, angrily brushing her tears away. She could not give up her dream. Would not. It was the only thing she had to hold on to.

Nelson would not have the last laugh.

Chapter 8

OUTSIDE KATHY'S BEDROOM DOOR, Jade raised a hand to knock, then paused. Instead, she listened for sound. Hearing none, she realized Kathy might still be sleeping and wondered if she should wait until later.

No, she decided. She wouldn't wait. Their argument two days ago weighed heavily on her mind, and Jade wanted to resolve the issue. Ever since their disagreement, she and Kathy had carefully stayed out of each other's way to the point where you'd think they were two strangers living together. Now Jade wanted to heal the rift between them. Kathy was her best friend and she needed her.

Hoping that Kathy was ready to talk, Jade knocked.

"Come in," Kathy called softly from behind the closed door. She obviously wasn't sleeping.

Placing her hand on the knob, Jade slowly turned it. Kathy sat cross-legged on the bed, still dressed in silk pajamas. For a moment, the two merely stared at each other, then after several seconds, a tentative smile lifted Kathy's lips. Relief washing over her, Jade smiled and walked into the room.

Kathy scurried to her feet, meeting Jade halfway. Arms outstretched, she offered her a hug, and Jade readily accepted it.

"I'm sorry."

"I'm sorry."

They spoke in unison. After a moment's pause, the two looked at each other, then burst into laughter.

"Come here, you." Taking Jade's hand, Kathy led her to the bed. They both sat. "Jade, I'm sorry. I didn't mean to pry into your life."

"No, Kathy, I'm the one who should be sorry. I didn't mean what I said. That kinda just came out, and it came out the wrong way."

"But you're right. I guess in a way I have been looking for comfort with different guys. I thought I was over him, but Sheldon still has a piece of my heart."

Jade squeezed her friend's hand. "I figured that."

"I'll get over him. I know I will. But sometimes it's just really hard to forget your first love, ya know?"

Instantly Terrell's sexy image invaded Jade's mind. She pushed it aside. "Kathy, you're a grown woman. I hardly have the right to tell you what to do with your life."

Kathy smiled, seeming to appreciate that comment. "I know. But as stubborn as I can be sometimes, I actually value your opinion. I hope you value mine."

"I do."

"I know I was out of line, but when I mentioned that you should have taken a chance on Terrell, I had the best intentions at heart. I know that man really loved you, unlike your ex."

Deep in her heart, Jade knew it, too, but she didn't like being reminded. She looked away.

"There I go again. Prying."

Jade's eyes met her friend's. "No, you're not. I suppose it's a touchy issue only because it's true. I should have at least given Terrell my number, but I got scared." She shrugged. "Well, there's nothing I can do about it now. I don't know how to reach him. He doesn't know how to reach me."

If Kathy wanted to make a comment, she didn't. Instead, she said, "So we're cool again?"

Jade hugged her. "We're cool."

"Great. I hate it when you're angry with me."

"Hey, you were angry with me."

They both giggled.

Kathy spoke first. "Are you working tonight?"

"Not tonight. I switched shifts with someone else." She told Kathy about the walkout. "So, I'm not really in the mood to—"

The phone beside Kathy's bed rang, and Kathy grabbed it before it could ring a second time. "Hello?... Oh, sure. She's right here."

"Who is it?" Jade whispered.

Covering the mouthpiece, Kathy said, "A woman."

Jade took the phone from her. "Hello?"

"Jade!"

"Cassandra." Jade turned in time to see Kathy walk out of the bedroom. "What's up, girlfriend?"

"You got the job!"

Jade's stomach fluttered. "I did? I got it?"

"Yes!" Cassandra squealed with delight. "Jeff loved you."

"Oh, my God." Jade could hardly believe her ears. "You're not playing, are you?"

"Girlfriend, I am dead serious. I don't think it really mattered to Jeff one way or another, but after he met you he was really impressed. He said you're beautiful, nice, and easy to get along with."

Jade's heart was pounding so fast, she thought it would burst out of her chest. "Thanks so much, Cassandra. This is just the news I needed." After last night's disaster at work, she needed a sign that she still had a shot at her dream. "Thank you!"

"No problem. I just want to help you any way I can." She paused, then said, "Now the shoot's gonna take place next Monday, the tenth. Is that okay for you?"

It wasn't, as Jade was scheduled to work, but she'd get out of it. "Sure, it's cool."

"Good. The crew is going to do the shoot at my place in Greenwich Village, and it'll be early: nine A.M."

"That's hardly early."

"Ugh. It is for me."

Jade chuckled softly. She remembered all too well how hard it was for Cassandra to make it to the salon before eleven in the morning. "You'd better be up. After all, you're the star."

"Yeah," she replied softly. "I am." Snapping out of her wistful moment, she said, "All right. Jeff's gonna call you with the monetary details. I believe it will be a flat rate. Something like five hundred dollars."

Five hundred dollars! Silently, Jade mouthed "Yes!" Man, could she ever use that kind of cash.

"It's not much, but Jeff did say that if he liked your work, he might hire you for future shoots."

Not much? It was certainly fine by her. But Jade did understand the point Cassandra was making. The bigger picture was getting more jobs. The pay, at this point, was a bonus. "Cassandra, I'm just so thankful for the opportunity. You're the best."

"Just make sure you do one heck of a job. I have a good feeling about this."

"So do I, Cassandra." She also felt totally nervous, but nerves she could handle. "I look forward to Jeff's call."

When she hung up the phone, Jade ran into the living room, anxious to share her good news. For the first time in a long time, things were looking up for her.

"You're sure?" Terrell asked, holding the cell phone to his ear.

"There's no listing for any J. Alexander."

She wouldn't still be using her maiden name, would she? "Try J. Crumm. C-r-u-m-m."

Her heard the clicking sounds of the operator's fingers hitting the keyboard. Seconds later, she said, "I've got an N. Crumm on West Fifty-seventh."

"That's not it." If Jade had been living there with Nelson, she certainly wasn't now. And he didn't imagine she'd still have a phone listed under his name.

"Anything else, sir?"

Terrell clucked his tongue. "No. That's all, thanks."

Using his chin, he flipped his cell phone closed, then tossed it onto the passenger seat. He'd told himself he wouldn't do this, that he would forget about Jade. What point was there in dwelling on a woman who wanted nothing to do with him?

Terrell slowed, then turned onto a residential street. The scene before him was as picturesque as a postcard. The tall pines and maples, covered with a good two inches of snow, looked majestic beneath the street and moonlight. Yesterday New York and northern New Jersey had been hit with a sudden winter storm, blanketing several cities with inches of snow. The white Christmas was late, just like it had been the last few years.

If he was smart, he would be at home in front of a fire

instead of in his car, making the trek to Maplewood, New Jersey, but Terrell didn't want to miss his mother's birthday. The drive could have been worse. At least he'd given himself plenty of time to get to his destination.

Seconds later, Terrell turned into the driveway of the two-story Cape Cod–style house on Crowell Place, maneuvering his Jeep carefully in the thick snow. His brother's Chevy Blazer was parked behind his parents' Ford Explorer. They all drove sport utility vehicles; Terrell had made sure of that. In winter weather, he wanted to know his family was as safe as possible on the roads.

Once outside his vehicle, Terrell gingerly lifted the large, gift-wrapped box from the backseat, then nudged the door shut with his hip. Snow continued to fall, and he carefully made his way to the front steps. He had seen his family over the Christmas holiday, but even now as he rang the doorbell, he smiled. He would never tire of them.

His mother, a short, heavy-set woman with graying hair, opened the door. Her eyes lit up in that special way that always warmed his heart. "Terrell!"

"Ma," he said, stepping into the vestibule. Leaning forward, he planted a wet kiss on her cheek. "Happy birthday!"

The pounding of small feet caught his attention, and Terrell looked up in time to see his niece and nephew charging toward the front door. "Uncle T!" Their voices mingled as one.

"Hey, Sadé. Hey, Kwame."

"You two wait until your uncle has taken off his shoes and coat," his mother scolded. But she had a smile on her face.

Sadé turned and ran toward the living room, followed closely by her younger brother. When they were gone, Terrell passed the gift to his mother. "Here you go, Ma."

"Is this for me?"

"Uh, I'm not sure. I might auction it off to the highest bidder, earn myself some extra cash." Her face twisted in a playful scowl, and he chuckled. "Of course it's for you."

"Oh, it's heavy. I wonder what it is."

"Don't open it yet." Terrell loved surprising the people he loved. "Wait until after dinner, at least."

Mrs. Edmonds tried shaking the package, then frowned when that didn't tell her anything.

"After dinner." Terrell hung his leather jacket on the coat tree.

His brother, Drew, stood as Terrell entered the living room. Though Drew was the older brother, Terrell was the taller one. Drew hugged and patted him on the back. "Hey, Big T."

"What's up, D?" Glancing over his brother's shoulder, he saw Lena sitting on the sofa. "Hey, Lena."

"How you doin', Terrell?"

"I'm keeping busy." Terrell moved away from his brother and toward his sister-in-law. He sat beside her, kissing her on the temple.

"He needs to settle down. I tell him that all the time, but he doesn't listen to his mother."

Glancing at his mother, he saw her standing before him with a stern look and folded arms. "Where's Dad?"

"In the basement. Says he's finding just the right wine."

"Uncle T, come see what I got for Grandma!" Sadé tugged at Terrell's arm, and he rose. When his knees cracked, she giggled. "Why do your knees always do that?"

"I'm an old man. That's what happens when you're old."

"It's because he's double-jointed," Kwame said proudly. He was five years old going on twenty.

Eight-year-old Sadé rolled her eyes. Terrell waited for her comeback, but instead she said, "Come on, Uncle T. It's upstairs so Grandma won't see it."

"I'm coming."

As she held his hand and led him up the stairs, her ponytail bopping up and down, Jade suddenly crept into his mind. If they had married years ago, they'd probably have children of their own by now. His mother certainly would be thrilled about that.

Forget Jade, he told himself. He didn't have her but he had his family. It was enough. It had to be enough.

Later Terrell and Drew sat in the parlor, both with a warm brandy in hand. Laughter from the other room drifted over them as the rest of the family played a board game. The fireplace was alive and with his elbows resting on his knees, Terrell watched the embers and flames dance.

Drew sipped his brandy, then leaned back in the recliner. "Man, as much as I love my family, it sure is nice to finally get a moment's quiet. Sadé and Kwame just don't know when to quit."

"Ah, kids will be kids."

"And turn me old and gray before my time."

Lifting the snifter to his lips, Terrell slowly sipped the amber liquid, letting the flavor play on his tongue. "At least you won't grow gray alone."

"I guess not." Terrell felt his brother's eyes on him, and he faced him. "So, Big T. You gonna tell me what's bothering you?"

"I already told you. I'm thinking about work, everything I have to do."

"That's all?"

Terrell turned back to the fire, watching the flames fight over each other. Being only two years apart, he and his brother had always been close. In fact, Terrell considered Drew his best friend. "No, there's something more."

"Something good? Bad?"

Running a hand over his hair, Terrell blew out a ragged breath. "I don't know."

"Doesn't sound good. You're not sick, are you?"

Maybe he was—just not the way his brother meant. "Remember Jade Alexander?"

"How could I forget her? Thanks to her, you were sulking around for weeks. What about her?"

"I saw her again. New Year's Eve."

Intrigued, his brother raised an eyebrow. "You're kidding?"

"She's no longer married."

"Really?"

Terrell nodded. "Really. And man, I thought I was over her. I mean, it's been six years. But one glimpse of her and *bam!*"

"You still love her."

Terrell and his brother hadn't talked about matters of the heart since the day Jade married another man. But now Terrell found himself opening up. He needed to get all thoughts of her off his chest. Maybe this was the best way to do it.

"I didn't think I did."

Drew flashed him a who-are-you-kidding look.

"It's true."

"And you thought the reason you've remained single until now is because…?"

"Because I wasn't ready to get married. It isn't a crime."

"All right." But his tone clearly said he didn't believe his brother.

Maybe Drew was right. Maybe on a subconscious level Terrell had always loved Jade. But he'd been too crushed after her marriage that he'd had to forget her, which meant blocking all thoughts of her from his mind. It was the only way he had been able to go on. Seeing her at the Marriott on New Year's Eve and feeling the familiar longing for her return, he'd known then that he'd never stopped loving her. "It took seeing her again to realize what my heart already knew. But that's not the problem."

"Then what is the problem?"

"She left without giving me her number." He frowned, remembering. "We talked, we danced. I *thought* we got close again, then she told me she was going to the washroom and never came back."

"Ouch."

Concentrating on the brandy, Terrell sipped the liquid. That and the fire were the only things that offered his soul any warmth at the moment. "And I feel like a fool again. I mean, was she playin' cool but looking for the first chance to get away from me?" The possibilities were endless, and thinking about her reasons frustrated him more than supplied any true answers. He stood. "This is stupid."

"I don't know what to say. I know she's the only woman who ever meant anything to you, but if she…" When Terrell threw back his head and downed the brandy, Drew quieted.

"I need another drink."

"That ain't gonna help you, Big T."

"No, but it will help me forget."

"Man, you've got it bad." When Terrell didn't respond, Drew rose to meet him. A thick hand clamped down on his shoulder. "Don't sweat it, Big T."

"Easy for you to say. You already have the wife and kids. I'm pushing forty and I'm not even close."

Sadé and Kwame shrieked loudly as if on cue. Drew rolled his eyes heavenward. "Is that what you want—a wife and kids? Hey, take mine anytime you're ready."

Despite the melancholy Terrell felt, he cracked a smile. "Like you could live without them."

A slow smile spread across Drew's face. "Ain't that the truth."

If Drew wanted to say anything more about Jade, he didn't. Terrell was thankful for that, because the fact that he'd gotten his feelings off his chest actually had him feeling worse.

Crossing his wrists behind his back, Terrell walked to the window and looked outside. Snow continued to fall, but not as heavy as earlier. Still it was enough to make him dread the trip back to Manhattan. "I'd better get out of here. The roads aren't getting any better and I still have work to do."

"I should have known that was coming."

"Hey, someone in this family has to bring in the big bucks." But he smiled.

"Look, if there's anything I can do…"

"There isn't."

Jade was Terrell's problem. Only he could get her out of his heart.

Chapter 9

"Wow." Cassandra leaned forward in the chair, looking at her reflection with awe. "How'd you do that?"

Behind Cassandra, Jade stood, a smile playing on her lips. "Do what?"

Cassandra fluffed her shoulder-length black hair with both hands. "Give me so much volume. My hair has never looked so healthy."

If Jade had had the supplies and more time, she might have considered adding a piece to Cassandra's hair for the shoot, but as it turned out, the conditioners and mousse she'd used had done the trick. "I'll never tell."

Cassandra shook her head lightly, smiling as she watched her hair bounce around her shoulders. "I can't believe it's me."

"It's definitely you." Sifting her fingers through a section of Cassandra's hair, Jade added, "What I can't believe is that I did this."

Cassandra glanced at her by way of the mirror. "Oh, stop. You're a fabulous hairstylist."

"I've been out of practice."

"But it's like riding a bicycle—you never forget how."

"I guess not." And it had felt great doing someone else's hair again. At first she'd been so nervous, certain she would somehow forget everything she'd learned over the years. But once she'd found her groove, the nervous energy had become creative fuel.

"Wow." Carefully Cassandra fingered a soft curl that fell over her forehead. "Can I hire you full time?"

"I think that can be arranged."

Swiveling around in her chair, Cassandra faced Jade head-on. "Girlfriend, things are gonna be all right. Nelson may have set you off course temporarily, but you're gonna have the last laugh."

The words made Jade feel much better than she would have expected. For a time, Nelson had had too much power over her life. That was going to change.

As she'd styled Cassandra's hair, Jade had confessed what Nelson had done, how he'd betrayed her, how she'd had to start over from nothing. With her hands in her old friend's hair, baring her soul had been like therapy.

"I know I'll have the last laugh," Jade said in response to Cassandra's comment.

There was a knock at the door, and both Jade and Cassandra looked toward it. Beyond them, Jeff, the editor-in-chief, and Eve, the article's writer, stood in the living room of Cassandra's loft. Jeff hustled to answer the door.

As he opened the door he said, "Ah, the photographer has arrived."

And then Terrell Edmonds stepped into the room.

Jade's heart fell to her knees.

"Look who it is," Cassandra said, rising.

Instantly Terrell's eyes moved in their direction and he saw them. Saw her. His smile never wavered, but there was a spark of surprise in his eyes.

Jade held a hand at the base of her throat as she turned to Cassandra. "Why didn't you tell me that Terrell was going to be here?"

"I didn't know." Rising from her chair, Cassandra practically floated into the living room. "Terrell. So nice to see you."

"Wow. You look great." He hugged her, but his eyes locked with Jade's over Cassandra's shoulder.

Her mind scrambling to accept the situation, Jade glanced nervously away. Terrell was the photographer? He'd been an aspiring one years ago. Did he make his living doing this, or did he get a lucky break as she had?

"Jade did my hair," Cassandra announced. The high-pitched voice pulled Jade from her thoughts. "She's the best."

"No doubt."

Jade's pulse went wild as Terrell's eyes held hers, as he moved from Cassandra and strolled toward her. Instinctively she took a step backward and bumped into the makeup artist's bag. She stumbled, but regained her footing before she fell flat on her butt. Her face flamed.

Terrell's smile broadened, but it wasn't a mocking one. He was genuinely happy to see her. "Hello, Jade."

"Terrell. I didn't know you were going to be here."

"Life is just full of surprises."

"It is."

The sound of clapping hands alerted them, shocked them out of the mesmerizing hold their eyes seemed to have on each other. As Terrell spun around, Jade released the breath she didn't know she was holding.

"We'd better get started."

Terrell walked toward Jeff, and Jade felt a weird sense of loss. "Sure. A couple guys are bringing up the lights from downstairs, but let me take a look at the room. Did you have an idea where you wanted to do the pictures?"

"I was thinking we could move the sofa next to the window," Jeff replied. "With the…"

Jade tuned him out. Her mind seemed capable only of hearing the intense beating of her own heart.

Before January first, she hadn't seen him in over six years, yet only days into the new year she was seeing him a second time. What kind of game was fate playing with her? And instead of being angry that she had deserted him at the party, he genuinely seemed happy to see her. Which puzzled her— and, she had to admit, warmed her. Terrell's special brand of warmth had been her weakness years ago.

She watched as he gestured around the room, as he held up a lens and peered through it, as he instructed his assistants as to where they should put the various lighting. Every so often, he would glance her way, and a blush would spread from the base of her neck over her face. Embarrassment or desire? Right now she couldn't be sure.

Right now she couldn't help thinking that he was truly gorgeous. His movements were smooth, sexy, and mesmerizing. In jeans and sweater, he looked as attractive as he had in his jazzy suit on New Year's Eve. If he was a photographer, then he no doubt dealt with hundreds of women, no doubt had hundreds of women propositioning him. So why was he still unattached?

The only woman I wanted broke my heart. His words echoed in her brain, and she felt an odd tingling span the length of her arms.

"Ooh, he's fine."

The sound of Lynda's voice startled her. Feeling as guilty as a child who'd been caught with her hand in the cookie jar, Jade faced the makeup artist. "Yes, he's very attractive."

"DDGF: drop dead gorgeous fine." She enunciated each word as her eyes drank in the sight of him. "God, I hope he's not gay."

"He's not," Jade immediately replied. Like Lynda, she was unable to draw her eyes from his lean, muscular form.

"How do you know?"

"I…I know him." She didn't know Lynda well and hoped she wouldn't ask for more information than that. "He's definitely straight."

"Good." Lynda chuckled. "Not that it matters…but at least it doesn't ruin the fantasy."

Lynda was right—women would definitely consider Terrell a fantasy man. Tall, gorgeous, with enough sexual presence to intimidate Don Juan, Terrell was certainly pinup material. Not that she'd have had to settle for a pinup. She could have the real thing. But she'd let him go.

Jade wondered again why he wasn't involved with anybody. According to him, she'd broken his heart. Had he really been that hurt by her rejection?

Jade had heard her share of lines, had dealt with her share of players. Terrell, she knew, wasn't a man who played games.

As Cassandra conversed with Jeff and Eve, Terrell approached Jade. "You're not leaving, are you?"

Why was it that when he stood near her, the air seemed electrified? "No. I…I have to stay."

"Good." His deep voice sent ripples of desire over her. "Because you're not going to get away from me this time."

Now Jade understood why people who worked in theater and film were paid so well. If she hadn't witnessed it with her own eyes, she never would have believed that taking a few pictures would take all day.

She was exhausted. And exhilarated.

"Hey, guys," Jeff said as he snapped his briefcase shut. "We're going for a brew. Wanna come along?"

Jade was about to speak, but Terrell, who stood beside her, stepped forward and said, "No, that's okay. Jade and I have plans."

Her head snapped up. "We do?"

"Yes, we do," he responded, not even bothering to glance at her as he dismantled the flash from his camera.

A tingle of desire raced down her spine at Terrell's command, and for the nth time Jade wondered why her body had such a hard time resisting him when her brain knew that she should.

Cassandra approached Jade, gave her a big hug. "Thanks so much for everything today. You too, Terrell. I'm sure the pictures will look fabulous."

"I know they will," Terrell said, smiling.

He seemed more confident than he'd been years ago, and his confidence was like a magnet that drew her to him. Despite what she tried to tell herself, she couldn't ignore the fact that she was attracted to him.

But she didn't have to act on it. There was too much baggage between them, too much that would weigh them down if they ever pursued a relationship. How could he ever really trust her, and how could she ever really trust a man again? Even if the man in question claimed he'd only ever loved her.

When Cassandra turned to walk away, Jade said, "You're leaving?"

"I'm heading out with Jeff and Eve."

Her gaze moved to Terrell. "Oh, then we should hurry—"

"Don't worry about it," Cassandra said, dismissing that thought with a wave of her hand. "The door will lock automatically when you leave, so stay as long as you want." She spun around and ran to the door. "See you later!"

"Later." As Jade spoke the words, Cassandra disappeared. Terrell put down his camera bag and moved toward her. The realization that they were finally alone made her heart race. "Terrell," Jade quickly began. "I'm not sure this is a good idea. You and me…"

"Say what you want, Jade, but this time I'm not giving you a choice."

Her stomach fluttered at his words, yet she squared her jaw, feigning a woman who had total control of her emotions. "Oh, that's real nineties of you."

"It isn't the nineties."

His comment threw her for a loop. But then Jade realized he was right. And as much as she wanted to continue staring at him with defiance, she couldn't help cracking a smile.

"That's better. Jade, you have no reason to fear me. I've never hurt you before and I'm not about to start now."

Heat enveloped her face as she realized he couldn't have spoken truer words. Why *was* she afraid to spend time with him? He couldn't force her to do anything she didn't want to. The only thing running like a scared puppy would prove was that she wasn't immune to him.

And he certainly didn't need to know that.

"How about we go to my place?"

"I, uh, I…"

He moved to stand before her. "No, I'm not propositioning you. I just want to talk."

"Then what about a bar? A restaurant?"

"I want no distractions." When she merely stood paralyzed beneath his gaze, he added, "If not my place, then how about yours?"

"No." Kathy might be home. "No, definitely not."

"Then it's settled."

Maybe this wasn't such a good idea, Terrell thought as he looked down at Jade from the upper level of his loft. She sat on his leather sofa, her hands folded in her lap, her eyes darting around the place like a terrified cat's. Could someone look less thrilled if they were heading to the gas chamber?

Turning, Terrell walked into his bedroom, where he unloaded his bags, then stripped off his sweater down to the white T-shirt he wore beneath. Maybe it was the fact that Jade was downstairs, but his eyes strayed to the king-size bed, and his mind floated to an image he'd long ago buried. More times than he cared to admit, he'd pictured her lying there, wearing one of his T-shirts that reached her midthigh. He'd pictured her lying on her side, one leg provocatively draped over the other, a sexy smile playing on her lips.

The fact that Jade sat downstairs on his sofa, looking like she'd rather be anywhere but here, definitely ruined the fantasy.

Maybe he shouldn't have pushed her to join him tonight. But Lord knows, if he didn't, he would never have a moment's peace. Since he'd met her again, all he could think of was her and whether or not fate was finally giving him the chance he'd always wanted.

Pushing his thoughts aside, Terrell descended the wooden steps to the main level, watching with interest as Jade looked up at him. She didn't smile, just stared, and his heart sank.

"Can I get you a drink?" he offered. "I've got brandy, some wine. A bit of vodka."

"If you have some ginger ale or club soda, I'll take a wine spritzer."

"White wine okay?" He never did like red wine, and he dumped the contents of the bottle Keisha had brought after she'd left.

"Sure."

Jade watched as he walked away, admiring the view of his broad, well-sculpted back. She wished she wasn't so tense. Maybe the spritzer would help her relax.

Minutes later, Terrell returned with two drinks—a brandy for himself and a spritzer for her. He handed her the drink then sat beside her.

Not sure what to say, he merely sat and sipped his brandy, wishing Jade would say something—anything—to let him know he hadn't made a big mistake. He wished he didn't, but he still had deep feelings for her.

"Nice place," Jade finally said.

Terrell looked at her. It wasn't much, but it was enough to break the ice. "Thanks. I really love it here."

"So photography—that's what you do now?" Jade knew the answer to the question already, but still had to ask. One look around Terrell's home and she knew he was a professional photographer. Large black-and-white photos as well as color ones of people and places hung on every wall. The photos were spectacular. A black-and-white of a black man holding a tiny pale baby in his arms was the most striking of the pictures.

"Yeah, that's how I make a buck."

"I'm sure you love your job. At least, looking at these pictures that's the impression I get."

"I do. I'm very lucky."

"I'm happy for you. You were always ambitious about photography, so I'm glad you made it happen."

"Thanks." He paused, sipped the brandy. "And what about you? What happened to your salon?"

Oh, God. He knew. Her eyes must have conveyed her terror, for he said, "I know your salon isn't there anymore. I… What can I say? I just know. Did you move it out of Manhattan?"

"Not exactly."

"I don't get it."

Jade filled her lungs with air, emptied them. Found the courage to continue. "Other than today, I haven't done hair professionally in over a year."

"Why not? That's what you love doing, isn't it? So why sell your shop?"

Surprising herself, Jade told Terrell the truth. "I didn't sell it. I…I lost it. It's one of the reasons I'm no longer married."

"Really?"

"Yeah. Let's just say I trusted Nelson with the books, but he wasn't a very trustworthy man. I didn't really know him."

"I'm sorry to hear that."

"I'm sorry, too."

Silence fell between them. But curiosity got the better of Terrell and he asked, "And the reason you're not married? *If* you want to tell me."

Jade brought the wineglass to her lips and took a sip. She let the liquid slowly make its way down her throat.

Clearly she didn't want to talk about it. "Forget I asked."

"No. I don't mind telling you." Which was almost as much of a surprise to her as was seeing Terrell on New Year's Eve. "Nelson…he…he left me for another woman."

"What?" Terrell's mouth fell open.

Jade sighed deeply. "I found out a ton of money was missing from the salon's account, and I asked him about it. He said the bank had made some mistake. I went back to the bank, took a look at the records, saw that more money was going out than coming in. I wanted to believe that it all went to pay bills, but then I found out the bills hadn't been getting paid. Still Nelson denied any knowledge that anything was wrong. But I kinda suspected he was lying, and he must have suspected that I suspected that, 'cause a few weeks later, he left me a note and moved out.

"Weeks later, he finally called me. He confessed to *borrowing* the money to support his gambling habit. I never knew. All those times I figured he was staying late at work, he was really off in Atlantic City, and God knows where else. I was hurt, shocked, angry. He promised that he'd get help, that he'd pay me back every dime. And he asked if he could come home. I feel like a real idiot, but I said yes. I thought that's what a wife is supposed to do, stick by her husband. But a couple of weeks later he left me another note and took off again. And this time, he dropped a bombshell. He told me that…that he and his new girlfriend were going to have a baby."

"Ah, Jade."

"I was stunned, Terrell. Literally paralyzed with grief and anger. And I felt like such a fool." Jade finally stopped, noted that her hands were shaking. Terrell took the wineglass from her, placed it and his own glass on the table, then cupped both her hands in his. She averted her eyes, wondering why she'd just shared the most painful events of her life with him. "I don't know why I'm telling you this."

"Because you know you can trust me. You do know that, don't you?"

She did. Instinctively she did. She'd always known that. Just like she'd always known in her heart that Terrell had been right, that if she married Nelson she would be marrying the wrong man. "I guess you have the right to tell me you told me so."

"And what would that accomplish? Truly, Jade, I never wished you and Nelson ill, I only wanted you to be happy."

"But you didn't think I could be happy with Nelson."

He shrugged. "No. I didn't."

Jade's eyes strayed to their hands, to the sight of her small ones in his large ones. "You were right."

"I didn't want to be right."

"It doesn't matter. You were. And I was a fool."

"You trusted him. You—" He broke off and Jade watched the rise and fall of his Adam's apple. "You loved him."

He released her hands, but kept his eyes glued to hers for a long moment, as though asking her to tell him otherwise. Jade said nothing, and Terrell suddenly looked away. He was asking for more than she was ready to give, more than she was ready to ask of herself. But the crushed look she saw in his eyes made her remember that night in her salon, made her feel again like she was breaking his heart. She didn't know why but she wanted to give him something, perhaps let him know he hadn't been crazy to think there was something between them. "I…I'm not sure I did. Not when I really think about it."

His eyes bolted to hers, hopeful. "You're not sure you what?"

She had already opened the can and may as well spill its contents. "I'm not sure I loved Nelson. I mean, maybe I was really in love with the idea of him, of us. I don't know. I only know that soon into the marriage I felt I'd made a mistake."

"Because of—"

"I don't know why." She cut him off before he could ask that question. Truth be told, on many nights when she'd faced Nelson's back with tears in her eyes, she had thought of Terrell, had thought of his warning, had thought of the explosive passion she'd experienced when kissing him. She was too embarrassed to admit that Nelson never made her feel that way. "I don't want to talk about Nelson anymore."

"Neither do I." Nelson was a thing of the past, and if he'd messed up his relationship with Jade, then that was his loss. What mattered now was that Terrell had a chance with her. "Let's talk about us."

Us. Was there really a chance for that? Suddenly Jade didn't know what to think, didn't know what she wanted. Sitting this close to Terrell, it was hard to breathe, let alone focus her thoughts. "Us? I'm not sure what there is to say."

"You don't get it, do you?" He seemed genuinely perplexed.

She should get it; in fact, she was sure she knew exactly what he was trying to say, but a part of her didn't want to hear it.

"Jade…"

She stood. "Terrell, I don't know…"

He stood to meet her. "Dammit, Jade, I let you go six years ago. I sure as hell don't plan on letting you go again."

"But I've changed, you've changed…"

He ran a finger down her arm. "What I feel for you hasn't changed, Jade. In fact, just being near you has proven to me what I've always known to be true. You're the only woman for me." He touched a finger to her chin. "Jade, I never stopped loving you."

"Terrell, don't—"

"Why not? It's true. Jade, I know you feel it. If what I'm feeling is this strong, it can't be one-sided."

"I don't know what I feel." Wrapping her arms around her torso, she walked toward a floor-to-ceiling window and glanced out at the snow-covered SoHo Street.

He was close, so close. Close to getting Jade to admit that she felt something. Close to proving he wasn't crazy for obsessing over her. Slowly he strolled across the hardwood floor, stopping about a foot behind her. "Do you ever wonder?" he asked softly. "About me and you, what it could have been like?"

Maybe it was the trust they'd just reestablished, maybe it was the new year, but Jade lost all reason as she turned around and blurted out, "All the time."

He took another step toward her, almost closing the distance between them. A hand reached for her, but he pulled it back. "God, you don't know how many times I've imagined you here, standing before me the way you are now, lying on my bed—"

"Terrell," Jade whispered. She'd meant it to be a warning to stop, yet her low tone had sounded sultry and inviting instead.

This time his hand found her body, reaching around her waist to pull her against him. God, this felt so right. He pressed his nose to her hair, inhaling its delicate scent, letting the breath out on a sigh. "Jade, you don't know how many days I drove myself crazy, thinking about you with Nelson." He brushed the tip of his nose against her cheek. "You don't know how many nights I couldn't sleep, imagining what you two were doing."

It didn't make sense, but his words turned her on. Her body thrummed with a desire she'd never known before, and it was totally overpowering. Tentatively she pressed a hand against Terrell's firm chest, enjoying the sound he made low in his throat. Terrell made her feel so alive. "Terrell, I'm sorry…"

His hands framed her face. "I don't know what it is about you, but you made me crazy from the first time I saw you and you're making me crazy even now."

She didn't know what to say. She wanted to tell him the things she'd felt, but she had repressed her feelings for so long it was hard to express them now. "I didn't mean to make you crazy."

"Sweetheart, this is a good kind of crazy."

His mouth neared hers and she stiffened. Not because she didn't want him to kiss her, for she did. But because she knew that kissing Terrell would be so completely different than kissing Nelson had been. Because kissing Terrell could lead her to a place she wasn't sure she wanted to go.

Slowly his mouth moved to her ear, his breath warm on her face. "Say my name. Let me know this is real."

"Terrell…"

He moaned his satisfaction, then covered her mouth with his. Jade practically melted in his arms. It felt so good, like tasting water again after a terribly long drought. It felt so incredible, so right. With an urgency Jade didn't expect, she threw her arms around Terrell's neck and surrendered to the kiss with reckless abandon. So what if he was dangerous? She'd played it safe her whole life and she now craved the excitement Terrell was offering.

Boldly she opened her mouth for him, forcing her tongue into his. This must be what the forbidden fruit tasted like, hot and sweet. She wanted more of him, had always wanted more of him, and that thought scared her.

He pulled away, looked into her eyes with surprise. "Jade…"

"Don't say anything," she whispered. "Just…just kiss me."

"I want to do more than kiss you."

"Then stop talking and do it."

Her eyes fluttered shut as his tongue found her neck. She lolled her head backward, arching to give him as much access to her body as he needed. While his tongue trailed a fiery path to her earlobe, one hand cupped her breast. A long, soft moan escaped her lips. She wanted to rip her shirt off. Touching her through her clothing wasn't enough.

"Oh, Jade." He nibbled on a spot behind her ear and she gasped.

He pulled away, looked into her eyes. "What did I do?"

"Nothing…wrong." She paused to catch her breath. "It's just that…well, I didn't know my ear was so sensitive."

"Right here?" Terrell flicked his tongue over the spot it had recently been.

"Oh, yes."

His hands framed her head as he nipped at the smooth skin along her jawline. The soft mewling sounds that came from her throat made him crazy, made him want to do whatever it took to please her, to see her wild with desire.

"Ooh!"

"You like that?" Once again, he flicked the tip of his tongue into her ear.

She dug her nails into his biceps. "Mmm."

"I'll take that as a yes. I wonder where else you're sensitive."

He felt her sharp intake of breath when he pulled down the zipper on her shirt. His gaze fell to the soft, honey-brown flesh that spilled from her bra. She was beautiful, perfect. Slipping a hand beneath the fabric, he ran his fingers over her stomach up the fullness of one breast, enjoying the way she quivered beneath his touch. She was soft and warm and so completely irresistible. But like over six years ago when only a piece of her wouldn't do, he wanted more than a piece of her now. "I've always wanted you, Jade. You know that."

"Yes."

"This isn't about sex."

"I know."

"So stop me if you can't give me what I want. Because I want you, Jade. All of you. Body and soul."

Chapter 10

"TAKE ME, TERRELL." Jade couldn't stop the words. She didn't want to. Right now she craved Terrell more than she'd ever craved anything in her life, and for once she was going after what she wanted. Whatever happened tomorrow, she wanted tonight. She wanted now.

"Jade." Her name was a breathless whisper on his lips.

"Shh." She placed a finger on his mouth, silencing him. She didn't want to talk; she wanted to act. She didn't want to think about it, whether this was right or wrong. She just wanted to do it.

His tongue flicked over her finger, and the simple action was so utterly erotic that for a moment Jade couldn't breathe. Then he held her hand to his lips, kissing her palm, taking her thumb into his mouth, gently suckling. Jade thought she would die of the pleasure.

It wasn't enough. She tipped until she was on the balls of

her feet, stretching to reach Terrell's sensuous mouth. He framed her face and guided her to him. But he stopped a hairbreadth away from her lips, torturing her for a moment, his mouth hovering over hers, his warm breath gently framing her face. Then slowly he extended his tongue, ever so lightly tracing the outline of her lips.

Oh, God, what this man could do to her! One touch and he made her so hot, so excited, she'd let him do anything he pleased with her. Right now she was his. She wanted him to take her, wanted to feel her body against his, skin to skin. Placing her hands between them, she yanked the shirt from his pants and reached beneath the thin fabric. His skin was warm and smooth. His stomach was flat and muscular, just as she'd known it would be. Up and down she ran her fingers along his skin, hoping that she had the power to drive him as crazy as he was driving her.

He moaned, then his mouth smothered hers. His tongue delved into her mouth, insistent, urgent, and unrepentant. Jade's hands found their way to his back and as he gripped her even more tightly, she dug her long fingernails into his skin. She couldn't get enough of him.

"Jade, I've waited so long for this."

Their eyes met, held, and Jade felt the warmest of sensations wash over her. "I know."

"I don't want to disappoint you."

"You won't."

"It's been a while."

"It's been a while for me, too. I don't want to wait any more."

Nudging her cashmere sweater off her shoulders, Terrell brushed his lips over her skin. Instantly heat engulfed her body. He replaced his lips with his fingers, trailing them downward to cover a breast. Her nipple jutted out to meet his palm.

"You like that?"

"Yes." Her eyelids fluttered shut.

He kissed her again, then tweaked the nipple through the fabric of her bra. When she purred into his mouth, letting him know how much she wanted him, fire shot through his veins and pooled in his groin.

"Jade, you feel so good."

"Don't stop."

Urgently he pushed the lacy material of her bra aside. Lowering his head, he brought his hot tongue down onto her swollen peak and suckled hard.

"Oh… Oh!" Gripping his shoulders, Jade arched her back. Sweet sensations rippled through her body from her breast down to the center of her womanhood. Nothing had ever felt as wonderful as this. She hardly recognized the passionate cries that came from her lips.

Terrell brought his mouth to her other breast, this time circling the tip with his tongue. It contracted and hardened and Jade thought she would surely explode.

She couldn't take any more of his exquisite torture. She pulled at his T-shirt and he held up his arms, allowing her to take it off his body.

Then he stood before her, his strong, muscular upper body naked and in all its glory. Reaching out, she fingered both his nipples and watched him close his eyes in delight. So he was sensitive there, too. Smiling, she pressed her lips to his chest, kissing the warm, smooth skin. A deep groan rumbled in his chest.

He tangled his hands in her hair, then pulled her away from his body. Confusion flashed in her eyes as she looked up at him, and he gently stroked her face to let her know that nothing was wrong. Then he stepped back and let his gaze wander over her flesh. He wanted to see her, appreciate her.

Maybe he was staring at her too intensely, for she covered both breasts with her wrists.

"No...don't."

Her hands fell to her sides.

God, she looked so beautiful, half-naked before him. Her bra was bunched up under her full, pert breasts, creating a wickedly enticing vision. She had the kind of body men paid to see, the kind a man would never tire of, and his mind filled with lurid thoughts of how he would mercilessly please her. Reaching for the front clasp of her bra, he unsnapped it. Jade untangled herself from the bra and shirt, letting both drop to the floor.

"You're perfect." His hands covered both breasts, tweaking the nipples, making them pucker and harden. Her entire body thrummed with a sexual energy she'd never experienced before. When Terrell's hands moved to the button of her pants, quickly unfastening them in one smooth move, heat pooled between her legs. He took control as if they had made love hundreds of times before and weren't timid with each other. He slipped her pants over her hips, letting them fall around her heels. She stepped out of them.

She should feel self-conscious beneath his gaze, but she only felt heat. She felt wanted. She felt appreciated. And when he wrapped his arms around her again, she felt like more of a woman than she'd ever felt in her thirty-four years.

His hands gripped her hips, pulling her against his groin. He was hard and large. And she wanted him. She undid his jeans and helped drag them off his long, lean legs. Then she watched with admiration as he stood before her in white bikini briefs, the evidence of his desire for her bulging beneath the cotton material.

Then they were in each other's arms, exploring, tasting, enjoying. Catching up on all they'd missed. Though overwhelmed with happiness, Jade couldn't help but feel sadness that she'd ended things between them so many years ago. She never should have married Nelson.

Terrell whispered in her ear, "Let's go upstairs."

"Quickly."

He scooped her into his arms, carried her up the stairs and to his king-size bed. When he placed her atop the sheets, he stood above her and slipped his fingers beneath her panties, slowly dragging them off her legs. Then his dark eyes holding hers, he took off his own briefs and joined her.

Jade wanted to tell him how she felt, that she was sorry for the way she'd hurt him, that she missed what they hadn't had. But then his lips were kissing her calf, her knee, her thigh…and she stopped thinking altogether. His mouth was driving her delirious, taking her to new, unexplored heights.

Lying on his back, he pulled her onto his body. She placed a leg on either side of his strong hips. Though she'd blocked out all thoughts of Terrell years ago, she had dreamed of this moment several times. Times when she knew that marrying Nelson had been a mistake. Now she couldn't believe she was really going to experience what loving Terrell could be like. She couldn't believe how much she wanted to experience this. More than anything, she wanted to be with him, to give him all her soul had to give.

Terrell framed her face with one hand. "Jade, you know I want you, but if you're not okay with this, we can wait."

She paused, drew a shaky breath, then said, "I'm okay."

"Come here." Terrell sat up, wrapping her in the comfort of his arms. "Baby, I'm sorry."

"No. Don't be." Jade pulled back and stared into Terrell's dark eyes. She was suddenly aware that her own eyes had filled with tears.

"Damn, you're gonna cry."

And then the first tear escaped. She wished she could hold it back, but she was so overwhelmed with so many emotions that she just couldn't control them.

"I've rushed you."

"No, you haven't. This is…six years overdue."

He ran his hands through her hair as he held her face to his. "Then why the tears?"

"Regret. Regret that I didn't listen to you."

"Shh." Releasing a sigh, he rested his forehead against hers. "Get dressed."

His concern for her feelings and his gentleness were as potent as any aphrodisiac, causing desire to consume her and wash away the melancholy. "No. I want you." She kissed him softly, letting her mouth linger over his lips. "Make me forget, Terrell. Make me forget."

He kissed her slowly, as if making sure she was really ready. She savored the feel of his full lips, the taste of them. Their lips picked up speed, their breathing grew heavier. And finally his tongue entered her mouth, hot and sweet and demanding.

Jade slipped her hands between their bodies, pushing Terrell away from her, silently urging him to lie back. He did, then ran his hands down the side of her arms to her hips. She felt him harden once again beneath her and she closed her eyes as sweet sensations washed over her.

Terrell guided their bodies together. Jade cried out as he filled her with one hard thrust. He paused, and Jade opened her eyes to find him staring at her. She said nothing, but covered his hands with hers and gyrated her hips. In response, he thrust upward slowly, once, twice. She moved her hips in tune with his. As they found their rhythm, Terrell's strokes grew faster, harder. He gripped her hips, holding her in place, pushing deeper.

Jade arched her back as she met his thrusts, moving her body to the magic of his. Nothing had ever felt this good before. The pleasure came not only from the physical, but from a place deep inside that for once in her life seemed satisfied.

"Jade…"

Her name on his lips was the sweetest sound. She cried out as he thrust even harder, deeper, as his hands tightened on her hips to anchor her in place. And then she was lost as her body exploded, as the most exquisite sensations sent her flying to another world.

Terrell tensed as his own release came, and then he was crying her name and gripping her back and forcing her body down onto his. He held her to him and ravaged her lips until she whimpered and finally broke free for air.

They stayed like that for several minutes, Jade on top of Terrell, their breathing ragged, their bodies slick and spent but satisfied. Then finally easing her off his torso, he settled her beside him.

Wrapping an arm around her, he snuggled her close, then brushed his lips over her forehead. "You okay?"

A smile spreading across her face, Jade answered without hesitation. "I've never been better."

Chapter 11

THE NEXT MORNING, after waking early to make love again, Jade and Terrell lay on the bed, Jade resting her head in the crook of his arm. Slowly she trailed a long fingernail over the grooves of his smooth, almost hairless chest.

"Baby, if you keep doing that, we'll never make it out of this bed."

"Promises, promises."

He placed a hand on hers, stilling it. "Was it what you expected?"

Jade propped her head up to meet Terrell's eyes. "No." When his eyes widened, she smiled. "It was more. Much, much more."

"So it was worth the six-year wait?"

"Definitely."

"Yeah," he agreed softly. "It was for me, too."

As though Jade suddenly realized that they couldn't stay

in bed forever, she bolted upright. The clock read 10:33 A.M. "Oh, no. Is that the time?"

"Holy—" Terrell sat up. With Jade in his arms, work had been the last thing on his mind. "I've got an appointment in half an hour."

She giggled as he scrambled out of the bed. Her eyes roamed over his naked body, settling on his firm butt. Instantly her body warmed, remembering how incredible their lovemaking had been.

She watched as he stood before his dresser, the sunlight from the nearby window bathing his magnificent form as he searched the top drawer. She was tempted to sneak behind him, trail her tongue along his spine and feel him shiver in delight. She'd learned last night that he had a few unexplored erogenous zones as well.

"I don't mind if you stay here," he said, then closed the drawer. He approached her naked and in all his glory, underwear in hand. "But I'm gonna be a while."

Jade swallowed at the sight of him, then watched as he tossed the underwear onto the bed. What was she going to say? Oh, yes. "Uh, I've got to get going. I have to work at noon."

"Where are you working? I never did ask."

"At The Red Piano."

"On the Upper East Side. Will you be able to make it home in time to get ready for work?"

"Never. I live in Brooklyn."

He swore softly. "I wish I could give you a ride—"

"Don't worry about it. I always keep a uniform at work." She stood, meeting his naked body with her own. Her body grew warm as she watched desire spark in his eyes. "If you don't mind, I'll shower here." She gasped softly as he embraced her, pulling her against his hard muscles. "Then, I'll, uh, leave."

"I don't want you to leave."

"I can come back."

"Then do that."

"What about the shower?"

"Let's go."

Jade laughed as Terrell scooped her into his arms and carried her to the bathroom en suite. She'd never made love in the shower before.

She was looking forward to it.

"Would that be okay?"

Terrell, whose mind had drifted to memories of Jade, looked at the young man before him. "Sorry, what did you say?"

"I asked if you would mind me changing into another outfit."

"I usually do three outfits for three rolls of film."

"I know," the man said, walking toward him. "But I wouldn't mind doing some in my biker outfit. I'm not sure how they'll turn out, but if they look good, I hope my agent will start sending me out for more types of auditions. I'm tired of just playing the clean-cut guy."

Terrell was tempted to say no. In fact, he normally would say no. Three outfits was plenty and he allotted only so much time for each session. But he was just so darn happy today that he saw no need to be so hard-nosed.

"That'll be fine. Just change as quickly as possible. I've got another appointment after you."

"Thanks, man." The man hurried to the change area.

A smile on his face, Terrell walked toward the window. The smile had been there ever since Jade left. Instead of thinking about work, about the film he had to develop, about who was coming next, he kept remembering the feel of her in his arms. He wondered if she would return tonight.

He planted his hands on his hips as he watched a car cut through the snow. Despite the weather, there were cars and people everywhere. New Yorkers were tough—they didn't let a little bad weather keep them down.

Jade was tough. After what she'd gone through with her ex, she was determined not to let that keep her down. But was she ready to jump into another serious relationship? Just being with her, Terrell knew he wanted nothing less from Jade than a commitment. He'd always wanted that from her.

But the fact that they'd been apart for more than six years could not be forgotten. Though they'd made love, they were a long way off from saying "I do." They needed to get to know each other, to build their relationship like they'd have been able to do if she hadn't married Nelson.

"I'm ready."

Terrell turned at the sound of the young man's voice. "Let's do this."

For the first couple of hours, Jade had been busy enough that she could forget the angry look in her boss's eyes. But by the time lunch rush was over, it was impossible to ignore the fact that he was totally peeved with her.

Five minutes earlier, he'd told her that he wanted to see her when she had a moment. Since that time, she'd slowed down with her last few customers, not yet ready to face an angry Pierre. When she thought about it, the stress she had to deal with on this job was making it less and less worth it.

"There you go," she said cheerfully as she handed change to the lone elderly woman. "Make sure you come back again soon."

"This is for you," the woman said, firmly placing two quarters in Jade's hand.

"Thank you." Jade smiled. The tip was far less than ten

percent, but she knew that some people couldn't afford to be as generous as others. She was a firm believer in the "It's the thought that counts" motto.

The two women at her other table were busy chatting, hardly noticing the desserts before them. Darn, she wished she could offer them more coffee, more water, more *anything,* but she'd already done that twice and they'd insisted they were fine.

That meant she really couldn't put off the inevitable meeting with Pierre. Frowning, she left the dining room floor and headed into the kitchen.

Pierre stood at the opposite end and when he saw her enter, he waved her over impatiently. Knowing that she had to face his wrath eventually, Jade gritted her teeth and approached her manager.

She already knew what he was going to say. He'd specifically forbidden her to change shifts with Mandy yesterday, but Jade had done it anyway. As far as she was concerned, one server could easily replace the other and she didn't think it was a big deal that she hadn't worked, as long as her shift was covered.

"Inside," Pierre said.

Jade had a sinking feeling of déjà vu. She followed her boss inside the small office and took a seat opposite him. Her nerves were frayed but she tried not to show it as she sat quietly, waiting for him to speak.

"What happened yesterday?"

Slowly Jade met his eyes. "Pierre, I explained to you that there was something important I had to do—"

"And I told you not to change shifts with Mandy." He almost shouted the words.

Instead of flinching, as Jade was sure he hoped she'd do, she squared her jaw. "What was I supposed to do? Anybody else who wants to switch shifts with another server can do so, so why can't I?"

Pierre's face reddened. "Do you want this job or not? Because right now, I am this far away from letting you go." He held up a thumb and forefinger with very little space between them.

She wanted to get up and walk out, to leave this crappy job behind her once and for all. Oh, she did, and she was certainly tempted to do just that. But how could she leave this job when she needed it so badly? "I'm sorry, Pierre. I just figured that since people exchange shifts all the time, it wouldn't be a big deal."

"It was a big deal. Mandy is nowhere as experienced as you are."

"I'm sorry," Jade repeated, though it killed her to do so. Pierre was notorious for exaggerating any situation.

"I don't want this to happen again. Consider this your first warning." When Jade didn't reply, Pierre said, "Did you hear me?"

"Yes." She stood. "I've got tables to serve."

"I'm not stopping you. As long as we have an understanding."

"We do."

"Good."

At first Jade had considered going home after work. The meeting with Pierre and the feeling that her days at The Red Piano were numbered had her in a foul mood. She didn't want to see Terrell this way.

But after calling him, after hearing his reassuring voice, she quickly forgot all about Pierre and The Red Piano and the fact that she barely had two dimes to rub together. She could think only of Terrell and last night. That and the fact that she wanted more than anything to see him again.

Instead of heading to Brooklyn, she went to Duane Reade Pharmacy and bought a toothbrush, then to Daffy's where she bought some underwear and a new outfit. Not that she planned on spending the rest of the week at Terrell's or anything, but she wanted to be prepared.

Just in case.

Last night with Terrell had been incredible. She didn't know where this new relationship would lead, but she was at least inclined to keep her options open. And while she wasn't ready to commit to anything other than her career, she was willing to admit that maybe Terrell could still factor into her life on some level.

By six, she was knocking on his door. When Terrell responded to her knock, she smiled at the sight of him. Or maybe it was the way he looked at her like she made his day that made her smile. Whatever, she knew she'd done the right thing by not going home.

"Hi." Leaning forward, he planted a soft kiss on her lips.

"Hi yourself. Can I come in?"

"You better."

Giggling, she entered the foyer. But her smile faded when she looked behind Terrell and saw the stunning Asian woman. It was the shock of realizing they weren't alone more than jealousy, but still she was taken aback. "Uh, if you're busy…"

"No, I'm finished."

The Asian woman smiled tightly at Jade and made her way to the foyer. "Thanks, Terrell."

"Give me a week. If you don't hear from me by then, give me a call."

She flashed him a genuine smile. "Thanks. I will."

Several moments later, she was in her coat and boots and out the door.

"She's very beautiful," Jade commented when the door clicked shut, not sure why her chest felt so tight.

"Are you jealous?" Terrell slipped his hands beneath her coat and around her back.

"Should I be?"

"Not at all."

Jade relaxed against him, feeling silly for even having felt a niggling of discomfort. "Good." Wrapping her arms around his neck, she tipped on her toes. He lowered his face to meet hers, thrilling her with a deep kiss.

Terrell was the one to pull away. "Take off your coat and stay awhile." When he saw her shopping bags, he asked, "Does this mean you're planning to stick around?"

She didn't know if he meant tonight, or forever. She replied ambiguously. "For a bit."

He helped her out of her coat, then headed to the living room. As she slipped out of her boots, she noticed that the bright lights in the living room dimmed. Studio lights.

Then as she walked into the room to meet Terrell, the bright lights came to life once more. Terrell appeared before her, a devilish smile on his lips and in his eyes.

"What?" Jade asked cautiously.

He produced a camera from behind his back. "I want to take some pictures of you."

Jade spun around. "Oh, no. Terrell, I don't look good."

"You're beautiful."

She faced him and gestured to her clothes. "My clothes are hardly glamorous enough."

He winked. "Then take them off."

Tilting her head, she gaped at him. "I don't think so."

Terrell took her hand. "I just want to do a couple black-and-whites of you. For me."

Jade fussed as he led her to the sofa, but sat where he placed her. Without notice, he began snapping shots.

"Terrell, I'm not ready."

"Then smile."

He moved to one side, then the next, the flash going crazy, as he took shot after shot. Finally, deciding that she didn't want to look like a loser in all the pictures, she smiled.

"That's it." Moving closer, he bent on one knee so that the camera was eye-level with her. "Oh, yeah."

Jade brought a hand to her face, rested her chin in her palm.

"Beautiful. Make love to the camera, baby."

She giggled. "Stop."

He lowered the camera from his face. "I know, that was lame. People love to say that in books and in the movies, but I *never* say that."

Jade raised an eyebrow. "If you said make love to the photographer, well, *that* would be something I might consider."

Terrell shot her just as her tongue flicked over her lips. Then he placed the camera on the floor and edged toward her on his knees. "Would you?"

"If I had the right incentive."

"And what would that be?" He placed his hands on the outside of her leg and trailed them along the length of her thighs.

"Oh, I don't know." Her eyes closed as his fingers caressed her inner thighs. "I, uh, I think you're on the right track."

She was incredibly beautiful and her need for him was a major turn-on. But he wanted more than a sexual relationship. Instead of continuing to tease her, he joined her on the sofa.

"What… Oh, you tease!"

With a finger, he traced the outline of her jaw. "No. Just giving you something to look forward to. Tonight."

He smothered her protest with a kiss. It was a kiss that left her wanting more. When he pulled away, she asked, "Since you obviously don't want me now the way I want you, what did you have in mind."

"How about dinner? I'm starved."

"I've been running around all day. I was hoping to stay in and relax."

"Then relax. I'll cook."

Jade flashed him a suspicious look. "You? Cook?"

"What's that supposed to mean? Because I'm a man, you don't think I can cook?"

Jade shrugged. "Something like that."

"Talk about sexist."

"I'm sorry, but I've never known a man who could cook a decent meal. Not my father, not my brother, not my hus—" She stopped abruptly. "Sorry."

He placed his hand on her leg. "No problem. I can't pretend you weren't married."

"But I'm not trying to compare you—"

He placed a finger on her lip, silencing her. "I didn't think you were. Now as for my culinary skills, you never got to know me well enough back then, but I've been able to cook since I was twelve. My mother made sure of that."

Jade shifted on the sofa, bringing a leg up with her. "Well, I could get used to this. Do I get to know what's on the menu, or is it a surprise?"

"You've got a choice of stir-fried chicken with vegetables and rice, or pineapple chicken breasts."

"This is for real?"

He took her hand, linked their fingers across his thigh. Jade liked the way their hands looked together, his dark skin against her lighter skin tone. "One thing I don't kid about is my food."

"In that case, I'll go for the pineapple chicken breasts."

* * *

The chicken tasted absolutely delicious. If Jade hadn't seen Terrell prepare it from scratch with her own eyes, she would have wondered if he'd ordered in. Clearly he was talented in more ways than she'd ever imagined.

As Terrell took the last bite of dinner, dropping the fork against the plate, Jade bolted to her feet. "Let me get your plate for you."

His fingers wrapped around her wrist. "Don't worry about it. Sit. Enjoy your wine."

"Let me at least do something."

"You're not used to sitting back and relaxing, are you?"

The truth undeniable, she shook her head. She had waited on Nelson hand and foot, trying to be a good wife, trying to make him love her when she doubted he ever did. "No."

"Well, get used to it."

Jade eased back onto the chair. "Okay. I'll try."

Lifting the bottle of Canei, Terrell filled Jade's glass. It was a light-tasting, sweet wine, to which she didn't need to add any ginger ale. He'd bought it just for her.

Terrell sat back. "I didn't want to ask you this earlier, but why's a woman who's as talented as you working in a restaurant? Not that there's anything wrong with working in a restaurant, but for you, doing hair is as much a passion as photography is for me."

"I don't have a salon anymore, remember?"

"I realize that. But you can still do hair. You can work for another salon." Terrell saw a quick flash of unease in Jade's eyes and knew that was something she'd never considered. "Why not?"

"You don't understand. After having my own salon, it would be the hardest thing to work for someone else. Every day would be a constant reminder of what I'd had, what I'd lost." Which is exactly why, even though the thought had crossed her mind on occasion, she'd always dismissed it.

"But at least you'd be doing what you love. I know you." At her wide-eyed look, he took her hand. "Yes, Jade, I do. I know you better than you think I do. And I know that you're miserable."

They'd made love once and he knew this much? "How?"

With her hand in his, he brought the two to his chest, over his heart. "I feel it here."

"You're…a mystery."

"I'm not that hard to figure out." His eyes held hers.

Jade cleared her throat, pulled her hand away. "I didn't want to consider working for another salon before, but now…" Now she was desperate. "Now I don't know. You're right. I'm miserable at my current job. My boss is a jerk. I'm not making much money."

"If it's another salon you want to open, let me help you."

"Help me? How?"

"I have money, Jade."

She knew he did. He was clearly successful. But she wouldn't take a handout from him. "No, Terrell. I don't need that kind of help."

"I could loan you—"

"No." She gave him a stern look. "I won't even consider it."

Terrell ran a hand over his face, wondering why she was so adamant about not taking his help. Because she was too proud, or because she didn't have plans to stick around in his life that long? He finally said, "I know someone with a salon. Sherry McIntyre. If you want, I can introduce you to her. I'm sure she could use someone as talented as you."

Uncomfortable with the whole idea, Jade averted her gaze

and squirmed in her seat. She didn't know what to think, what to do. Saying she was ready to work in a salon that wasn't her own and actually doing it were two different things.

"And if you like, you can work for me."

Her eyes shot up. "For you?"

Terrell nodded. "Yes. I use freelance hairstylists and makeup artists for the models and actors who come for pictures. Not always, but sometimes. It depends on the person; sometimes they like to do their own hair and makeup. But if you're interested, you could make anywhere from fifty to seventy-five a session."

"If I were just a friend, would you offer me this position?"

"You're not a friend."

"I don't know, Terrell." She was thankful that he even considered her, and she squeezed his hand to let him know that. "I think I have to get used to us before I'd consider working for you."

"Which is why I suggested Sherry's salon first."

How had she ever married Nelson after meeting a man like Terrell? "Thanks. I'll let you know when I'm…ready."

He stood, stepped toward her. "Are you ready for what I promised you earlier?" Though he wanted more than a sexual relationship with Jade, it was hard to be near her and not think about making love again.

Pushing back her chair, she stood to meet him, a smile dancing on her lips. "What exactly are we talking about now?"

Leaning forward, he whispered in her ear.

Jade giggled and playfully punched Terrell's arm. "Oh, you're bad." Then she slipped her arms around his waist. "Well, what are you waiting for?"

He scooped her into his arms and headed for the stairs.

Chapter 12

LIKE ALL GOOD THINGS, Jade's romantic escapade with Terrell had to come to an end. As much as she enjoyed being with him, she couldn't spend the rest of her days at his place and pretend the real world didn't exist.

Though she wished she could. For the piece of the world he'd offered her was more wonderful than the one she'd known. If she had to stay at his place forever, she knew she could and never get bored.

Her lips curled in a smile as she approached her apartment door. Remembering the wondrous way Terrell's kisses made her feel would always make her smile. Remembering his thoughtfulness, his concern for her, would always warm her heart. And remembering what they shared in his bed would always make her body hot.

She slipped her key into the lock and turned it. But before she could push the door open, it opened on its own.

"Jade!" Kathy exclaimed.

Jade tried but failed to make the smile on her face disappear. "Hi, Kathy."

"*Hi, Kathy?* You disappear for two nights, three days and all you have to say is 'Hi, Kathy'?"

Nonchalantly Jade shrugged. "What am I supposed to say?"

Kathy's mouth fell open as she stared at Jade with disbelief. "Oh," she finally said. "I get it. I'm prying."

Jade nodded, then that silly smile broadened. "But that's okay. I have to tell someone."

Kathy grabbed Jade by her coat sleeve, pulling her into the room. "Get in here and don't leave out a single detail."

"I don't believe it." Kathy pulled a leg onto the sofa, then rested her arm across her knee. "I just don't believe it."

"You're the one who's always telling me I need to live a little."

"Yeah, but I didn't think you'd actually listen to me!"

Kathy laughed, and Jade did, too. She'd left out the private details, but had shared with Kathy the fact that she and Terrell had spent two incredible nights together.

"So," Kathy began, "what does all this mean? Sure you're over your dry spell, but…?"

"It means we're talking again."

"Talking? You're doing a bit more than that, hon."

"Oh, stop. You're making me blush."

"Don't. I'm thrilled for you. You and Terrell—it's about time."

"Maybe you're right."

"Girlfriend, you know I am." Tilting her head, Kathy stared at Jade through narrowed eyes. "And what about love?"

Jade hadn't wanted to think about love. She wasn't ready

for that. "I want to take things one day at a time. I mean, I loved Nelson and look where that got me."

"But Terrell is different. He always was."

Bringing both feet onto the sofa, Jade crossed her legs. "I made myself a promise over a year ago. I promised myself I would open another salon by the year 2000. Now I'm nowhere near keeping that promise, and the last thing I need is a distraction. As far as Terrell is concerned, I want to get to know him again, spend time with him, but my career has to come first. I can't compromise that."

Kathy's mouth opened as though she was going to speak, but then snapped it shut. She patted Jade's forearm instead. "I understand. But what about Terrell? Does he understand?"

"He certainly can't expect marriage. It's too soon."

"But he was always crazy about you. Now that your relationship is sexual, you have to accept that he may want a commitment."

"He hasn't said anything."

"Maybe not, but he's always loved you."

The thought disturbing her, Jade frowned. "You think I should tell him I want to take things slowly?"

"I don't know. I'd just hate to think you're leading him on."

Jade would hate to think that, too. Was she leading him on? How could he realistically expect a commitment at this stage of their relationship? She'd known Nelson for three years, had married him, and their relationship had ended disastrously. Getting to know Terrell, discovering whether or not he was the right man for her would take time. This time Jade would take things very slowly. Not only was she not ready for a serious relationship now, she knew she wouldn't be until she reopened Dreamstyles.

With a wave of her hand, she dismissed Kathy's concern.

"I doubt it. Terrell understands as much as I do the necessity in taking things slowly."

"I hope you're right."

"I am." She stood. "And now as much as I'd love to stay and chat, I have to get ready for work."

It was too soon to start making wedding plans, but Terrell felt as elated as any groom must be. The two nights he'd spent with Jade were undoubtedly the best two nights of his life. He'd expected a level of discomfort, of unease the first time they made love, but to his surprise, Jade had been more than comfortable. Her need for him had been as great as his need for her.

He missed her. She'd been gone less than a day, yet his loft already seemed empty without her. How would he sleep in his bed tonight—alone? The scent of her body, though welcome on his sheets, would make him miss her all the more.

He was tempted to go to her workplace tonight and order a meal, but the truth was, he needed the time away from her to get some work done. With Jade around, his focus had shifted. Instead of his photography, he'd been concerned only with her. As a result, he'd fallen behind.

As he climbed the stairs to his darkroom, Terrell tried to shake the image of a smiling Jade from his mind. How could he concentrate on work when he could think only of her?

He pictured her naked, lying on his bed. "This is impossible," he said aloud. He could no more get Jade out of his mind than he could get her out of his heart. Like over six years ago, he knew he was in love. And that wasn't something that could be helped.

He could only hope that love wouldn't affect his ability to develop film.

Much later that evening, after actually getting a lot done, Terrell gave in and called her.

"Hello?" She sounded slightly breathless as she answered the phone.

"Hi." To his own ears, his voice was deeper than it usually was.

"Oh, hi."

Glancing at the clock, Terrell lay back on the bed. It was just after 11:00 P.M. "Is this too late to call?"

"No. It's fine. I'm just getting in, actually."

"How was work?"

"Could have been better. What about you? How was your day?"

"Let's just say I couldn't concentrate much on work."

"Really?" Her voice lowered an octave. "Why not?"

"Probably because I couldn't stop thinking about you." Pause. "I miss you."

"Do you?" He could hear a smile in that sexy voice.

"Mmm-hmm. I wish you were here tonight. My bed just won't be the same without you."

"Is that so."

"Mmm-hmm."

Pause. "Well, you know what they say about absence."

"I do. And I can't wait to see you again."

"Me neither. I've got to work the next few nights, but how about I come over on Saturday night?"

"So I'll have to dream about you until then?"

"I'll have to dream about you, too."

Terrell's eyes closed. Man, he wished he could hold Jade in his arms right now, sleep with her warm, soft body next to his. "All right. Saturday night. Early or late?"

"I work Saturday night as well, but I've got Sunday off. So it'll have to be late."

Late was better than never. "Okay, Jade. I'll see you then."

"Good night, Terrell." Pause. "Sweet dreams."

"Oh, they will be. Now that I've heard your voice." He blew out a contented breath. "Good night, sweetheart."

Only when Jade hung up did he replace the receiver. Then he turned off the bedside lamp, lay on his side, and closed his eyes, knowing that their reunion on Saturday night would be incredible.

"C'mon, sleepy head. Wake up."

Groaning, Jade dragged a pillow over her head. She'd been having the most pleasant of dreams and didn't appreciate the interruption. "Go away."

"Is that what you want me to tell your mother?"

Instantly Jade tossed the pillow aside and sat upright. Kathy stood in the doorway. "My mother's on the phone?"

Her friend nodded. "Yep. And she says it's an emergency."

Brother, Jade thought, but said, "Okay." She loved her mother dearly, but knew from experience that what her mother considered an emergency and what the rest of the world considered an emergency were two different things. "Thanks."

When she picked up the phone on her night table, she wondered what the problem was this time. With her family, she never knew. Life with the Alexanders certainly was never dull.

"Mama," Jade said into the receiver. "Hi."

"Jade, I swear I don't know how much longer I can put up with this."

"With what."

"Your father. I swear, that man will send me to an early grave."

Jade crossed her legs and asked what her mother expected. "What has he done this time?"

"He could be dead or alive for all I know. He didn't come home last night!"

"He didn't?" It wouldn't be the first time. When her parents argued, her father often spent the night at a friend's to allow a cooling-off period. "Did you two fight?"

"I guess we did. I know I shouldn't have gotten so angry with him, but that man gets on my last nerve sometimes."

Like you could ever live without him. "What happened?"

"Last night when I went into the kitchen to start dinner, your father had made a mess of the place. Said he wanted to surprise me with some fried chicken. He knows I do not like any of his surprises. Lord knows, my heart can barely take it. There was flour all over the place and he was baking the chicken at two hundred degrees. Two hundred degrees! That man will kill me with salmonella poisoning one day, I tell you."

"It sounds like he was trying to be thoughtful."

"Thoughtful. Hmm. He should fix the windows like I'm always telling him if he wants to be thoughtful. Or build me a new bookshelf. But he should stay out of my kitchen. He doesn't have a clue what to do when he's in there."

Smiling, Jade shook her head. Her parents were always like this—bickering over every little thing the other one did. But deep down, they were happy together.

"Kathy said this was an emergency."

"It is an emergency!" her mother exclaimed, her New Orleans accent getting heavier as her voice rose. "My husband's gone. Oh, Jade, what if he's hurt?"

"Mama, I'm sure he's fine. Did you check Mrs. Tracey's? You know how he and Dick are."

"Not yet." Her mother's voice softened.

"Give her a call, Mama. I'm sure there's nothing to worry about."

Mrs. Alexander let out a long-suffering moan. "Oh, I hope

not. Lord knows, I still need your father. With B.J. engaged and you gone, if I didn't have your father I don't know what I'd do."

"I know, Mama. Give Mrs. Tracey a call."

"We miss you," her mother continued. "Both your father and I. It was nice having you home for a few days."

"Yeah, it was nice," Jade agreed. She'd had a good dose of melodrama, but had enjoyed seeing her parents and her brother again. She'd even had a chance to meet Buttons, her brother's latest fiancée.

"Wait a second." After a moment, her relieved mother spoke. "Your father just stepped in the door."

"See," Jade said, surprised to find she was also relieved. "I told you he was fine."

"Well, he won't be when I get through with him. That man, I swear! Making me worry like this."

"Tell him hi for me."

"I will. You take care, honey. We'll talk later."

"And give him a kiss for me."

"A kiss? Hmm. I'll give him something all right."

"Mama," Jade said sternly. "Promise me you'll be nice. Daddy loves you and you love him. Remember that."

"Oh, all right. I'll give him a kiss for you. But that's all."

The other line beeped. "Mama, hold on a sec. I've got another call." As she clicked over, Jade hoped it was Terrell. "Hello?"

"Hello. Uh, I'm looking for Kathleen Small."

Disappointment tickled her stomach. "Oh, sure. Just hold on a sec."

"Mama," Jade said as she clicked back over to that line, but heard only a dial tone. Shaking her head, Jade hit the Hold button on the phone. Her poor father. He was definitely in for an earful.

Jade found Kathy in the foyer, slipping into her coat. "Oh, Kathy. There's a call for you."

"Who is it?"

"I don't know. A man."

Kathy looked to the living room, then back at Jade. For a moment, Jade thought she was going to ask her to take a message. Then Kathy said, "Okay. Thanks."

Turning, Jade headed back to the bedroom. Thinking of Terrell most of the night had kept her tossing and turning. And even when she had slept, Terrell had appeared in her dreams.

Now was a perfect time to catch up on her sleep. And if she dreamed of Terrell again, well, she thought with a smile, so be it.

Chapter 13

CLEARLY TERRELL KNEW Jade better than she thought. And the man was nothing if not thoughtful. When she'd arrived at work for her evening shift, Jade had been in a foul mood for no other reason than she had to spend another day waiting tables when she really wanted to be doing hair. But when she'd walked through the front door of the restaurant, the hostess had presented her with an envelope.

"This arrived for you by courier a couple hours ago."

It was a regular letter-size envelope. Terrell's address was neatly printed in the top left-hand corner, and it was addressed to her in care of The Red Piano. Jade had looked at the hostess with curiosity, but Mary had merely shrugged.

In the change-room, Jade couldn't deny the excitement she felt at receiving a letter from Terrell. Who would have thought a simple envelope could set her heart racing? And then she'd felt warmth like she hadn't known when she'd read the short note.

> My Dearest Jade,
> I know you said you didn't want to consider working at another salon yet, but I hope you've had time to give it some thought. If you have and you want to call Sherry, here's the number to the salon. 555-9800. I hope you'll give her a call. The name of her salon is Simple Pleasures.
> I miss you. Can't wait to see you Saturday.
> Terrell.

Jade had held the letter to her chest, able only to think of how special Terrell was. And his letter had come at the right time. Knowing she couldn't handle much more of working at The Red Piano, she was ready to give Sherry a call.

But because she was a chicken, Jade was finally calling Sherry about 9:00 P.M. As she dialed the number to the salon on the old phone in the small staff room, she prayed the salon had an answering machine.

Someone picked up on the third ring, leaving Jade momentarily startled. "Uh, hi." Darn, she'd wanted to leave a message. "Um, I'm looking for Sherry McIntyre."

"This is Sherry."

Jade tried to gulp down her nervousness. It didn't work. "Uh, Sherry. My name is Jade Alexander."

"Oh, hi, Jade." To a stranger, it would sound like Sherry knew her. "Terrell told me you might call."

"He did?"

"Yep. And I'm glad you did. I need a new stylist and you come highly recommended."

For a moment, Jade was speechless. Terrell was full of surprises. "Really?"

"Really. Like desperately. What's your availability like tomorrow?"

Tomorrow! "I'm not sure if Terrell told you, but I already have a job—"

"He did. But if you can spare some time tomorrow, I'd love to meet you, show you the salon."

It was like this was all meant to be. Though her New Year's dream was to open another salon, she'd been given two wonderful opportunities to get back into doing hair in less than two weeks. It was impossible to ignore the possibility of a higher power at work. "Sure. I can come by in the afternoon."

"Great." Sherry sounded relieved. "Let me give you the address."

Minutes later Jade hung up, unable to believe Sherry had been so receptive to the idea of her working for her. In fact, Sherry made it sound like she already had the job.

Maybe the year 2000 was going to be her year after all.

Thanks to Terrell.

If the weather was nice enough, Terrell usually skipped his Thursday evening workout routine in his apartment's gym in favor of a jog through Central Park. However, tonight he didn't have even an hour to spare for a workout because he was behind on his workload. He'd had to call a few clients and tell them that their pictures would be ready early next week, not tomorrow.

This wasn't like him. As a single man, his rigorous work schedule wasn't a problem. As a man who wanted to spend time with the new lady in his life, he knew he'd have to cut back on a few hours.

Which wouldn't be a problem. His mother had been telling him for ages that he worked too much and that if he didn't slow down his "wife" would pass him by. Before New Year's Eve, he hadn't cared if he ever settled down. Not that he didn't want to—family was important to him. But the only woman he'd ever considered settling down with was Jade, and when he'd lost her, he hadn't given marriage a second thought.

After doing fifty pushups on his living room floor, the only workout he could do today, Terrell sat, his breathing ragged, and wrapped his arms around his knees. His eyes strayed to the newly mounted photo of Jade. It was the shot where she'd just started to smile, and the look the camera captured was both innocent and seductive. He'd enlarged the photo to an eleven-by-seventeen size, mounted it on a black wood backing, then placed it in the center of his living room above the sofa. With Jade's picture on the wall, he'd always feel her presence.

Speaking of pictures, Terrell rose, stretched his muscles, then headed for the stairs, determined to develop more photos. He usually developed his own film but sometimes brought it to a lab in SoHo that he trusted. It cost him more that way, but he'd have to bring a few more rolls there tomorrow, if he wanted to stay on schedule.

Halfway up the stairs, Terrell stopped, turned, descended instead of ascending. With the sudden urge to call Drew, he headed straight for the living room phone.

He sat on the sofa and picked up the receiver. Holding it to his ear, he punched in the digits to his brother's East Orange home. Drew answered on the first ring.

"Hey, D," Terrell said, referring to his brother by the simple nickname he'd earned growing up.

"Big T? Wow. This is a shock."

"Don't start."

"Hey, you and I know that you never call during the week. Something must be up."

Stretching his long legs before him, Terrell crossed his ankles. "Not something. Someone."

"Jade."

"Yeah. Jade."

"Well, at least you sound like you've stopped crying."

"Gimme a break." Terrell's lips twisted in a wry smile. "I wasn't that bad."

"Yeah, right. Anyway, what's changed this week? I thought you weren't in touch with her."

"You won't believe this, but she ended up working on a shoot I worked on. Talk about a small world."

"And now you're either over her or you've slept with her."

"Hey, hey, hey."

"I'm guessing the latter."

"We're talking."

"Mmm-hmm."

"It's that obvious?"

"Hey, I think it's great. My only advice: keep things in perspective."

"D, things are gonna work out this time."

"For your sake, I hope so."

"They will. We talked. I know why she ran, why she didn't want me to call her. But we've worked that out."

"Well, then, I'm happy for you. As long as you know what you're doing."

Sensing something was bothering his brother, Terrell asked, "What's up, Drew?"

"I'm a little preoccupied."

"Anything I should worry about?"

"Naw…I hope not, anyway. Mom's just been feeling a little under the weather."

"Really?" He should give her a call. "It's not serious?"

"No. She told Lena she fainted, and I guess I'm just a little worried. After her heart attack last year…"

Drew didn't have to explain. "I know." Terrell wondered if this was serious. "She didn't say anything to me."

"Nor to me. It was probably just woman talk that brought it out, anyway. You know women. There's no issue they leave unexamined."

"Yeah." But Terrell's mind wasn't on women and what they talked about. His mother was sixty-five, an age where he was very concerned about her health. "I'll call her."

"I'm sure it's nothing to worry about."

"Probably not, but I'll call anyway."

"Give her my best."

"Will do."

"And Terrell?"

That his brother didn't refer to him as Big T made Terrell's nape tingle with worry. "Yeah?

"Good luck with Jade. I hope it all works out for you."

"Thanks. Later."

"Later."

After speaking with both his mother and father, Terrell felt a tremendous sense of relief. His mother was her regular cheery self, and his father seemed happy as well. His mother had flat out told him that she felt fine, that she'd fainted only because she'd skipped breakfast one morning. She knew it was silly, but she'd been absorbed in sewing an outfit for Sadé and hadn't realized the time.

Terrell loved his parents. If anything ever happened to

either of them, he didn't know what he'd do. They'd given him so much and he was glad that his success as a photographer had allowed him to give something back.

He'd almost lost his father three years ago. On the drive home from work to his home in East Orange, New Jersey, his father had been accosted by a thug with a gun and ordered to get out of his car. His father had complied and the thug hadn't hurt him, but Terrell knew how lucky his father was to have escaped the carjacking with his life. Some people didn't think any more of killing another human than they did of squashing a spider.

The moment he'd had the chance, Terrell had bought his parents a home in Maplewood, New Jersey, a much quieter area. Anything could happen anywhere, but in a more mature neighborhood, Terrell was praying his parents would be safe.

Since their move two years ago, they had been. And Terrell worried less about them. But his mother's heart attack a year earlier had scared him more than anything.

She was okay now. A change in diet had worked wonders for her. And until now, he had forgotten that anything could happen to her.

He would visit his parents this weekend. And if Jade was ready, he'd bring her with him.

Chapter 14

JADE HAD EXPECTED to find Kathy awake and before the television as she did on many a morning, but instead, she found Kathy in her bedroom. That she wasn't her normal happy-go-lucky self worried Jade as she pushed open the door and stepped into the room.

Kathy sat cross-legged on the bed, her elbows resting on her knees and her chin resting in her palms. Instantly concerned, Jade hurried to her side.

"Kathy, what's wrong?"

Kathy didn't move or respond. It was as if she was in her own world.

Jade's concern increased. "Kathy?"

"He called me. After eight years, he called me."

"Sheldon?" It could only be him.

Sitting up straight, Kathy nodded. "The one and only. And you won't believe what he said to me."

"What?"

"That he's sorry. That he's back in town. That he wants to see me."

By Kathy's reaction, Jade could only assume that was bad news. "How...how did he get this number?"

"He called my brother. Those two were always tight."

Jade wondered why Kathy's brother would give out her phone number but didn't ask. "Are you gonna see him?"

Kathy flashed Jade a not-on-your-life stare.

"Dumb question."

"You know, it wouldn't have been so bad if he'd at least told me what was going through his mind before he left. If he'd let me know why he was suddenly so afraid to marry me. Maybe I could have forgiven him then, but not now."

"Is there anything I can do?"

"Other than make him disappear? No."

Jade stood. "I was going to tell you something, but if you want to be alone, it's okay."

"No." Bringing her knees to her chest, Kathy wrapped her arms around them. "What is it?"

"I might soon be working at a hair salon. Do you believe it?"

"That's great." Kathy forced a smile, but it wavered as she repeated, "Just great."

Jade dropped onto the bed beside her. "Kathy... Oh God, you're not going to cry..."

But she was. Twin tears rolled down each cheek as her lips puckered in a frown. "I'm sorry."

This was the first time Jade had seen her friend cry, and it left her feeling helpless. She offered the only support she knew how—she gave Kathy a hug.

"I didn't think he still mattered to me."

"Clearly he does."

"But I don't want him to."

"Maybe you should talk to him. Hear him out."

"No. It's too late for that."

It was amazing how completely right Jade had been about Kathy. All the other men, the flirting, the dating, the never having a dull weekend—it all meant nothing because in her heart she'd never really gotten over Sheldon.

Finally Kathy pulled out of Jade's embrace. She wiped at her tears with the backs of her hands. "I'm okay."

"You sure?"

Kathy shrugged. "If I'm not, there's nothing you can do to help me."

"I can listen."

"But that won't change the facts. I just want to forget Sheldon and finally move on. That's the only thing you were right about. I never did move on because there was never any closure."

"That's why it wouldn't hurt to talk to him."

"We did talk," Kathy replied succinctly. "Now it's time for me to move on." And then as though nothing had happened, Kathy hopped off the bed and skipped to her closet. "I think I'll call Tyrone. At least he's not into games."

Behind Kathy's back, Jade blew out a hurried breath, worrying about her friend. If Kathy was going to start dating Tyrone again, then she was hurting more than she was ready to admit to herself.

Kathy disappeared, leaving Jade sitting on her bed. Knowing there was nothing she could do to help her friend, Jade made her way back to her own bedroom.

It was time to get ready to head to Simple Pleasures.

* * *

The familiar sights, sounds and smells of a busy Manhattan hair salon overpowered Jade as she entered the large building in uptown New York. She knew she'd missed doing hair, missed running Dreamstyles, but until she'd stepped into Simple Pleasures, she didn't realize just how much she missed it all.

"Can I help you?" a dark-skinned receptionist asked.

"I'm here to see Sherry."

"Just take a seat. I'll get her for you."

As Jade sat on a vinyl seat near the window at the front of the salon, she looked around the shop. Like the days when she'd had her salon, Friday was clearly a busy day. Water gushed from the sinks in the back of the shop, almost every dryer was in use, and stylists crimped and curled hair at every station. The air was filled with the perfumed scent of relaxers, conditioners, and hairsprays. Some customers sat and read quietly beneath dryers or in the waiting area, while others gabbed and laughed.

It was a beautiful sight.

"Hi," a woman said, and Jade looked up at the very fair-skinned black woman with frizzy red hair. She wore a smock over a black T-shirt and black leggings. She extended a hand. "You must be Jade."

Standing Jade shook the outstretched hand. "That's me. Sherry?"

"Yep." The woman's grin was genuine. "Pleased to meet you."

"Likewise."

"Would you care for a coffee? Tea?"

"I'm fine," Jade said.

"Please, let me take your coat."

Jade slipped out of her leather jacket and handed it to Sherry. "This is a great salon."

"Thanks."

It was larger than Dreamstyles had been and in an upscale neighborhood. The women seated in the chairs all looked liked professional people. Jade had served professionals as well as artists and students.

"Let me introduce you." Jade followed the woman as she headed toward the back of the shop. Pausing at the reception desk she said, "Jade, this is Sabrina."

Sabrina and Jade acknowledged one another.

"This is Judy," Sherry said, gesturing to a short, attractive woman curling a patron's hair.

Jade said, "Hi."

"This is Marla. Gwen."

Jade greeted them, noting that Gwen's stomach was as large as a house, then followed Sherry to the back of the salon. "Rachel, this is Jade."

The tall, skinny woman smiled her greeting, then returned to washing a customer's hair.

"And finally, this is Susan."

"Hi," Susan said happily as she towel-dried an elderly woman's hair.

"Hello," Jade replied. So far everyone seemed friendly.

Sherry had introduced Jade to the members of her staff as though she was introducing a new employee. Jade didn't bother to remind Sherry that she hadn't accepted a job yet.

When Sherry stepped through a door marked EMPLOY-EES ONLY, she placed Jade's coat over the back of a chair. "The staff washroom is right here. And there's a small eating area. Not that we get much time for lunch around here."

"I can imagine," Jade said, remembering how crazy her own salon had been most of the time.

"We're open Monday to Saturday, ten till whenever. I'm not here Mondays though."

For years, Jade had opened her salon only Tuesdays to Saturdays, until the demand was so great she'd started opening Mondays as well. Unlike Sherry, she hadn't been able to take the day off.

"Sometimes I open earlier," Sherry continued. "Especially if I have a weave or braids to do."

"Mmm-hmm." She had done the same.

"I understand you had a salon."

"Yes. Dreamstyles on West Thirty-fifth."

"Ah yes. I saw the magazine you published. What a great idea—putting together a magazine to showcase your salon."

"That was a while ago. I've been out of business over a year," Jade added, wishing the lump in her throat would disappear. When would it ever get easier to discuss her salon?

Sherry simply nodded, for which Jade was grateful. "Now I'm essentially looking for another stylist to replace Gwen. I'm sure you noticed that she's pregnant."

"I did."

"Well, she's due in a month, but from the size of her, I'd say she could give birth any day now. Anyway, I know your work and would love to have you on staff."

Just like that. It was like looking a gift horse in the mouth. "I'm flattered."

"Now I offer a fairly competitive salary, plus you'd get tips on top of that. You probably have more experience than Gwen, and I'm prepared to pay you extra for that."

"Okay." Folding her arms over her breasts, Jade considered the information.

"Other than that, I may look for someone else as well. Just for Thursdays, Fridays, and Saturdays. My clientele continues to grow and I could use the extra help on those days."

"But you'd want me for full-time work?"

"Yes."

Was this really happening to her? Though she'd been too proud to consider working for another salon before, the idea now seemed wonderful.

"Sherry!" someone called from the front of the salon.

"Give me a second," Sherry said to Jade. "Help yourself to some coffee and cookies until I return."

Instead of heading to the small food tray, Jade slowly walked through the door and back into the salon. With interest, she looked around the room, knowing instinctively that she would enjoy working here. As her mother would say, Sherry seemed like "good people."

Minutes later Sherry hurried back toward her. "Feel like showing me what you can do?"

Startled, Jade stared at Sherry with her mouth open.

"Not like a test," Sherry quickly added. "I could really use the help."

"I...uh."

"Even an hour would be a great help."

An hour. Jade glanced at her watch. It was two now and she had to be at work at five. She could make it.

"I'll pay you."

"In that case," Jade began, smiling, "you're on."

The sixty extra dollars in her pocket—fifty for the hour and a half of work and ten dollars in tips—were hardly of consequence to Jade. Instead, she could only think of how wonderful it had felt to get back in the groove of doing hair.

When she officially started, she would be strictly a stylist, but today she had applied a relaxer to a client's hair, put that same client under the dryer with a treatment, then went on to style another woman's hair in a French roll with soft curls framing her face. By the woman's own account, she'd never seen her hair looking so good. Even Sherry had seemed genuinely impressed.

Jade had left with a definite offer of employment. She promised to let Sherry know as soon as possible when she could start.

She'd be a fool to turn this opportunity down. As the saying went, everything in its time. Well, it was her time to do hair again and she was ready.

"What is it?" Kathy asked. "What's wrong?"

Tyrone reached over her body to turn on the lamp. "I don't know. You tell me."

"Nothing's wrong with me." Kathy ran a fingernail along Tyrone's chest. "You know I want you."

Covering her hand, Tyrone forced it to still. "Just two weeks ago, you wanted nothing to do with me. Remember that?"

With her hand beneath his, Kathy ran her toes up and down one of Tyrone's calves instead. "Did anyone ever tell you that you talk too much?"

He silenced her with a look. "I told you before. No more games."

Kathy didn't want games, either. She wanted what Tyrone was best at: sex. Maybe then she could forget the fact that Sheldon had called and asked her to give him another chance. Maybe then she could forget what it felt like to be a fool for love.

"No more games." She shifted so that her body half covered his. Slowly she traced circles along the base of his neck.

She was rewarded with a low, rumbling moan. "Woman, you are too much."

She moved over him completely, kissing his chest, then his belly. "What were you saying?"

"Shut up and kiss me."

As he pulled her upward, her breasts grazed the hair on his strong chest. Tangling his hands in her hair, he guided her mouth to his. Then he kissed her long and hard, letting her know how much he wanted her.

She kissed him back, wishing she wanted him half as much.

After taking out the dinners to the table of ten, Jade hurried to the kitchen for a much-needed break. She'd been running around on her feet for hours, fetching water, ketchup, beer, more water. She could stand all day in a salon and never feel as burned-out as she did after a shift at the restaurant.

Glancing around, she saw that the other servers and staff members were occupied with their own lives. Satisfied that nobody had noticed her, she slipped into the staff room and closed the door.

Nobody was inside. Thankful, Jade pulled out a fold-up chair and sat next to the phone. Terrell hadn't been home when she'd tried him earlier, and she hoped he was home now. She wanted to thank him for referring her to Sherry.

After four rings, the machine came on. Just hearing Terrell's smooth, deep voice made her smile. She couldn't wait until tomorrow when she could see him again. She might not be ready for a commitment, but she wanted to spend time with him.

Maybe she was just horny. Before this week, she hadn't made love in well over a year and it had felt good to finally be with a man again.

Not just a man, a voice told her. *Terrell.*

Ignoring the voice, she left a message. "Terrell, it's Jade. I was hoping to catch you home. Anyway, I just want to thank you for—"

"What the hell is going on?"

Jade literally jumped out of the seat at the sound of Pierre's angry voice. A hand on the base of her throat, she stared at her boss with a mixture of anger and disbelief. "You scared the life out of me."

"What are you doing back here?" Pierre's pale face was red with anger. "I am not paying you to sit back here on the phone when the restaurant is packed!"

Pierre had gotten on her last nerve. "I only came back here for a second. Don't you dare imply I'm slacking off."

"Excuse me? You're the one sitting back here on the phone when you've got a table of ten who needs your service. Or don't you care?"

"They've been taken care of!"

"You know, Jade, I really tried to be nice to you, but I've had it up to here with your insubordination." He raised a hand above his head.

"Insubordination?"

"Shut up. You let me talk now."

Her back stiffened with angry indignation. Not even her parents talked to her that way. There was no way Pierre Lamont would and get away with it. "You know what, Pierre?" As she spoke, she untied her apron. "You can take this job and—" She stopped herself before she said something crude. Instead, she shoved the apron in Pierre's hands and stormed out of the staff room.

He called her name, but she didn't stop until she reached the change-room. To think she'd actually felt a measure of guilt at the thought of quitting this job to work in the salon! Well, Pierre had just made the decision easy.

Jade changed into her street clothes and stuffed her dirty uniform in her gym bag. Thinking better of that, she took the clothes from the bag and left them in the small locker that she'd used while working here. She wouldn't need them anymore.

As her hand closed around the doorknob, the corners of her lips twitched. And then she smiled, knowing that she was doing the right thing.

For the first time in a long time, she felt more sure of herself than she'd ever been.

Chapter 15

WHEN JADE STEPPED OUT the front door of The Red Piano, she didn't look back. She didn't want to. That miserable chapter of her life was over and she was glad.

Clutching her purse and gym bag to one side, she walked quickly in the night. She had hoped to reach Terrell, maybe even surprise him with a visit before tomorrow night, but he wasn't home. Oh, well. One more day wouldn't kill her. Besides, she wanted to see how Kathy was doing.

"Hey, Jade."

The voice startled her, and she turned, stopped. Facing her was Milton Madden. "Milton. Don't you know you should never sneak up on a woman?"

Casually he shrugged. "Hey, we're friends."

Jade didn't know if it was the strange look in his eyes, the calm voice he spoke with, or the fact that with each step he was invading her space, but instantly she felt goose bumps pop out on her skin. "What do you want?"

"I was coming in to see you when I saw you heading out." He took another step toward her. "I just wanted to say hi."

Spinning on her heel, Jade turned back the way she was originally heading and started walking. "It's late, Milton. I'm on my way home."

He kept pace beside her. "Why don't we go for a drink?"

How many men would ask for a second date after a woman had more or less called him a slug? Only crazy ones, Jade was sure. "I…I can't."

"Why not?"

Jade was distinctly aware of the fact that she was practically alone on the street with Milton, not a situation that comforted her. "I just can't. Maybe another time."

Grabbing her forearm, he pulled her to him forcefully. "Tonight, Jade. Now I've put up with your flirting, your hard-to-get act, and I'm tired of it all. I'm going to give you what you really want."

Jade was so horrified, she stared at Milton with a stunned expression before she thought of screaming. In the instant she had wasted time, he covered her mouth with his hand and began dragging her toward a car. She tried fighting, kicking a foot backward in hopes that it would connect with his knee, but he was too strong for her.

"Don't fight me, Jade," he warned. "It will be easier this way."

Oh, God, what did he have in mind? Forcing her mouth open, Jade tried to take a bite out of his hand just as she heard Milton's agonized cry. The next instant, he released her, and Jade steadied her footing. She spun around in time to see Terrell level a punch at Milton's gut.

Milton, shorter than Terrell and clearly no match for him,

cried out again as he doubled over in pain. Terrell grabbed the man by his coat and hurled him toward the brick wall of a closed submarine shop. Hitting the wall head-on, Milton crumpled to the ground, moaning in pain.

"You're not so tough when faced with a real challenge, now are you?" Terrell asked, taking a step toward Milton.

Jade placed a firm hand on his arm, holding him back. "No, Terrell. That's enough."

Seeming to forget Milton even existed, Terrell turned and wrapped her in his arms. "Are you okay?"

"Yes." Thank God Terrell had arrived at the right moment. "Where did you come from?"

"I missed you," he explained, pulling out of the hug to frame her face. "I thought I'd come by and see you at work. I saw this jerk bothering you as I parked my car. I didn't know it was you at first, but I'm not the kind of guy who can walk away when a woman's in trouble."

No, he wasn't. Terrell not only was honorable, he had guts. She threw her arms around his neck. "Oh, I'm so happy so see you." She saw a flash of movement behind him and screamed, "Terrell!"

Terrell turned in time to see Milton wielding a rock that he no doubt intended to smash on his head. In one smooth movement, he pushed Jade behind him and deflected Milton's blow. The rock went flying. Jade heard the sickening sound of a jaw cracking as Terrell's fist connected with Milton's face.

"Son of a—" Milton yelled, gripping his injured jaw.

"Let's go," Jade pleaded, pulling Terrell away from Milton. "Please get me out of here."

Terrell rarely fought and his hands shook from a surge of adrenaline. He'd like nothing more than to teach Milton a lesson he'd never learned before, but as angry as he was right now, he knew that wasn't wise. Besides, Milton wouldn't be bothering anybody else now.

Turning to Jade, he wrapped an arm around her. "Let's go," he said, and led her to his Jeep.

"I'm fine," Jade repeated in a singsong voice, though she enjoyed lying on Terrell's sofa and being pampered. "Honest."

His butt resting beside her legs, Terrell held her forearm gingerly, fingering the blackened spot on her skin. "Look what he did to you."

"It's only a bruise. It will heal."

"Still…"

"It's over. And it could have been worse, but thanks to you it wasn't."

"Who was that guy, anyway?"

Jade frowned, remembering, wondering if there was any way she had encouraged him. "Just a guy who came into the restaurant from time to time. I always knew he was a jerk, but I didn't expect this."

"He liked you."

"If you want to call it that. He always came on a little too strong, didn't know how to keep his hands to himself. I told him I wasn't interested—"

"But he didn't listen. I know how that can be."

"You do?"

He nodded. "With my job, I guess it comes with the territory. Some women do the most incredible things."

Curious, Jade faced Terrell head-on. "Really? Like what?"

"Worst-case scenario—get naked and try to seduce me."

Jade's stomach lurched, though she shouldn't be surprised. Terrell often worked one-on-one with models and actors. And women were so bold these days nothing would shock her.

"Get naked, hmm?" She tried to laugh off her sudden insecurity. "Most men wouldn't mind beautiful women taking off their clothes for them."

"I'm not most men."

His tone was frank, and Jade instantly regretted what had come from her mouth. She'd meant it as a joke, though it had had a ring of truth. She'd been curious. "I'm sorry. That was insensitive."

"Photography is a job, Jade. It's what I love to do, and I don't appreciate unwanted come-ons any more than you do. I have a reputation to uphold. All it takes is one scorned woman spreading lies, and my reputation is as good as dirt."

"I didn't think about that."

"Most people don't. They think men are such animals that we enjoy sexual harassment, that women are the only real victims."

This was the first time Jade had seen Terrell so fired up about a subject. There was anger in his eyes, bitterness in his voice, and she knew there was a reason. "What happened?"

He told her about Darlene Simpson. And then she really felt like a fool. She slapped a hand to her forehead. "I am so, so sorry. For what you went through, *and* for being so simple-minded."

His expression softened. "Thanks. And don't think twice about it. I'm just a little passionate on the subject."

"Understandably." The talk of models and photography—and the fact that they needed a breather from their serious conversation—made Jade glance up at the enlarged photo he'd taken of her. Terrell certainly was talented, she thought, still unable to believe he'd actually made her look beautiful on film.

"You never did say what you thought of the picture."

His voice startled her, that's how caught up she was in looking at her image. His gentle tone told her he wasn't mad at her, and she was glad. "I love it," she replied truthfully. "I love the black-and-white look, the way you captured so many different emotions with one shot. I look coy, sexy, innocent. Like me, but not me. I can't believe I look so…"

"Beautiful?"

She nodded.

"Well, the camera doesn't lie, and that's no trick photography. You are beautiful. You have to know that."

Maybe, but it wasn't something she thought about. It certainly wasn't something that had given her a better lot in life.

"I can't believe it. You're blushing."

Was she? Though African-American, her pale complexion did tinge with reddish hues when she was embarrassed. "I guess I am."

"No need to be embarrassed, sweetheart. You're gorgeous and you should be proud."

His words warmed her heart, for she realized she'd rarely heard them from Nelson or anyone else, at least not in a way that was meaningful. "Thanks."

He smiled, then his gaze fell from her face to her arm. He gently ran a finger over her bruise. "You want some ice for this?"

"No." Jade shook her head. "But you could…kiss it better."

A smile flashed in his eyes. Lowering his mouth to her arm, he softly kissed the fair skin. "Like this?"

Instantly Jade felt the stirrings of desire. "That's a good start."

"Hmm." He trailed kisses down her arm, to her hand, to her thumb. Lifting her hand, he pressed her palm to his lips.

Jade could hardly catch her breath. What was it about Terrell that made her so hungry for his touch? She'd been married to Nelson for five years and had never felt this way with him.

His other hand moved to her leg and he bent it at the knee. Jade cried out—and not from the pleasure.

"What'd I do?"

"My ankle…it hurts. I twisted it when I was struggling with Milton."

"Come here." Carefully Terrell eased her legs up so that he could maneuver his body beneath them. He rested her legs across his lap, then slipped an arm under her back, lifting her upper body toward his. "Is that okay?"

"Mmm-hmm."

He held her firmly yet gently, resting his chin atop her head. Being with her like this, taking care of her, felt right. They didn't have to make love tonight. He just wanted to hold her, be with her.

"You know," Terrell began, "there's a lot I don't know about you."

It was true. They knew they were attracted to each other, that they enjoyed each other's company, that they were compatible in bed. Still, Jade asked, "Like?"

"Like your family, your favorite food. Your hobbies— other than me."

She smirked. "It always boils down to that, doesn't it?"

"Your insatiable sexual appetite?"

"Mine?"

"There's no need to be embarrassed," Terrell said, then yelped as Jade pinched his arm. "Okay. So it's mutual." Pause. "All right. Let's start with something simple. My favorite color is black. What's yours?"

"Black is not a color."

"So they say. It's still my favorite. What about you?"

"I love red."

"The color of passion."

Jade shrugged. "I guess so."

"Tell me about your family."

"My family is crazy," Jade replied without hesitation.

"Ah. Well, that explains it."

She pinched him again. "You need to stop."

Lightly he brushed his lips over her temple. She'd expected some type of rebuttal...not the simple yet stimulating caress of his lips against her skin.

"I thought we were talking."

"So talk."

"I...I can't...not with you..."

She heard his sharp intake of breath as he rested his face against hers. He wanted her, yet he was able to hold his desire at bay. It had taken thirty-four years, but she finally felt completely comfortable in a man's arms.

"You were talking about your crazy family."

Jade's hand covered his. "I love them. They're the only family I have. But they are crazy. My brother's been engaged so many times I can't even remember. My parents—" she paused "—they love each other, but they're always bickering over some little thing. I spent Christmas with them. Talk about talk-show material!"

"But I'm sure you wouldn't know what to do without them."

"True." They were all she had and she loved them to death.

"Your family's in New Orleans, right?"

"You remember that?"

"Sweetheart, you may think you sound like a born-and-bred New Yorker, but I still hear that Southern drawl in your voice sometimes." He ran the pad of this thumb over her wrist. "Besides, I remember a lot about you."

There was no mistaking the change in his tone, the way his voice deepened to that bedroom baritone, and Jade remembered Kathy's concern that Terrell might want more from her than she was willing to give. For this reason, she folded her hands in her lap and changed the subject. "What about your family?"

"They're in New Jersey. I've got one brother. And my parents are still together. In fact, I don't know a happier couple."

"Certainly not my parents."

"They must love each other if they're still together."

"I guess so." As a child, Jade had wondered if they truly did love one another. Now as an adult she realized that the bickering was just part of the way they communicated. "It's just that I wish they could be normal. Happy the way other couples are. No more bickering and fighting."

Terrell didn't know from firsthand experience, but he believed that arguing was at least better than silence. "They both sound very passionate."

"Maybe. But that kind of passion scares me."

"Why?"

"It's too…volatile. Did I tell you that my mother left my father once?" When Terrell didn't respond, she continued. "I'd just turned fifteen. She just packed her bags one day and left. Two days later she called to say that she was running off with a man who would finally give her what she needed."

"Really?"

"Mmm-hmm. My brother and I were devastated. Our family was falling apart and there was nothing we could do." Just remembering that insecure time in her life made her stomach tighten painfully.

"That must have been awful for you." He ran a comforting hand along her thigh. "What happened?"

"My mother came home a week later. She and my father had it out. It turned out she'd been at a friend's place—not on some rendezvous with another man—but had just wanted to make my father jealous. Is that nuts or what?"

"A little extreme," Terrell agreed. His parents had been the opposite—lovey-dovey, always holding hands or sneaking kisses to the point where it had embarrassed him as a child. He shared that with Jade.

"That would have been wonderful," Jade said, punctuating her thought with a loud exhale of breath.

"Well, at least both our parents are still together. They must have done something right."

Jade was silent.

"You don't agree."

Softly she said. "You don't know what it was like growing up with them. And after my mother left that one time, I was always afraid she would leave again. No child should have to feel that way.

"I think if my parents had been normal, not so *passionate* as you say, I wouldn't have married Nelson. He was just so different from what I was used to—quiet, mild mannered—I thought he'd be the perfect husband."

Terrell had the distinct feeling he was on the hot seat with the way she'd exaggerated the word passionate, and defended his position. "I don't think there's such a thing as too much passion. As long as it's with the right person."

"I don't know about that."

For a fleeting moment, Terrell had a sinking feeling in his gut. He wondered if his own emotional intensity, the way he'd let her know exactly how he felt about her without hesitation, had scared her right into Nelson's arms more than six years ago. And he wondered what Jade's view of passion and love would mean for them now. Terrell was a passionate person, believed in loving intensely and not holding anything back. But by Jade's own account, that kind of passion scared her.

She'd had a bad marriage, had seen her parent's up-and-down relationship. He wondered if she'd ever seen a "normal" couple—and suddenly wanted her to meet his parents.

"What are you doing tomorrow?"

"Well, I'm not working." She'd told him earlier how she'd quit her job.

"How about coming to New Jersey with me? I'm going to my parents' for dinner." He felt her stiffen in his arms, and he wondered if the mere idea of visiting his family was so intimidating. "What's wrong?"

"I...I think it's too soon. Don't you?"

"No."

She sighed. "Terrell, we're just getting to know one another again. Going to your parents' is a big step."

"If I like you, they'll like you."

"Is that supposed to make me feel better?"

Yes. But he said, "I can introduce you as a friend, if you want."

She took a moment to consider the option. Or maybe she needed time to think of the perfect reason to turn him down. "Maybe another time, Terrell."

Though he wanted to, he didn't push the issue. If Jade wasn't ready, she wasn't ready. But he had to wonder if there was more to it. "Another time, then."

Swinging her legs to the floor, she moved out of Terrell's arms. Then she yawned. "I'm kinda tired. Do you mind—"

"No," Terrell replied quickly. Perhaps too quickly.

Leaning forward, she planted a chaste kiss on his lips. "Good night."

"Good night."

Then Terrell watched her swaying hips as she walked away from him, an ache building in his heart. As she climbed the stairs without even a glance back in his direction, he had to wonder what had gone wrong.

Chapter 16

JADE COULDN'T EXPLAIN the tension she felt around Terrell, but she couldn't deny it, either. For most of the trip to Brooklyn, they talked about insignificant things like the record snow Manhattan had gotten this year and the fact that the world hadn't come to a sudden end because of the millennium bug.

Terrell felt it, too, she was sure. Sometimes when she felt him looking at her and she'd glance his way, he'd look back at the road. He didn't make a move to take her hand. Sure he was driving, but he was such an affectionate guy that his lack of physical contact seemed out of character.

She supposed she could have placed a hand on his leg or his arm. But she hadn't. Did he feel as confused as she?

And the darn thing was, she didn't know what had happened to change things between them.

Maybe their relationship was dying a natural death. Maybe not even the sex was enough to keep him interested anymore.

"Turn right here," Jade said; almost as Terrell was at the intersection. Sharply he hit the brakes, and she gripped the sides of the seat as he made the turn.

"Don't worry, Jade. This Jeep can handle a lot. Trust me."

Trust him? Why had he added that? So she wouldn't feel afraid on the snow-covered roads? Or was he making a commentary about their relationship?

"It's my fault. I should have been paying attention."

Terrell nodded. "Which way?"

"Left at the corner." Was it colder outside or in this Jeep, Jade wondered. "It's the second building on the right."

Moments later Terrell pulled up to the curb. After a moment, he turned to face her. "Can I call you later?"

"Sure." Pause. "About your parents—"

"It's okay." He smiled, but it didn't reach his eyes.

"I wish you weren't angry with me."

"I'm not angry." He shrugged. "Maybe a little disappointed."

There it was…out in the open. And she supposed he had a right to be disappointed. She didn't mind making love with him but she couldn't meet his family…? Maybe she was sending him mixed messages.

As though he sensed the direction of her thoughts, he said, "We'll talk later."

"Okay."

He leaned forward and kissed her. Jade savored the brief contact, then before they ended things on a worse note, she opened the car door and hopped out.

The moment she closed the door, Terrell started off. Jade waved at the departing vehicle, but he didn't seem to have noticed.

Or maybe he did but he just didn't want to wave back.

* * *

Of all the times for Kathy not to be home, Jade wished this wasn't the one. She needed her. She needed someone.

Maybe Terrell had finally realized that their relationship was moving too fast for her and that's what had him in a bad mood. If that was the case, then it was better that he accept the truth now rather than later.

But if she was so relieved about it, then why did remembering the forlorn look in Terrell's eyes make her stomach churn? Why did the thought of slowing things down make her feel worse than she'd thought it would?

"This is crazy," she said aloud, then dropped herself onto her bed. It was still early and after having only coffee at Terrell's, she was hungry, but she sure wasn't in the mood to fix something to eat. What was wrong with her anyway?

She needed something to do. Rolling off the bed, Jade dragged her feet to the living room. She'd check the answering machine.

Two messages were flashing. Extending a finger, she pressed the Play button with a fingernail.

The first message wasn't really a message. She could hear the sound of jazz in the background, as though the person who'd called had considered leaving a message, but had hung up instead.

A loud beep pierced the air, then the second message began. "Hi. This is a message for Kathleen. Kathleen, please give me a call. It's Sheldon. We need to talk. I'm in Brooklyn. 555-8376."

Jade jotted down the number on a piece of paper by the phone, though she wondered how Kathy would react to the message. According to her, she wanted nothing to do with Sheldon, but Jade could tell she still loved him.

Love. It was a tricky game to play, and more often than not, both players got hurt. She didn't know if she could handle getting hurt again.

Determined not to think about Terrell or love or anything stressful, Jade went to the washroom and started the bath. Hopefully a hot bubble bath would help relax her.

"Ma, what is it?" Terrell asked when he heard her long moan. Immediately he rushed to her side.

She blew out a breath and placed a hand on his shoulder. "I suddenly felt a little out of it."

"Why don't you sit down? I can watch the rice."

"Maybe I will."

"You've got to take it easy," Terrell told her. "You're always telling me I work too much. It's time you take your own advice."

As Mrs. Edmonds sat on the upholstered sofa in the neighboring living room, she chuckled. "You've been talking to your father."

"I've got eyes, Ma. It's obvious you need to rest."

"Listen to your son," Mr. Edmonds said, and both Terrell and his mother faced him as he walked into the living room. "I have been telling her over and over that she needs to slow down, but she's too stubborn to listen."

"Oh, hush," Mrs. Edmonds said, reaching for her husband's hand. Taking it, he sat beside her.

"You won't do any of us any good if you run yourself into the ground. Literally." Mr. Edmonds planted a kiss on her cheek.

"I'm not the first person to feel a little tired, Melvin. Must be my old bones."

Terrell smiled at that. It was something he liked to say about himself. "Can I get you anything?"

"Some water, please. I'm thirsty."

"Okay." Turning, Terrell disappeared into the kitchen. First he lifted the lid on the pot and checked the rice, then poured a tall glass of distilled water for his mother. Minutes later he handed her the glass.

"Thank you."

"Dad, I promised Ma I'd finish the cooking. Care to help?"

"I'll be there in a minute." His father was clutching his mother's hand.

It would have been good for Jade to see this, he thought as he walked back to the kitchen. What was wrong with two people being passionately in love? Nothing. Passionate did not mean emotionally unstable, as Jade seemed to believe. He wanted more than anything to prove that to her.

Scooping the lettuce from the countertop, Terrell brought it to the sink. Like he'd seen his mother do a million times, he broke the lettuce into sections and dropped it in a bowl in the sink. When he was finished, he ran the water over it, washing it carefully.

"Don't you two burn down the kitchen," he heard his mother call, and looking over his shoulder, he saw his father.

A smile playing on his lips, Melvin shook his head. "After forty-one years, you'd think she'd trust me by now."

"You know she does."

Bending, Melvin opened a bottom cupboard and withdrew a pot. He filled it with cold water pouring over the salad, then moved to the stove.

"Is Ma okay?" Terrell asked, his hands pausing.

"She says she is." Melvin turned on a burner.

"Yeah, but does she seem it?"

"She's tired all the time now. Doesn't have as much energy as she used to. But she's probably right. That's old age."

"Is she taking vitamins, seeing a doctor?"

"You know your mother. She's as fit as an ox and no one can tell her otherwise."

A smile touched Terrell's lips. "Yeah."

Melvin walked to the fridge and opened the freezer door. As he withdrew a package of frozen corn, he said, "She's working too much. You know Mrs. Bell down the road?"

"Mmm-hmm."

"Well, her granddaughter is getting married on Valentine's Day and your mother is making the bridesmaid dresses. That on top of the children she tutors each evening. I keep telling her she's just doing too much, but she won't listen."

Ever since his mother's retirement four years ago, she'd kept herself as busy as someone with a full-time job. She'd taught in New Jersey's public school system for forty years and couldn't get the job out of her blood. Each evening, she tutored children from kindergarten to high school. She was also active in her church. She loved to sew for herself and other people. No wonder she was exhausted.

"I am no doubt my mother's child," Terrell said, shaking the water off the lettuce.

"You saying I'm lazy?"

Wrapping an arm around his father, Terrell chuckled. "Not at all, Dad. You both worked hard all your life. Too hard. That's why I want to see you take it easy now. Retired means relax. In fact, how about a winter getaway? Hawaii? Aruba?"

"Oh, I don't know. You spend so much on us already."

That was true, but it was the least he could do for the parents who had given him so much. "Because I love you. So tell me, where do you want to go?"

* * *

The sound of the lock turning forced Jade awake. Rising instantly she reached for the nearby lamp and turned it on. Her eyes fought to adjust to the light, and she realized just how long she must have been asleep. As the door creaked open, she stood and walked to the doorway to greet her friend.

Looking like she was carrying the weight of the world on her shoulders, Kathy entered the room. Startled to see Jade, she said, "Oh. Hi."

"Hey, girl."

"I'm surprised you're home. I thought you'd be with Mr. Loverboy."

Though Kathy was being her regular tongue-in-cheek self, her tone was flat. "Kathy, are you okay?"

Her face twisted in a scowl as she removed her coat. "I've been better."

"Maybe this isn't a good time to tell you this, but Sheldon called for you a few times."

Panic flashed in her eyes. "What did you tell him?"

"Nothing. But he sounds pretty desperate to talk to you."

Kathy hung her coat on the coat tree. "Well, he'd better not hold his breath."

Not sure what to say, Jade followed her friend into the living room. "Kathy, I've never seen you like this. I don't want to tell you how to live your life, but maybe you need to see him." When Kathy opened her mouth to protest, Jade held up a hand. "At least to tell him it's over. Then maybe he'll stop calling."

Dropping onto the sofa, Kathy laid her head back and groaned. "Jade, not too long ago you told me not to pry in your life..."

What could Jade say to that? Absolutely nothing. She

moved to stand in front of the sofa where Kathy sat. Her friend didn't look at her or respond. "I'll, uh, be in my room."

"No, wait."

Stopping midpivot, Jade turned back to Kathy. She'd never seen her looking so sad in the seven years she'd known her.

"I'm sorry. This isn't your fault."

"Look, I'm certainly no expert in the love department."

Kathy patted the spot next to her. "But you're my friend. That counts for something."

At Kathy's urging, Jade sat. "If you want—"

"I'm back with Tyrone," Kathy blurted out.

"What?" The words escaped before she could stop it.

Sighing, Kathy dropped her head backward, then raised it to look at Jade. "I know what you're thinking. But I was wrong. He's sweet, he's willing to commit…"

"And you wanted him for one thing—his body."

"You're the one who kept telling me I wasn't giving him a chance," Kathy pointed out, pinning Jade with a level stare.

"Yeah, but that's when…" She stopped before saying that that was before she realized Kathy was still in love with Sheldon. Instead, she asked, "Why is it never easy? This love stuff?"

"Don't ask me. Speaking of which, why aren't you with Terrell?"

Why indeed? Jade shifted so that she sat sideways on the sofa, facing Kathy. "I…I really don't know." She wouldn't bother mentioning Milton. "Well, that's not really true. We started to have this conversation about love and passion and commitment, and let's just say I wasn't as enthusiastic about it as Terrell probably wanted me to be. I think you were right— he just wanted to pick up where we left off over six years ago."

"And you finally told him you want to slow things down?"

"I didn't have to. I think he figured it out. He doesn't seem too happy." And for some reason, neither was Jade. She enjoyed spending time with him and wanted to continue to do so. Was it wrong to want to take things slowly?"

The phone rang. Both Jade and Kathy looked at each other. "If that's Sheldon, I'm not here."

"I'm not getting it," Jade countered. She wasn't ready to deal with Terrell's disappointment in her.

"Fine." For the first time since she'd arrived home, Kathy smiled. "Let it ring."

Chapter 17

HE'D BEEN LEANING TOWARD saying no anyway, but his concern for his mother's well-being was what influenced his final decision. He would not go to Milan. Though Mr. Carracciolo's offer was the kind that came probably once in a lifetime, Terrell's family came first. They were irreplaceable.

Despite having made the decision, Terrell dreaded calling the man. Mr. Carracciolo was nothing if not persistent, and he knew that the Italian designer would do whatever possible to talk him out of his decision.

But when he'd called the successful design house in Milan, he'd reached an answering machine. The message was in Italian, and Terrell didn't understand a word, but he knew enough to leave a message after the beep. Briefly he left a message stating he was grateful to be considered for the position of house photographer but that he had to decline.

He'd thought that was the end of it, but when an hour later

his phone rang, he'd learned otherwise. Hearing Mr. Carracciolo's voice, Terrell knew he was in trouble. It was, he admitted to himself, flattering to be sought after by a successful designer, and part of him wished he could accept the job. "Mr. Carracciolo. How are you?"

"I am not doing very well, Mr. Edmonds. I just received your message."

In other words, Terrell's message was responsible for Mr. Carracciolo's negative mood. Terrell said simply, "You did."

"Mr. Edmonds, I am disappointed. But I am also not a man who easily takes no for an answer. Can I not persuade you to reconsider?"

"I'm sorry, Mr. Carracciolo. I truly appreciate the offer, but… Well, to tell the truth, I've got a few family concerns here." Not to mention Jade.

"Oh. I do hope everyone is all right."

"Yes, they are. For now. But my mother… I'm concerned about her."

"You do not need to explain, Mr. Edmonds. I understand. But as I said before, I would love you on my team and I am willing to wait for you. Take the time you need now, make sure your mother is okay. Then when you are certain everything is fine, if you still want the position, give me a call."

Terrell was truly surprised. "Mr. Carracciolo, I don't want to mislead you."

"I understand. Mr. Edmonds, do not worry about me. I believe that when you want something, it pays to wait."

As he said the words, Terrell thought of Jade. Though he wouldn't have thought it that August day over six years ago, Jade had been worth the wait. In fact, he'd come to accept that if they'd pursued a relationship back then, things might not have worked out. For one thing, Jade would have been racked with guilt and that would have hampered their developing relationship. At least now, though she'd broken his heart, she was unattached and free to build a new relationship with him without Nelson anywhere near the picture.

"I agree," Terrell said. "Again I'm not making any promises. To tell the truth, I don't know if I'll change my mind."

"Nothing is impossible."

Again Terrell thought of Jade. "No, Mr. Carracciolo, I guess it isn't."

"Good. So please do keep in touch, Mr. Edmonds. *Buon giorno.*"

"Buon giorno," Terrell repeated, then hung up.

Jade's sleep was restless. Her stomach was alive with nervous energy and her thoughts were all over the place.

She still couldn't believe she'd quit her job. The prospect of starting another one had her both scared and excited. But more than anything, she didn't know what to think about Terrell.

The time she'd spent away from him seemed like forever. Was this normal? She'd loved Nelson, yet she hadn't missed him near as much when they weren't together as she now missed Terrell.

Maybe what bothered her was the fact that though they'd seemingly parted on good terms, there had been too much tension between them.

Frowning, Jade rolled onto her back and covered her face with a pillow. What did she want, anyway? She liked Terrell; she always had. But did she want to go headfirst into another serious relationship?

The only commitment she was ready to make was to her job. Terrell was sweet and kind and thoughtful and sexy, but he wanted too much from her. She knew that now.

But even as she thought that, she knew it would be hard to

resist him when they met again. How could she live without his gentle kisses and sweet caresses? He made her feel alive in a way she hadn't before.

"Oh, get Terrell off your mind," she told herself. She grabbed the pillow off her face and abruptly sat up. Instead of thinking about Terrell, she'd think about work.

Picking up the receiver from the phone beside her bed, Jade dialed the number to Simple Pleasures with the intention of leaving a message for Sherry. She'd committed it to memory.

"Simple Pleasures. Sherry speaking."

For a moment, Jade was surprised. Sherry had said she didn't work Mondays. "Hi, Sherry. It's Jade."

"Hello, Jade. I am so happy to hear from you. Please tell me you're calling to accept the job."

"Actually I am."

"Oh, thank God. Can you start right away? As in today?"

Jade hesitated for a second, then said, "Sure. Why not?"

"Great."

Already Jade was rising, moving to her drawers to search for something to wear. "It'll take me about an hour to get there."

"Just get here when you can. Gwen's officially on maternity leave."

"Already?"

"She went into labor over the weekend. She had a baby boy last night."

The thought of a new baby boy seeing the world for the first time made Jade smile. How wonderful for Gwen. "I'll see you soon, Sherry."

After two days of hoping she would call, it was apparent she would not. Finally late Monday evening, Terrell gave in and called her.

"Hello?"

"Jade."

Silence. "Terrell, hi."

"Jade, I was hoping we could talk."

"Go ahead."

She wasn't making this easy. "I meant in person."

"It's late, Terrell. I've got to work tomorrow. If you have something to say, why not say it now, on the phone."

Clearly he didn't have a choice. "All right. What's happening to us? One minute we were fine, getting close, having fun…the next, there's this tension between us and I don't know why."

She paused, then said, "You're moving too fast."

"*I'm* moving too fast? Not so long ago, you were the one seducing me."

"I'm not talking about the sex," she said softly. "It's everything else. Me being part of your life, me meeting your family… It's all too much right now."

"I'm pressuring you."

He heard her sigh. "I'm sure I led you on."

His stomach lurched. He didn't like where she was going with this. "Exactly what are you saying?"

"That we should slow things down. Terrell, as much as I'm attracted to you, I am not ready for another relationship. Maybe I never will be. I have to concentrate on my career."

"Why can't you do that and still see me? I set you up with Sherry—I want to see you succeed."

"And I owe you, right?"

"I didn't say that."

"Then what are you saying?"

Frustrated, Terrell ran a hand over his hair. "Don't be like this."

Silence. "I'm not trying to be like anything," she said, her tone softer than Terrell had expected. "Terrell…I don't want to hurt you."

"You're hurting me now." He hadn't wanted to put any pressure on her, but the words came out without thought. "Jade, all I want is a chance."

"I didn't say we couldn't have that chance. Just maybe not as the same pace as before."

Terrell had heard the "let's slow it down" speech before. He'd used it himself when he wanted to end relationships that weren't working out. Yet if what he felt for Jade was so strong, how could it be unrequited? Or was this relationship only about sex for her? She certainly didn't mind sharing his bed.

Maybe all she needed was time. "All right," Terrell said, though he wanted to find her and kiss some sense into her. "We'll take it slowly."

There was a long silence, then Jade said, "Thank you."

"You have my number. When you're ready, give me a call."

If Kathy hadn't been expecting a call from her brother she never would have answered the phone. Now as much as her mind told her to hang up, she found her heart wouldn't let her do it.

"Kathy, don't hang up."

"What do you want?" Her throat was suddenly dry.

"To see you. We need to talk."

"You had your chance to talk to me eight years ago, Sheldon, but you didn't then and I don't see the point now."

"That's what I want to explain."

"*Explain?*" Kathy's heart pounded furiously in her chest. She wished he didn't make her feel anything. "Like you can explain away eight years. Good-bye, Sheldon."

Before she lost her nerve, she hung up. Seconds later the phone rang. She let it ring.

She wasn't ready for this. Sheldon's reappearance in her life was just too sudden for her to deal with rationally. Maybe when she had enough time to get used to the fact, she would be able to see him face-to-face and hear what he had to say.

But in the meantime, she had resolved to finally get on with her life—without him. Unlike some couples, Kathy knew that she and Sheldon could never be friends.

When Terrell heard the phone ring, he sprinted from the darkroom to his bedroom and grabbed the receiver before the machine picked up. "Hello?"

"Hey, Terrell. This is Jeremy Schlick."

His brain had known that Jade wasn't going to call, yet still his heart was disappointed. "Hi, Jeremy."

"I'm wondering what your time is like from Wednesday to Saturday."

Jeremy was an independent film producer who did everything from documentaries to dramatic features. On the few occasions Terrell had worked for him, he'd enjoyed doing so. "What do you have in mind?"

"I've got a crew heading to Toronto to film a promotional video. I'd love to have you as the stills photographer."

"Wednesday." That was very short notice. "I've got photo shoots scheduled from now till Friday."

"Anything you can reschedule?"

He probably could, but he'd rather have Raymond, an assistant he used on bigger shoots, pick up his slack. If Raymond was available. He performed in a jazz bar in the evenings and his days were usually free. "I can look into it. When do you need to know?"

"Yesterday."

"Okay. Let me make a couple calls, then I'll get right back to you. Where can I reach you?" Terrell jotted down the phone number. "All right. I'll call you soon."

He wanted to do this, he realized. Needed to. Getting away from New York and Jade was a must for his sanity.

Maybe Jade was right—they needed some distance between them. If Terrell was out of town, he wouldn't be tempted to drive to her place and make a total fool of himself.

Two hours later, Terrell had spoken with Raymond and had made the necessary arrangements. Lucky for him, Raymond was available and willing to pick up his workload. Though Raymond wasn't as experienced as Terrell, he trusted the younger man would do more than a decent job with the head shots.

And hopefully when he went to Toronto, he'd leave his thoughts of Jade in New York.

Chapter 18

BY FRIDAY, WHEN JADE HADN'T heard from Terrell, she realized he wasn't playing. He really wasn't going to call; he would wait for her to make the first move. Though she'd told herself that she didn't miss him, her heart told her otherwise. She missed his laughter, his warm smile, the feel of his strong body wrapped around hers in an embrace.

"Here you go," the patron said, slipping a bill into the pocket of Jade's smock.

"Thank you," Jade replied absentmindedly.

"You all right?" the woman said, gazing at Jade with a concerned expression.

She had to snap out of this! She forced the best smile she could. "I'm fine. I was just thinking how great your hair looks."

Turning, the woman looked in the mirror, then caressed her short do. "I love it. I admit I was a bit afraid of how I would look without all that long hair, but this is great."

"I'm glad you like it."

The woman's smile made Jade feel like she'd performed lifesaving surgery. "It's fabulous."

As the woman headed to the front to pay, Jade took advantage of this moment to go to the back room and call home. Maybe Terrell had left a message for her.

Kathy wasn't home, and the machine picked up after four rings. Jade punched in the code to retrieve her messages and listened.

There were three messages from Sheldon, one from Cassandra, but none from Terrell. To her surprise, Jade felt a niggling sense of disappointment. What had she expected?

Holding the receiver between an ear and shoulder, Jade punched Terrell's number into the phone. After three rings, the machine picked up. She disconnected without leaving a message. It was too awkward to talk to his machine and not to him.

She decided to call Cassandra, who had left a message to call right away.

Cassandra was home. "Hey, Jade. You got my message."

"Yeah. What's up?"

"Let me first apologize for the late notice. But I'm hoping you're free tonight. I've got two front-row tickets to my play and I thought you might like to come. I might add that Jeff from *UpClose* will be there...a great opportunity to schmooze."

"Tonight?"

"Mmm-hmm. Eight o'clock. I can leave the tickets for you at the box office. Please say you'll come."

"I'd love to, but—"

"Then do it."

"Oh, why not?" It wouldn't hurt to see Jeff again and

remind him that she existed. Other than that, a night out would surely help take her mind off Terrell.

"Let me give you the address of the theater." When Jade had scribbled it down, Cassandra asked, "Will you bring Terrell?"

Almost instantly a lump formed in Jade's throat. Man, she missed him. She wanted to see him. If she could only reach him, she'd ask him to be her date tonight. "I'll see."

"Oh, great. I can't wait to see you."

"How dressy should I be?"

"Not at all, unless you want to. Jeans and a T-shirt is fine."

"Perfect. See you tonight."

When you started to feel like a prisoner in your own home, you knew you were in trouble.

And that's exactly how Kathy felt now. Every time she turned, Sheldon was calling. She'd had to resort to not answering the phone and was even cautious when entering or leaving her apartment.

Today she'd realized that this had gone too far. Though she'd spoken with Sheldon a couple times and had asked him to stop calling her, he wouldn't listen. He claimed that once she met him face-to-face and heard him out that he'd leave her alone.

Yeah, right. Like she'd lost her mind.

Her traveling bag packed, Kathy glanced around the apartment to make sure everything was in order before flicking off the light switch. She'd left instructions for Jade to tell Sheldon she had moved out, but she'd really just be spending the next week or so at her brother's place.

Satisfied that all was in order, Kathy exited the apartment and locked the door.

* * *

Not even one message from Jade.

Gritting his teeth, Terrell disconnected the line, but held the receiver in his hand for several moments.

Replacing the receiver, he sat on the firm mattress in his hotel room. He was crazy. It was Friday night, he was in Toronto with a great crew, and all he could do was sit in his room at the Sutton Place Hotel and think of Jade?

The knock on the door pulled him from his thoughts. Jumping off the bed, he hurried to answer it.

Jeremy stood before him. "Hey, Terrell. Marty, Linda, and I are going across the street to the Bistro 990 for a few drinks. Want to join us?

Jeremy couldn't have come at a better time. "You bet. Just give me a minute to get ready."

Clearly Jade hadn't given him a second thought this week, as she hadn't even called him. The least Terrell could do was make a concerted effort to put her out of his mind.

As the audience hooted and applauded even more loudly, the cast of *Through the Wrong Door and Up the Wrong Tree* ran back onto center stage. Holding hands, they bowed in unison, then ran off to the wings for a last time.

The show, about a thirty-something woman looking for love in all the wrong places, was simply fantastic. And sadly enough, Jade could relate.

The applause quieted and Jade reached for her purse. It rested on the vacant seat beside hers. She'd tried but hadn't reached Terrell, and Kathy was nowhere to be found, either. Ultimately, she'd gone alone.

"Cassandra was magnificent, wasn't she?"

Securing her purse over her shoulder, Jade faced Jeff. "Yes, she was." Cassandra had always had a flair for the dramatic, but Jade hadn't known she was this good. "The reviews of her performance are all well earned."

Eve, Jeff's date for the evening spoke. "I'm very impressed. With a performance like that, she'll be on Broadway very soon."

Jeff turned to Eve and the two began chatting about the upcoming article about Cassandra. As she didn't know them, Jade felt a little uncomfortable intruding on their private conversation. Right now the fact that she had come alone was clearly evident.

Unable to stop her mind from drifting to Terrell, she wondered where he was. Maybe if she called him now and he was home, he'd let her come over.

Oh, what was she doing? One minute she told herself that the less time they spent together, the better. The next she couldn't wait to see him again.

"What are you doing now?" Eve asked Jade.

"Oh, uh, I…I'm actually supposed to meet a friend." She didn't want to mention Terrell's name, as they knew him. "She couldn't make it for the show, but promised to meet me afterward for a late dinner."

"Oh, that's too bad," Eve said. "We were hoping you'd join us for a nightcap."

"I'm sorry." She knew this was crazy; spending time with Jeff and Eve might ensure her future work. But she wanted to see Terrell. If she didn't mend the rift between them now, she might never get another chance.

"Perhaps another time," Jeff said.

"Sure." At least that sounded hopeful. Jade hoped it wasn't a subtle brush-off. But then New Yorkers weren't known for their subtlety.

As Jeff and Eve strolled down the aisle. Jade watched them go. After several seconds, she joined the crowd of departing guests, hoping that there was a pay phone somewhere in this theater.

Jade wouldn't have known it was possible to miss another person this much if she weren't actually missing Terrell terribly now. Maybe it was the fact that she was home alone, sitting in her darkened bedroom, but she truly felt like she had no one.

Kathy had practically moved out. At least the way her note had been worded, Jade guessed Kathy wouldn't return until she felt that Sheldon would no longer bother her. Judging by Sheldon's persistence, Jade figured Kathy wouldn't be coming home for quite some time.

So that left her alone…except for the occasional pigeon landing on her windowsill for company. But for some reason, whenever she approached one of the birds, it flew away.

So much for any company.

Just pick up the phone! a voice told her. *Call him.*

Her hands jittery from nervous energy, Jade reached for the receiver and punched in Terrell's number. If he wasn't home, she'd at least leave a message.

To her dismay, the answering machine picked up. It was after 11:00 P.M. Where was he?

The sudden thought that he might be out with another woman almost caused Jade to hang up the phone. Instead, she fought the urge and spoke. "Terrell, this is Jade. It's Friday night and I'm wondering where you are. Please call me. It doesn't matter how late."

Duh! If that didn't sound desperate, she didn't know what did.

But clearly she was desperate, for when the phone rang

minutes later, Jade grabbed the receiver as if her life depended on it. "Hello?"

"Jade. Hi."

Instantly the hairs on her nape rose. God, it couldn't be. But she'd recognize that voice anywhere. "Nelson?"

"It's me," he replied, his voice merely above a whisper.

Jade's breath snagged, and for a moment she wondered if she'd find her voice. After a long pause, she did. "W-why are…w-what do you…?"

"I know, this is a shock." Pause. "Jade, this is going to sound like a crazy request, but I was wondering if we could talk. Maybe meet somewhere."

Had someone zapped her to the twilight zone? Nelson had her number because of everything they'd had to settle after the divorce, but she hadn't heard from him in months. "You're right. That does sound crazy."

"I know, but I'm still hoping."

She blew out a frazzled breath. "I…I don't get it. Why?"

"It's a long story, Jade. I'd just really like to talk to you in person. Can you do that? Can you spare a bit of time for your husband?"

Husband? Had Nelson truly lost his mind? "*Ex*-husband."

"Ex. Whatever. C'mon, Jade. I really need to see you."

"This is…" She couldn't even get her thoughts out.

"Look, Jade, I'm sorry. I just want a chance to make it up to you."

With his apology, her brain began functioning normally. Nelson was one of the best apologizers on the planet. Whatever mind game he was trying to play now, she wouldn't give him the satisfaction of playing her for a fool again. "No. I can't see you."

"It's about the money."

Her stomach lurched. "What about it?"

"You know I want to find a way to repay you."

"Do you have the money you stole?" Jade asked before he could continue. As her husband and partner in the business, she'd had no legal recourse to go after Nelson the way she would have been able to go after a stranger who'd stolen from her. "Because if you don't—"

"I'm working at getting it back for you. Okay? Jade, you don't know how sorry I am for everything. I'm finally trying to get my life back on track."

Something else was going on, and Jade had the eeriest feeling. But the thought was so absurd, it couldn't be true. "Fine. When you get the money, you call me."

He didn't respond right away, and Jade wondered if she should just hang up. When she was about to do so, he spoke. "There's more, Jade. It's about my son."

"Nelson, I do *not* want to know!" She didn't have time for this.

"Amanda says he's not mine."

That silenced her.

"She says she lied, that she wants me gone. I don't know what to do."

The mention of Amanda and his son brought the bitter memory of his betrayal crashing down on her. "I don't care what you do. Leave me out of this."

"I made a mistake," Nelson continued as though he hadn't heard her. "I never should have left you. And if the baby's not mine—"

"That doesn't make a difference." At least not to her. How could it? The fact remained that he'd cheated on her. If he hadn't actually fathered the other woman's child, that was his business and not hers.

"Give me a chance," Nelson whined, as though his whole existence depended on it. "I...I love you."

Her heart beating frantically, Jade hung up. For a while, she was unable to move, unable to fathom what had actually just happened. Her stomach was churning so badly, she thought she would be ill.

Why? she wondered. Why now? And did she care? For a year she'd worked hard to forget what Nelson had done to her, and he had the nerve to call and say he loved her? He was insane.

But maybe she was, too, for even letting him affect her the way he had.

Maybe, just maybe, if Nelson had been a man and had dealt with his problems before, she could forgive his infidelity. *Maybe.* But to steal from their salon, to leave her almost penniless with an insecure future, the man had a nerve to expect to even breathe the same air she did!

Where was Kathy? Where was Terrell? For months, Jade had tried to tell herself that she didn't need anyone, that she was strong, that she could handle her problems on her own. Now sitting cross-legged on her bed, alone, she knew that wasn't true.

Chapter 19

As the saying went, there was no place like home, and right now Terrell agreed wholeheartedly with that. Though his four days in Toronto had been a nice escape, he was more than happy to return to his own space and stretch out his legs.

But if he'd been hoping to forget Jade, the enlarged black-and-white photo on the wall above his sofa made that impossible. Seeing her coy smile made him miss her with a force he hadn't expected.

Rising from the sofa, Terrell turned his attention from the picture to the large living room windows. He strode to them, opened the blinds, and looked out at the world below. Maybe it was the darkness, but he couldn't make out a single shape.

The truth was, he couldn't focus—not when all he could think about was what had happened to ruin his relationship with Jade. The distance between them weighed heavily on his heart and on his mind.

It wasn't normal, he was sure. But what hurt was the fact that he truly couldn't understand what had gone wrong. It was like having to go cold-turkey and forget that she existed, after having experienced the best moments of his life with her.

Softly Terrell swore, then turned from the window and marched to the kitchen. Opening the cupboards, he reached for a glass. He needed a brandy to take the edge off.

It was then that he glanced down at the answering machine, which rested on the counter near the fridge. The green light was blinking, indicating he had several messages. The need for a drink fleeing his mind, Terrell replaced the glass and hit the Play button on the answering machine instead.

After several messages, and his heart sinking lower with each one, when Jade's voice finally filled the air it was like music to his ears. Before her message finished playing, he picked up the receiver and called her number.

The phone rang once, twice…and Terrell wondered if all this anxiety was good for his heart. Was it possible to crave another person the way one craved chocolate? Apparently so, for his need for Jade was almost like an addiction.

After the third ring, someone picked up the phone. Terrell blew out a relieved breath. But his relief turned to shock when he heard Jade say, "Go away!"

Stunned, he almost didn't respond. "Jade? This is Terrell."

"Terrell. Oh…I'm sorry."

She sounded…stuffed up. Did she have a cold? The flu? Was that why she was irritable?

"Uh, I got your message. You said to call."

"This isn't a good time."

His heart sank. "Are you sick?"

"You could say that."

"Can I do anything for you?"

"No. I just…I'll have to call you later. Okay?"

Jade sounded horrible. "Are you sure—"

"Bye."

Terrell heard a dial tone before he had a chance to say anything else. Holding the receiver from his face, he stared at it with a puzzled expression, as though it could answer all his questions.

He replaced the receiver, certain of one thing: Jade needed someone. And Terrell had never been the type to walk away from a woman in need.

He hurried from the kitchen, grabbed his coat, and was out the door in a minute flat. On his way to Brooklyn, he'd stop at his favorite Manhattan deli.

The annoying sound of her apartment buzzer startled Jade, and she froze. Why was it that when one just wanted to curl into a ball and wither away, life handed you an interruption?

Blowing her nose, Jade glanced at the clock. Nine fifty-three. Who could be buzzing her apartment at this hour? It was too late for salesmen or Girl Scouts, and anyone else had no business calling on her now.

But when the buzzer sounded again, this time two quick blasts, Jade realized that maybe Kathy was downstairs. It wouldn't be the first time Kathy had lost her key.

With that thought, Jade scrambled from the bedroom and hurried to answer the intercom. She hoped it was Kathy and not some psycho-killer.

As if a psycho-killer would ever ask for an invitation.

"Hello," Jade said, pressing the Talk button. She would let Kathy in and retreat to her bedroom, hoping her friend would realize she was in no mood for conversation.

"Jade, it's Terrell."

Oh, my goodness! Jade thought, feeling suddenly trapped. Yes, she wanted to see Terrell, needed to see him, but not like this. She looked a mess. Her flannel pajamas were hardly flattering, and Lord how her face must look. "Uh, hi."

"Can I come up?"

She cleared her throat. "Uh, sure."

She depressed the button to release the front door, then ran to the washroom. Darn! She had no time to change, no time to freshen up. She had time only to splash water on her face and pass a comb through her hair. Man, her hair looked pathetic! It should be a crime for a hairdresser to have such limp, dull hair.

There was a knock. Jade took one tentative step, then another until she reached the door. She didn't have to, for she knew it was Terrell, but she looked through the peep-hole anyway.

It was him, and the sight of him stole her breath. Forgetting how she looked, she quickly turned the lock and opened the door.

Instantly she saw the brown paper bag in his hand and the concerned look on his face. "You *are* sick," he said, then stepped toward her.

Sick? And then it sank in, and she couldn't help but smile. A Kleenex was stuffed in her pajama top and her eyes were red from crying.

He thought she was sick so he'd rushed over to see her. She wanted to kiss him.

"Do you have a microwave?" he asked.

"Yeah, in the kitchen. W-why?"

"I stopped at a deli on my way over here. I picked up some chicken soup."

"Chicken soup?" She asked the question as if she'd never heard of the stuff.

"Well, you're sick. I thought I'd bring you some chicken soup. Always makes me feel better."

Was Terrell Edmonds real, or a figment of her imagination? He was too good to be true. With Nelson, she could have walked around with an IV pole for days and he wouldn't have even boiled her a cup of hot water. "You're not joking?"

"No. Why would I be?"

Jade could only manage to shake her head. "I can't believe you."

Misunderstanding her, Terrell said, "You didn't want me to come over."

Jade closed the distance between them, tentatively placing a hand on his arm. "That's not what I mean. I…I can't believe you'd actually do this for me."

"You know I—" He stopped abruptly, then continued. "Care about you."

A faint smile touched Jade's mouth. "I know."

"Where do you want me to put this?" He held up the bag.

"The kitchen."

He walked toward the kitchen, and still digesting the fact that he'd come over with chicken soup, Jade watched him in awe.

Several seconds later, he joined her in the doorway. "If you don't feel up to company…"

"I do." Jade sniffled. She didn't know why, but thinking that someone cared about her as much as Terrell apparently did overwhelmed her emotionally. Made her feel all weepy and sentimental.

His eyes narrowed as he looked at her, and then he realized the truth. "You…you're not sick, are you?"

Well, he was too perceptive. "No," she said softly, then felt like bursting into tears.

"You've been crying." Oh, man. Not a crying woman.

She simply nodded in response.

"Oh, Jade." Stepping toward her, he wrapped her in an

embrace. Relieved to have his arms around her again, Jade sagged against him. "What is it? What's the matter?"

"It's my problem." How could she share this with Terrell?

With his arms around her, he felt the tension between them melt away. He ran a hand over her hair. "Jade, you've got to know you can trust me by now."

She did. She'd always known. Terrell had always made her feel safe. "I do, but…"

"But what?"

She stepped out of his embrace. Moving away from him, she went into the living room and plopped down on a sofa. Terrell followed her, and she was glad. He sat beside her.

"This is about me."

"No," Jade answered quickly, facing him. The saddened look in his dark eyes made her heart ache. She hadn't meant to cause Terrell any pain. "I'm just not having a very good life."

"You mean day."

"No, I mean life."

"This is serious." As he said the words, his face twisted with a mix of emotions—confusion, concern, pain.

He didn't have to say he thought he was the root of her problems; it was written on his face. She'd wanted to spare him any talk of Nelson, but he no doubt needed to hear what she was going through. Besides, she wanted to tell someone.

"It's Nelson." Hearing the man's name, Terrell's jaw flinched. "He…he wants me back."

His stomach suddenly felt like he'd downed a pitcher of acid. "You're joking."

"No. When he called me yesterday, it was a shock. But he called me tonight again, begging me to see him."

"He called you?"

"Yeah."

"I didn't realize he had your number." Man, this was getting worse by the second.

"He does, but not for social reasons.'"

"I see."

Did he? If the muscles popping in his neck were any indication, Terrell wasn't pleased.

"He wants to get back with you."

"Yes."

He wished he could read her thoughts, but since he couldn't, he hoped she'd be honest with him. "Is that something you'd, uh, consider?"

Jade looked away, and his heart nearly imploded. Softly she said, "Yesterday, no."

She saw the nervous rise and fall of his Adam's apple. "But today?"

"Today I don't know."

Terrell let out a half laugh, half moan, then swore. "Jade, I don't get it."

"Neither do I." He didn't understand. Neither did she. She tried to explain. "I'm not saying I want to see him, but part of me wonders if I should."

"Why? After the way he hurt you?" And what he didn't say, Jade could read in his eyes: *Why would you go back to him and leave me again?*

"Hear me out." This was more difficult than she thought. "Terrell, I grew up believing that you get married once. That whatever problems you have, you work them out. My parents had a lot of problems, they worked them out. They're still together."

"Problems, I can understand. What Nelson did, that's a whole other category."

"I know." She did, so what was it that had her in such a dismal mood? "But—"

Abruptly Terrell stood. "Don't say it."

"You're not listening to me."

"Man, I'm getting a feeling of déjà vu."

She stood to meet him. "Please, Terrell."

"Please what?" He didn't want her to speak, to tell him she was leaving him for Nelson—again. "I can't hear this."

He turned from her and headed for the door, and frustrated that she couldn't express herself clearly, Jade said, "It's not what you think."

He stopped, but didn't turn. "Then what is it?"

"I just feel bad." He didn't respond, so she continued. "Nelson…he questioned my love for him, said that if I'd really cared for him I would give him another chance."

Terrell would have laughed—if it didn't feel as though someone had taken a sledgehammer to his gut. Was Jade actually considering reconciliation with her ex? Was that what this was all about, what her tears were about? Was she one of those women who never seemed to tire of the abuse some men liked to dish out in the name of love?

God, was she still in love with him?

Heaven help him if she were. He'd lived that nightmare once. After finally getting close to Jade, after having the chance to love her, Terrell didn't know if he could handle losing her again.

His gut clenched so tightly the pain was overwhelming, but still he turned and faced her. He had to ask, had to know. "Is…" He almost croaked, his throat was so dry. He swallowed, tried again. "Is that what you…want? Because if it is, Jade, tell me right now. Tell me and I'm out of your life forever."

Chapter 20

TIME STOOD STILL as she looked up at him, her eyes dark and mysterious, hiding the secrets of her soul. Terrell held his breath, praying she wouldn't utter the one simple word that could shatter his heart.

Then something flashed in her eyes as she took a step toward him. Desire, maybe? Man, he wished she wouldn't look at him that way, not if she was in love with someone else.

"No," she whispered. "That's not what I want."

"You don't?"

"No." She took another step closer.

"Then…" He swallowed, trying to ignore the heat in his groin. What was it about Jade that made him want her all the time? "What *do* you want?"

"You." Reaching out, she splayed a hand over his heart. Terrell released a long, slow breath and closed his eyes, enjoying the feel of her touch after what seemed so long. "Then why? Why the tears?"

She stepped to him, rested her head against his chest. "I feel bad, Terrell, not because I love Nelson, but because I'm not sure I ever did. I feel sad I wasted so many years with the wrong man. And I feel guilty—if I'd really loved him, wouldn't I give him another chance now?"

Terrell opened his mouth to speak, but Jade placed a finger on his mouth, silencing him. "For a brief moment," she continued, "I wondered if I should actually give him another chance, forgive and take him back the way I'd always been taught a good wife should do. But I can't, Terrell."

"Why?"

Her eyes held his as she said, "Because of you."

"Don't do this to me, Jade. Not if you don't mean it."

"I do." She ran her finger from his face down his chest, past his stomach, to the buckle on his belt.

He placed a hand on hers, stilling it. "Jade, I want more than this. I want all of you."

Her free hand crept around his waist. "I know. Terrell, I may be confused, but I'm not confused about this."

Tipping on her toes, she reached for his mouth and kissed him—and Terrell was lost. He threw his arms around her and held on for dear life. His tongue moved over her teeth, the roof of her mouth. Kissing her like this, tasting the passion in her wet, hot mouth, made him remember how right it felt to be inside her.

His hand moved down her back, over her round bottom. Cupping the soft flesh, he pulled her into him.

"Oh God, Terrell…"

There were too many clothes between them. Slipping a hand into the waistband of her pajamas, he nudged the material over her hips. Moaned when he found the treasure he was seeking, brushing a thumb over her most sensitive area.

Arching her head back, a passionate cry escaped her lips, and Terrell knew without a doubt that she was his.

He secured both hands under her arms, lifted her. Instinctively she wrapped her legs around his back.

"I never knew flannel was such a turn-on," he whispered.

Jade giggled. "I'll have to wear it more often."

"I'd rather see you out of it."

"Then what are you waiting for?"

He dipped his head and ran his tongue along her neck, tasting her delicate, womanly scent. She tightened her legs around him and moaned…and he could wait no longer.

"Which way to the bedroom?"

"Last door on your right," Jade managed to say, then slowly, seductively, ran a tongue over his earlobe. Clutching her even tighter, Terrell ran to the bedroom before his body exploded.

Though it was the hardest thing he had ever done, Terrell made a determined effort to take things slowly with Jade. Deep down, he sensed that that was what she needed. Like a butterfly emerging from a cocoon, she wouldn't realize how deep her feelings were for him until she was ready.

It was ironic—they were able to connect sexually like two souls who had been long denied the opportunity to love. She gave him her body wholly and completely, in a way that was purely honest. She hid no part of herself from him in bed.

He wished she could be as honest in examining her feelings.

But Terrell was nothing if not patient. For over six years he'd been in love with Jade. He'd never expected to reunite with her, but he still hadn't been able to get her out of his heart. Now that he actually had a chance with her, he didn't want to blow it.

So this week, he would set out to prove his love for her. It would be about showing her he really wanted a future with her.

No matter if it killed him, he wouldn't think about making love to her.

Okay, so he might think about it, but he wouldn't act on his thoughts.

He spent the next week courting her the old-fashioned way, as though they hadn't already been lovers.

On Monday he surprised her at work with lunch. When Jade had seen him walk in the door with a small picnic basket and a smile, she'd felt as though someone had lifted her to the clouds. He'd waited and watched her as she worked, always flashing her a smile when she looked at him. Jade had been more than a little flustered, and when they'd finally had a moment to go to the back and share lunch, she'd learned just how sensual eating grapes could be.

On Wednesday the first love letter arrived at the salon. When she'd seen Terrell's return address, she'd at first been confused. But she'd snuck to the back to read it, and when she had, Jade's body had been flooded with warmth like she'd never known. Terrell's sweet, romantic words warmed her heart.

She got another love letter on Thursday, and one on Friday. But also on Friday, he surprised her with a delivery of fifty long-stemmed red roses. Not only had Jade been the center of attention, she'd been overwhelmed by Terrell's romantic nature.

A girl could get used to this.

And more than anything, she wanted to see him. Since their lunch on Monday, they'd chatted on the phone in the evenings…but that was it. They hadn't spent any more time together because not only was she busy, but Terrell was busy. Now she wanted to see the man and assuage the hunger he'd been building inside her all week.

After numerous attempts to reach him today, he'd finally called her back. He promised to be at Simple Pleasures by nine, when she expected to be finished.

She wasn't ready when he arrived, so he waited for her. When they finally stepped outside, Terrell scooped her into his arms and kissed her until she was breathless.

"I have been dreaming of doing that since Tuesday," Terrell confessed.

"Me, too." Slipping a hand around his neck, she lowered his head until their lips met again. When the door to the salon opened and Carmen, another new stylist stepped out, Jade pulled away from Terrell.

"See you tomorrow," Carmen said.

"Bye." Jade suppressed the urge to giggle as she watched Carmen walk away. "Come on. Let's go to your place."

"Not so fast." Terrell took her hand. "Have you eaten?"

"I'm hungry for one thing only right now," Jade protested as he led her to his Jeep. "And it's not food."

He chuckled. "All things come to those who wait."

"I don't want to wait."

At the Jeep, he leaned her against the door and kissed her. She mewled and pressed her body to his, no doubt hoping that he'd take her straight to his place. He'd created a monster, it seemed. "How about a quick bite at the Motown Café? I promise, we'll have dessert at my place."

"All right," Jade agreed, but a small frown tugged at the corners of her mouth.

"Sweetheart, don't look so sad. I promise, the dessert will be worth the wait."

* * *

The quick bite turned into a full-fledged meal. As Terrell was driving, he didn't drink, but Jade had a couple glasses of zinfandel with her "Heat Wave" Spicy Chicken Pasta, one of the many entrées named after famous Motown songs and performers. The entertainment was fabulous, with four male performers doing a dynamite imitation of The Temptations.

But the entertainment aside, Jade wanted to go to Terrell's. She couldn't understand him. At times it seemed he couldn't get enough of her, yet now when he had the chance to get her home after days of being apart, sex seemed to be the last thing on his mind.

He applauded as the entertainers exited the center stage, and Jade merely watched him. When he stopped clapping and saw her staring at him, he reached across the table and covered her hand with his, brushing the pad of his thumb over her knuckles.

The simple gesture of affection nearly drove her mad—and made her wonder all the more why they were still here. "Terrell, please tell me you're ready to leave."

His eyes lit up like the torturing devil he was. "Well, I'm kinda enjoying watching how much you want me. And don't bother denying it, I can see it in your eyes."

"At least you're not blind. I was beginning to wonder." Jade smiled to soften the words. "C'mon, Terrell. Don't tell me you're doing this on purpose."

He had been, but not to get a rise out of her. On the contrary, he wanted her to know that they could spend time together without involving sex.

But even he was getting a little tired of holding out.

"I'm kinda enjoying teasing you. Makes me think the dessert will be that much sweeter."

"Just don't wait too long—until it turns sour." Jade flashed him a sardonic smile.

Then she sat back in her chair, crossed one leg over the other, and deliberately positioned her leg so that it was exposed beneath the slit in her skirt. It didn't matter that she wore leggings. The fact that she was being deliberately provocative had his groin getting very hot.

When he flagged the waiter seconds later, Jade smiled her victory. She knew she had him right where she wanted him, but he didn't care. The feeling was mutual.

Their bodies slick and hot, their breathing ragged, Terrell clung to Jade as he exploded inside her. She cried out as he thrust long and hard, digging her nails into his back, breaking the skin. But he didn't care. Jade could mark him as much as she wanted, prove to the world he was hers. Because he wanted only her.

Easing off her beautiful body, Terrell lowered his head and teased a nipple with his tongue, enjoying the way she arched for him and the sweet sounds that came from her mouth. She responded to his touch every time, and he couldn't get enough of her.

He moved his mouth from her breast to her lips and kissed her slowly, gently. Her lips were soft and supple and pliant beneath his. He finally broke the kiss. Brushing her damp hair off her forehead, he simply stared at her.

As if sensing his eyes on her, she opened hers. Softly she said, "What?"

Terrell didn't respond at first. His own body was trying to deal with the rush of emotions he felt just being with her. All at once, he felt desire, contentment, love.

She touched his face. "Why are you looking at me like that?"

"I love you," he said before he could stop the words. But saying them had been like easing a burden. "I love you," he repeated, then lowered his mouth to hers for a slow, sensual kiss.

Afterward he lay sideways, nestling Jade against him. It occurred to him only as he closed his eyes that Jade hadn't whispered the same three words back.

Chapter 21

WHEN KATHY OPENED THE DOOR of her brother's brownstone, her breath caught in her throat. For a moment, she thought her eyes must be playing tricks on her. But as soon as she realized it wasn't an illusion, she wished the floor would swallow her up.

Instead, she made a quick effort to close the door.

Too fast for her, Sheldon stuck his foot in the opening before she could slam the door shut. "Kathy, wait—"

"Get lost, Sheldon."

"I just want to talk to you."

"I don't want to talk to you."

Easily stronger than her, Sheldon eased the wooden door back and slipped into the house. Unable to do anything else, Kathy merely stood there and stared at him. As her chest heaved from their struggle and her anger, her eyes took in the length of him, passing over his tall, lean frame, noting that he'd grown a goatee since the time she'd last seen him. Of course, he'd had plenty of time to grow a goatee—eight years.

"How dare you come here?"

Sheldon didn't answer her at first. Instead, he let his eyes roam over her body the way she had just sized him up. Why was it that she felt warm beneath his gaze? It was her anger, of course.

"You think this is the way to get what you want by harassing me, bullying me?"

"You've given me no other choice."

She was such a bundle of angry nerves, Kathy's body shook. "*I* gave you no other choice? Hel-lo? You're the one who made your choice eight years ago. I've lived with it for that long. Now you deal with it."

He took a step toward her and instinctively she stepped back. Then regretted it. She didn't want Sheldon to feel he had any power over her.

"I have dealt with my decision, Special. And regretted it. You don't know how much."

Kathy's fluttered at the old nickname Sheldon used to call her. Swallowing, she straightened her back and gave him a level stare. "I want you to leave."

He shook his head, but thankfully didn't approach her again. "I can't do that, Special. Not until you give me a chance to explain."

If this wasn't her brother's home, Kathy would be tempted to run for the phone and dial 911. But it was and she wouldn't be responsible for bringing the cops here and making her brother's home the center of attention. She had to face the fact that Sheldon wasn't going to take no for an answer.

"All right," Kathy finally said. "Let's go somewhere and talk."

Finally after eight long years, she was going to give Sheldon Monroe a piece of her mind.

* * *

"Hold up!" the woman at Jade's station exclaimed, her eyes widening in horror. "What are you doing?"

Looking at the woman's expression, Jade's stomach lurched. Then she followed the woman's eyeline to the can in her hand. Good Lord! She'd been about to add a color spray to the woman's hair instead of the sheen she'd intended.

"I'm sorry," Jade said, then groaned loudly.

The woman's expression could kill the dead.

"I…" Jade suddenly felt unqualified to be a stylist, like a big fraud. A concerned expression on her face, Sherry approached her. "I don't feel well."

Placing the aerosol can in Sherry's hand, Jade hurried to the back of the shop and the washroom. She turned the lock then leaned against the door, closing her eyes tightly.

If she'd sprayed the gold color into the woman's hair, at least that could be corrected.

Her mind was somewhere else today. Darn, she'd never been like this before. In the past when anything bothered her she was always able to put it to the back of her mind and concentrate on her work. Why was it different now?

Terrell.

Jade crossed to the sink, turned the cold water faucet. As the water poured against the white porcelain, she cupped some and splashed it over her face. She was out of sorts because of Terrell. Though their night had been explosive and wonderful, his proclamation of love had changed everything.

And now just thinking of him, of where their relationship was going, had her doing a bad job at the salon. She couldn't afford to screw up here. She needed this job, this career. If she lost her head over a man to the point where it affected her career goals, then how on earth would she ever get her salon established once again?

There was a soft rapping at the door, then Sherry said, "Are you okay?"

Jade dried her face with a paper towel, then opened the door and faced Sherry. "I really don't feel well."

"Oh, my. You don't look too well, either. Why don't you take the rest of the day off?"

Jade was about to say no, that all she needed was some food in her stomach, but then decided that the afternoon off might be a good idea. "Are you sure? Saturday is such a busy day."

"Yeah, but what good will you be if you're sick?"

"True," Jade agreed, wondering if indeed she was coming down with something, or if she was just sick at heart.

Later she found herself on West Thirty-fifth Street in midtown Manhattan. The cold wind biting at her skin, she walked briskly past Fifth Avenue toward Sixth, clutching her coat collar around her face.

If she hadn't taken the walk from the subway often enough to know the exact spot where Dreamstyles had been, she might have walked past the place. In fact, when she did stop outside the large glass storefront she knew had been her salon, she paused, unsure. But she knew. The brown brick exterior was the same and it was still next to a Vicki's Flowers.

Though she knew the building would house a different business now, Jade was still slightly surprised to see a café and not her salon. For several moments, she stood outside, watching as several people sat and chatted over deli sandwiches and salads, coffees and desserts. The place was completely different.

When a passing pedestrian brushed against Jade, she

realized that she couldn't stand outside the shop all day. Well, it was a café open to the public. She decided to enter.

She hadn't come here since she had officially lost the salon to the bank. She hadn't wanted to. Now as she slowly stepped inside the café, she looked around and remembered the way it had once been.

At the back, where the shampoo area had been, encased glass kept fresh meats chilled. That's also where the cash register was. Behind that, a door led to a private shop area—the area she'd once used for her employees. The café had a fifties deli motif and feel, with large stools and counters and many booths. There was even a jukebox near the entrance, out of which some fifties song was playing.

"Can I help you, miss?"

Jade spun at the sound of the woman's voice. A young brunette, no older than her early twenties, stood with a menu in hand and a smile across her face. "Uh, I'd like a coffee."

"You can have a seat at the coffee bar, over there."

The woman pointed toward the left. A large semicircular counter adorned with chrome surrounded the coffee bar. Two cappuccino machines and an array of specialty coffees were available in that area. No hairdryers, no stylists. Swallowing a sigh, Jade walked toward it and took a seat on a corner stool.

Shrugging off her coat, she scanned the menu board. Sheesh, a mocha cappuccino was over three dollars. That was Manhattan for you.

"What can I get ya?" a man in white asked from behind the counter.

"A mocha cappuccino, please."

As he whirled around, Jade positioned herself on the stool, carefully draping her coat across her lap. Seconds later, the man placed the drink before her.

But she hardly noticed. Instead, she noticed the lump in her throat and the pain in her heart. This was her salon, her baby, and if it weren't for Nelson, she would still have it. Despite how much she wanted to forget that and move on, she wasn't sure she'd ever be able to.

"Terrell." His name fell from her lips on a sigh. And she suddenly realized why she'd been feeling so down today, so out of it. Because she felt guilty.

Terrell loved her.

Not that she hadn't known. She'd seen it in his eyes, had felt it in his touch. And she'd sensed his disappointment that she hadn't repeated the same words to him. He hadn't mentioned it, but Jade had known.

She reached for her drink and took a slow sip. It didn't help the lump in her throat, and she knew it never would. The truth was, she was confused out of her mind and didn't know what to do.

Terrell was a decent man, a wonderful man. He loved her. But…Jade closed her eyes, reopened them. Despite the attraction she felt for him, she didn't know if she loved him. What did she know about love? She'd thought she'd loved Nelson, and look how horribly that marriage had turned out. She wasn't about to put herself in that kind of position again, loving and trusting a man and giving him the power to destroy her.

As she sipped the warm mocha cappuccino, Jade considered what she wanted out of life. First and foremost, she didn't want a man to stand in the way of her dreams. That had happened once, and she would always regret it. Terrell, though completely different from Nelson, had already had her mind wandering from her career goals and work to him and more of him—which was definitely not good.

She wanted to continue seeing Terrell, that was certain,

but she wanted to take things very slowly. Maybe after a very long courtship she might even consider marriage—*if* she decided she ever wanted to go there again. But how could she ever realistically consider marriage to Terrell, knowing what she knew?

That, she sensed as her stomach took a nosedive, was the much bigger picture, the one thing she didn't want to face. Terrell was a family man and would no doubt want children, the one thing she couldn't give him. Was it really fair to continue this relationship, lead him on, then break his heart with the devastating news that she'd never make him a father?

Jade's eyes misted as she remembered Nelson's own disappointment, and she felt like a failure all over again. Was that why he'd turned to drinking, gambling? Was that why he'd run into Amanda's arms? She had to face it, she just didn't have anything to offer a man. And she couldn't handle disappointing Terrell the way she'd disappointed Nelson.

So this year had to be about her, about getting her life back on track. She could accept the fact that she'd never be a mother as long as she had her career. But the deeper she got involved with Terrell, the more she had to wonder if she'd end up putting her career on the back-burner. Though he was a welcome distraction at times, he had been a distraction.

Yet she couldn't bring herself to even imagine breaking off their relationship. And after his proclamation of love last night, how on earth could she tell him she wanted to slow things down without hurting him? It was too late to spare his feelings; he was in too deep. As she brought the mug to her lips for another sip, she had to face one other thing—*she* wasn't ready to slow down their relationship. Like him, she was in too deep as well.

But was she ready for love?

* * *

How Kathy ended up in Sheldon's bed when she should have been giving him a piece of her mind would always be a mystery to her. One minute they had been in his car, trying to figure out where they could talk. The next minute they'd been wrapped in each other's arms as though no time had passed, barely able to control their passion. As Sheldon had driven to his flat in Queen's, Kathy's body had thrummed with an awareness she hadn't felt since…well, since the last time she and Sheldon had been together.

Now her head resting against his strong chest, her fingers gently weaving through the curly hair on his chest, she asked, "How did you know I was at Wayne's?"

Sheldon trailed fingers up and down her naked back, causing her body to once again come alive with desire. "He called me. Said he'd be out in the afternoon but that you would be home."

"That jerk," Kathy said, unconsciously yanking on a chest hair.

Sheldon yelped. "Baby, at least it got us together, didn't it?"

To her own surprise, Kathy smiled. "Yeah, it did."

Lifting her hand to his lips, Sheldon kissed her palm. "Baby, what are you thinking?"

She was thinking that she loved it when he called her baby. But she said, "I don't know."

"You happy? Sad?"

"Confused."

"I know." He pulled her close. "This wasn't planned—getting you in bed, I mean. That's not what I wanted."

"It isn't?" But her voice was playful.

"You know what I mean. I didn't plan this. Baby, all I wanted to do was talk to you, make you understand that I still love you."

The words made Kathy's eyes mist with tears. She'd always only loved Sheldon and being with him now she knew she'd never stopped. But whether or not she could completely forgive him was another matter. "You don't know what I went through, your calling off the wedding like that. Sheldon, I was not only hurt but humiliated. For months we'd been planning the wedding, only for you to up and join the military to get away from me. If you didn't want to get married, you never should have proposed.

"Don't you think I know that?" He blew out a frustrated breath, but held her tighter, as though he didn't ever want to let her go. "Baby, I *did* want to marry you. But I don't know what happened. I suddenly didn't want to be a failure. My dad kept telling me I was too young, that I didn't have my life together…I don't know."

Kathy wanted to be mad at him, wished she could be. But she knew what he was talking about. Sheldon's father, at best, was cruel and sarcastic and had emotionally scarred all four of his children.

She said, "But you never made him proud, did you?"

"Naw. There was no pleasing him. I did everything he wanted, but it never mattered." Sheldon paused, then added, "He died last summer."

Kathy leveled her chin on his chest and met his eyes. "Oh, my God. Sheldon, I'm so sorry."

"These things happen," he replied nonchalantly. But Kathy knew that his father's death had hurt him, if for no other reason than Sheldon hadn't had the chance to make him proud.

"It's funny," Sheldon continued. "When my father died, I finally felt like I could come back. Like I'd been running and now didn't have to anymore." The hand on her back moved lower, splaying over her bottom. "I came back for you."

"I believe you." Kathy inched forward, planted a kiss on Sheldon's lips.

If she was a fool for love, then so be it.

Despite Jade's concerns earlier, when she met Terrell at his place later, there was no strain between them. She had wondered if there would be, had in fact felt stressed over it, but Terrell had simply greeted her with that smile that could melt butter when he'd opened the door. If he was disappointed that she hadn't told him she loved him last night, he certainly didn't show it.

For that Jade was glad. If nothing else, it made her realize that she could probably take things slowly with Terrell without feeling guilty about it.

"I called the salon today," he began as he settled on the sofa next to her. "Sherry said you'd left, sick."

"I...I wasn't feeling very well."

"Did you go home?"

"No...I just...hung around. Got something to eat. I felt better after that."

"Hmm."

"Hmm, what?" Jade asked, wondering what was on his mind. And she suddenly wondered if their relationship had gone to another level—one where Terrell felt she had to report her actions and whereabouts to him.

His answer surprised her. "You think you might be pregnant?"

"What?"

He placed a hand on her stomach. "That wouldn't be so bad, would it? If you gave me a son or a daughter? Lord knows my mother would be thrilled."

"Where is this coming from?" A nervous chill raced down her spine. "I—I'm barely getting my feet back on the ground financially. The last thing I need is a child."

She sounded convincing even to herself.

The spark that fizzed from Terrell's eyes made it clear he was disappointed. "I just wondered," he said. "Condoms aren't exactly foolproof."

Jade felt like the walls were closing in on her. Oh, God, Terrell wanted children. She should tell him now, let him know she could never be the woman he wanted. "Terrell, I—"

"Relax." He scooped her legs onto his lap and began massaging one foot. "It was just a question."

Jade didn't like the sour note, the small frown. Despite the fact that his hands worked on her feet like magic, she knew a part of him was disappointed. So she lied. "Maybe some time in the future, Terrell. Just not yet."

He flashed her a small smile. "I think I'll make a good father. But for now, let's just concentrate on us."

Guilt lodged in her throat, threatening to choke her. She should tell him the truth. Instead, she said, "I like the sound of that."

And as she sat forward, intending to wrap her arms around his neck, the phone rang.

Terrell rose and walked to the kitchen phone, picking up the receiver before his answering machine came on. Talk about timing. "Hello?"

"Terrell, it's Drew."

The serious tone in Drew's voice set off warning bells in Terrell's mind. "What is it? What's wrong?"

"It's Mom," Drew responded, and a cold wave swept over Terrell. "Get to Jersey as soon as you can. She's in a coma."

Chapter 22

AS TERRELL SPED HIS JEEP through the streets toward the hospital, Jade could only stare at his hands as they clutched the steering wheel. She wished she could do or say something to help erase the look of sheer terror in his eyes, but there was nothing she could do. She knew.

When her mother had called to tell her that her aunt Lizzie had found a lump in her breast, Jade had been so horrified she hadn't been able to actually digest the facts. And when Aunt Lizzie had died only weeks after receiving the death sentence—and before Jade had had a chance to make it back to Louisiana—she'd felt a profound sense of horror and loss that no words ever could have eradicated.

She was glad she didn't tell him she couldn't have children. He didn't need to deal with that tonight.

Terrell cursed loudly as he came to a screeching halt at a stoplight. Jade flinched, not from fear of him but from fear for him. Silently she prayed his mother would be all right.

And to show her support, she gently rubbed his forearm. He glanced at her for the briefest of seconds before his foot hit the gas and the Jeep accelerated. His lips were pulled in a tight line, and there were so many lines across his forehead that Jade had to wonder if it wasn't painful. But she understood. He wouldn't be all right until he knew his mother was all right.

Jade placed both hands in her lap. For a fleeting moment, she wondered if she should even be here, if Terrell shouldn't just be with his family at a time like this. But she pushed that thought aside, knowing that he needed her now. He'd always been there for her. The least she could do was be here for him now.

Reaching across the front seat, she placed her hand on his leg…and let it rest there.

After what seemed like hours, Terrell and Jade were finally at the U.S. Veterans Hospital in East Orange, New Jersey, rushing through the corridors of its emergency ward. As they rounded a corner and he spotted his father, Terrell felt a modicum of relief. Gripping Jade's hand, he quickened his pace, darting around hospital staff and anxious family members of other emergency patients.

Immediately his father approached him, his eyes red from crying. "Terrell."

"Dad, what happened?"

"It looks like your mother is in a diabetic coma."

"Diabetes?" For a second, Terrell thought there must be some mistake. "Mom doesn't have diabetes."

"Apparently she does." That was Drew who spoke and Terrell turned to face him. Lena, who'd obviously been crying, stood beside her husband, clutching a child to each side. "She'd been experiencing symptoms for a while, but ignoring them. Feeling lethargic, really thirsty, blurred vision, to name a few. You know she hasn't been feeling one hundred percent lately."

"I should have realized something was wrong," Mr. Edmonds said, fresh tears spilling from his eyes. "I should have made her see a doctor."

Releasing his hold on Jade, Terrell wrapped his father in a tight embrace. "It's not your fault."

"It's nobody's fault," Drew added.

When Terrell pulled back, he saw Drew's eyes travel between him and Jade. Instantly Terrell remembered Jade had never met his family. "Uh, Drew, this is Jade. Jade, this is my brother, Drew, his wife, Lena, and their children, Sadé and Kwame. This is my father."

Jade politely smiled at Terrell's family members, not sure what to say at a time like this. She felt like a fifth wheel—totally unnecessary and out of place. "I hope Mrs. Edmonds is okay."

Lean sniffled. The two young children, quiet and probably scared, clung to their mother. Only Drew seemed composed and in control of his emotions.

Jade couldn't help thinking that if it were her family here, they'd be bawling down the entire building.

Terrell's father flashed her a weak smile before his lips quivered. He brought a hand to his face, covering his mouth as he choked back the tears. Jade's heart broke for the man.

And then they were all huddled together, giving one another support, while she stood behind them all, watching and feeling like an outsider.

A short while later, the doctor, a short, middle-aged white man, faced them with a somber expression. Terrell's heart dropped to his knees. "My God. What is it?"

The doctor looked at the senior Mr. Edmonds. "I wish I had good news to give you, but I don't." There were collective wails of grief. "Your wife is still in a coma, and we're administering insulin to break down her sugar. Her blood sugar level was 760, several times above the normal range. She's older, and that's complicating things, but I'm hopeful. Of course, it doesn't hurt to pray."

Lena threw a hand to her mouth but that wasn't enough to stifle her sobs.

In a state of disbelief, Terrell closed his eyes. When he opened them, he put an arm around his father. Mr. Edmonds made no pretense of being solid as a rock. Tears streamed down the older man's face.

"It's too soon to tell if she'll make it or not."

More sobs from Lena. Terrell had to fight his own. Not his mother. Not the woman who had worked so hard her whole life and was only now beginning to enjoy it. Please God, not her.

The doctor added quietly. "I'm sorry."

Drew, who held a sleeping Sadé, pulled Lena, who held a sleeping Kwame, to him. For the first time his cool demèanor cracked as his eyes filled with tears. Terrell placed an arm on his father's shoulder, and Jade saw a tear roll down his face.

Quietly she took a step backward. Terrell didn't notice and neither did anyone else. They were all overcome with grief, clinging to each other for support.

She didn't know why she felt the sense so strongly, but she knew she didn't belong.

Turning, Jade headed for the exit. As she quietly walked away, she didn't look back.

Terrell had never doubted there was a God, but this was just further proof of his existence. Their prayers had been answered. Not only was his mother going to be fine, she was awake and talking about her experience. The night had been long and almost unbearable, but the sight of his mother alive and conscious warmed his soul.

His father sat on the chair beside her bed, and the rest of the family, including Sadé and Kwame, either stood or leaned against the mattress.

The only one missing was Jade. When Terrell had looked around last night, he'd discovered her gone. He understood that she wouldn't want to spend the entire night in the hospital, but why hadn't she said she was leaving? At the very least, Terrell would have arranged for a car to take her home. And there was no message from her on his answering machine or at the hospital.

It left him with a very bad feeling in his gut.

But now was not the time to think about Jade. His mother was what mattered now. He couldn't give God enough thanks for not taking her last night.

"I saw my mother," his own mother was quietly saying. "I swear, I saw her in a tunnel. Lord, it's true what all those people say. I saw my mother in a tunnel of light. She kept telling me to go back, that it wasn't my time."

Lena let out a small cry, and Mrs. Edmonds reached for her hand. "Save your tears, sweetheart. I'm still here. And I'm not going anywhere. Not yet anyway."

Mr. Edmonds, who had refused to even leave her side the moment he'd been allowed to see her, kissed her hand. "I love you."

"Boy, is this what I have to do to get you all to fuss over me?" She smiled weakly. "Please, someone smile. I can't take seeing all your gloomy faces."

Sadé edged forward and rewarded her grandmother with a wide grin. "I'm glad you're okay, Grandma."

Just before midnight, Drew had driven Lena and the children home, then returned to the hospital. While Drew had caught up on some sleep this morning, Terrell had picked them up and brought them back. All the while, he'd wondered why Jade had felt she couldn't even tell him she was leaving.

"Oh, my sweet Sadé." Mrs. Edmonds ran a hand over the young girl's head. "I am so glad to be okay, too."

"Can I get you anything, Ma?" Terrell asked. "Water? Juice? Food?"

She cleared her throat. "Water would be nice."

"No problem." Terrell walked to the small table in the room and lifted the glass pitcher. He filled a glass with water and brought it to his mother.

His father took it from him, then carefully placed it at his mother's lips. Lifting her head a little, she sipped.

"Mom," Drew began softly, "as much as we all want to be here, if you're tired, let us know."

Mrs. Edmonds looked at them each in turn, then finally said, "I wouldn't mind some time alone with your father."

"Absolutely." Terrell took Sadé's hand while his brother gathered Kwame into his arms. "We'll be outside."

As they stepped into the hallway, Sadé extended her arms, silently asking Terrell to lift her. He did, and she rested her head against his shoulder.

Lena went to her husband's side and sagged against him.

"It's going to be okay," Drew told her, wrapping one arm around her waist.

"I know. It's just that she's the closest thing to a mother I've ever had." Lena punctuated the sentence with the blowing of her nose.

"Hey, Terrell." At the sound of his brother's voice, Terrell looked at him. "Did you ever find out what happened to Jade?"

"No." And as far as he was concerned, he wouldn't be the one to call her. If the roles had been reversed, he never would have left in the face of her grief.

"Maybe you should give her a call. I'm sure she has a reason for leaving."

"Maybe," Terrell said, but knew that whatever her reason, it couldn't be good enough.

He focused on his family instead, on these few people in the world who mattered to him the most. It was about time he concentrated on them, instead of the fantasy he had that he and Jade might actually have a future.

Chapter 23

WHEN THE FIRST RAYS of sunlight spilled into the room, Jade rolled onto her back and dragged her forearm over her face. She'd felt too lousy to sleep and had hoped that at some point sheer exhaustion would claim her, but so far, she'd had no such luck.

She should have told Terrell that she was leaving the hospital last night, but she just hadn't known how. How could she have told him she was leaving in the face of his pain?

But she'd realized one thing. She and Terrell, they were so different. They came from totally different backgrounds. Seeing him with his family she could understand why he was so confident about relationships, why family mattered to him so much. Jade wasn't near as confident as him, and besides, could never give him the family he craved.

What point was there in continuing their relationship?

The sound of laughter coming through the walls made Jade sit up. Was Kathy home?

More laughter. Indeed, the prodigal Kathy had returned.

Scrambling from the bed, Jade supposed she was on the phone, but she didn't care. Right now, like a confessor with a priest, Jade needed to talk to her best friend.

Seeing that Kathy wasn't in the living room, Jade knocked on her bedroom door, then without waiting for a reply, opened it. And got the shock of her life.

"Oh, my gosh! I'm so sorry."

Jade pulled the door closed a little harder than was necessary, her face as hot as a neon light. Softly she cursed. Though she hadn't been the one caught butt-naked with a man in her bed, she felt as embarrassed as if the tables had been turned.

Jade had just hopped back onto her bed when Kathy entered her room, pulling the tie of her pink terry cloth robe.

"Kathy, forgive me. I don't know what I was thinking."

Giggling, Kathy sat on the bed next to Jade. "Don't worry about it."

"So…you're home."

"Yeah." Kathy replied in the most dreamy voice Jade thought she'd ever heard.

"And that's…" Having seen two naked forms, Jade hadn't hung around to see if it was Tyrone.

"Oh, you're not going to believe this." Kathy inhaled a deep breath and released it slowly. "That's Sheldon."

"Sheldon!"

Instantly Kathy covered Jade's mouth, then threw a glance over her shoulder. "Not so loud. And I know what you're going to say."

Jade tugged at Kathy's hand until her mouth was free. "You're darn right you know what I'm going to say! What on earth is going on?"

Kathy's sheepish smile explained everything.

"I don't believe it." Jade stood, eyeing her friend as though she were a stranger. "*You* and Sheldon? After the way you've been avoiding him like the plague? Kathy, you even moved out temporarily to escape him, and the first night you're back you…you bring him!"

Kathy stood to meet her friend. "Yes, and it's wonderful. I know I didn't want to have anything to do with him anymore, but we've had a chance to talk—"

"Have you really thought this through?" For the life of her, Jade didn't know why *she* was now the one who sounded like she opposed their reunion, after knowing Kathy had never stopped loving him. "You of all people should know that sex complicates everything."

Kathy's smile disappeared. "Who are we talking about, Jade, me or you?"

Jade swallowed, suddenly unsure. "I…" Her voice trailed off when she realized she couldn't answer the question.

"All right. What's up with you and Terrell?"

"It's more like what's *not* up with us."

"Uh-oh. Want to talk about it?"

Briefly Jade explained last night's events. "I just left, Kathy. I just walked away and didn't say a thing. I don't know why, other than I just felt like I was intruding. Oh, I don't know." When Kathy didn't say anything, Jade said, "I know, it was stupid. But Kathy, I just freaked. Seeing him with his family, seeing them all so distraught—what was I supposed to do?"

"You didn't want the emotional investment."

That stopped Jade cold. Man, Kathy was right. Jade said so. "It was like I suddenly realized how serious a step it was, being there with his family…it was like if I'd stayed, it would be telling Terrell I wanted to be a part of that. And I don't know that I want to be a part of that. Does that make sense?"

"Some. Especially after the way Nelson's family treated you."

"Yes." Jade agreed heartily, though she hadn't consciously acknowledged that that had been one of her fears. Nelson's mother, his sister and brother—they'd all been less than fond of her and had never let her forget it. Perhaps that had scarred Jade more than she'd ever been willing to admit.

Taking Kathy's hand, Jade dragged her onto the bed beside her. "I got scared, Kathy. And now I don't know if Terrell will ever forgive me."

"I'm not sure he will, either," Kathy replied softly. "Look, Jade, you have to talk to him. I know you don't want another man to stand in the way of your career, but Terrell isn't Nelson. You have to stop treating him like he is."

Jade's mouth opened in protest, then snapped shut. She felt the tears blur her eyes and only hoped that she wouldn't cry in front of Kathy.

Kathy wrapped her arms around her. "Jade, don't cry. Talk to Terrell. Explain what happened, why you're afraid. He'll understand. If Sheldon could finally get through to me—and you know how pigheaded I can be—then Terrell can get over his anger. As long as you tell him why."

Jade pulled back from Kathy's embrace and wiped at her tears. "So you and Sheldon are back together."

A smile spreading over her face, Kathy nodded. "Yeah. And you're not going to believe this, but we're getting married!"

Why did Kathy's announcement make Jade feel a jarring pain in her heart? "I… Already?"

"No, we were thinking of May."

"I didn't mean—"

"I know." Kathy smiled—and she looked simply radiant.

"I never stopped loving him. And though he was wrong to walk away from me eight years ago, he had a good reason. It's a long story," Kathy explained with a wave of her hand. "But the bottom line is, I forgive him and I want to spend the rest of my life with him. Making babies, doing the whole family thing."

Jade swallowed hard, hoping to dislodge the lump in her throat, but it seemed to grow instead. She made an attempt at humor. "It's about time."

"I guess it is. I'm not getting any younger."

Jade gave Kathy's hand a supportive squeeze. "I'm happy for you."

"Thanks. I'm really happy. Happier than I thought I'd ever be." She squeezed Jade's hand in return. "I want you to be as happy as I am, Jade."

"I think I may have blown my chance." And that, Jade realized, was her real fear.

"Call him, Jade. You two can work this out."

Hours later Jade called Terrell, but he wasn't home. She didn't bother to leave a message, knowing that words on an answering machine would never suffice.

No doubt Terrell was still at the hospital with his mother. She didn't know much about diabetes, but she did know that falling into a coma was serious.

Oh, God. What if Mrs. Edmonds hadn't made it? The thought caused Jade's stomach to tighten painfully. It felt as though someone was sitting on her chest—that's how hard it was for her to breathe. If Terrell's mother died, she could only imagine how he was suffering right now.

She had to know. If his mother had died, he would need her, and she was willing to try and be there for him. Picking up the phone, Jade dialed 411, then punched in the number to the U.S. Veterans Hospital. Minutes later she held the receiver to her chest, relieved.

Mrs. Edmonds was not only alive, but she'd come out of the coma.

Thank God.

"No way, Ma."

"I insist." Mrs. Edmonds pinned Terrell with a level gaze, then moved her eyes to each family member in turn.

"Well, you know I'm not leaving," Mr. Edmonds said.

Mrs. Edmonds squeezed his hand. "My love, you know I wasn't talking to you. Though you can't stay here forever, either."

"Maybe Mom's right," Drew said, stepping forward from the back of the group. "She's barely out of the coma, and she needs rest more than anything else. Now that we know she's going to be all right, we should give her some space. I'm not saying not to visit, but I am saying that we don't want her calling hospital security on us."

The last crack made Mrs. Edmonds smile—then she winced in pain. Her husband eased forward, brushing a hand over her forehead. "What is it?"

She settled against the pillow, her face relaxing. "I'm okay. I just want you all to get some rest. Please."

His mother was right, but Terrell didn't want to leave. Leaving meant he had to go home, had to face an empty bed.

Had to face a life without the woman he loved.

The way Jade figured it, Terrell had to come home sometime. She had resorted to leaving messages, apologizing for her thoughtless actions, but if he had retrieved them, he certainly hadn't called her back.

She couldn't blame him.

But when Monday afternoon she hadn't heard from him, she decided to make use of the key he'd given her. She went to his place after work and decided to wait for him.

It was weird, being in his place alone, waiting for him to come home the way she had once waited for Nelson.

"Forget Nelson," she told herself.

Hours later, like an intruder caught in the act, she bolted upright on his sofa when she heard the lock turn. As she swung her legs to the floor, Terrell stepped inside.

The only indication that he was startled was the brief widening of his eyes. But then they narrowed and he simply stared at her.

The tension between them was thick and tangible. But despite the fact that her heart was banging against her chest so hard she thought it would explode, she approached him. Then swallowed before she spoke. "H-how's your mother doing?"

"Jade, you do not want to go there right now."

He was angry. She had known he would be, that he certainly had a right to be; yet still Jade wasn't prepared for his wrath. A sudden chill sweeping over her, she hugged her torso. "Terrell, I'm sorry."

"Why, Jade? I just want to know why. You knew how much I needed you. My mother was in a coma. I've never been so afraid in my life. And when I turned around, you were gone."

"I'm sorry." What else could she say? There really was no rational explanation for her behavior. If she didn't understand her actions, how could she expect Terrell to understand them?

"Sweetheart, this is one of those times when sorry isn't enough."

"I...I don't know what more to say."

Terrell pursed his lips in thought as he weighed her words.

After a long pause, he spoke. "You know what I think? I think this is your way of telling me that you don't want a relationship. I guess I wasn't willing to hear you before, but leaving the hospital the way you did has made things clear to me now."

She didn't like the finality of his words. "It's not like that."

"Then what is it like, Jade? Tell me, because I don't understand."

"I don't know what I want," she said, exasperated. "Terrell, I've tried to give you what you want but the truth is I don't know that I want the same thing. I was married before. I only ever wanted to be married once. My marriage failed. I don't want to go there again."

"So you're going to punish yourself for marrying the wrong man for the rest of your life? I know you're smarter than that, Jade."

She squared her jaw as she stared defiantly at him. "You don't know me at all, Terrell. You think you do, but you don't."

"Because you won't let me get to know you. You've got these barriers up around your heart that are impossible to penetrate."

"Why can't you just admit that I'm not who you thought I was and let that be the end of it?" That would be so much easier than letting him know she'd never be the woman he wanted. "I'm trying, Terrell, I really am, but I just can't be the type of woman who runs heart first into another relationship. No matter how much I care about someone. This time, I have to look out for me first."

"Someone. Hmm."

"I didn't mean it like that."

Terrell shrugged. "You don't love me, do you?"

His question silenced her. She didn't know what she was feeling. "I…it's…" Knowing anything she said would sound lame, her voice trailed off.

"Jade, you know how I feel about you. You know that I love you. That I want a future with you, a family, but if you don't want the same thing, then I have to accept that. And I'm not going to chase you around for the rest of your life."

A nerve in Jade's jaw flinched at Terrell's words. She had known the words would come one day, but she wasn't prepared for the feeling of being lost. "Terrell, it's not that I don't care about you." *Tell him. Tell him what's really bothering you.* "I just need more time."

"Time for what? You either want to be with me or you don't."

"It's not that simple."

"It is for me. That it isn't for you says it all."

"I…" The words died on her lips.

"I'm going to be thirty-nine this month, Jade. I'm too old for games." Pausing, he blew out a frustrated breath. "Since you asked," he started in a much softer, pained voice, "my mother is alive. She'll probably be in the hospital for several weeks, however. When she's better, I may move to Milan."

"Milan?" Jade said, feeling a pain seize her heart.

Terrell hadn't planned to even mention Milan. Truthfully he hadn't changed his mind about Mr. Carracciolo's offer. But knowing that the life he'd always wanted here wasn't ever going to be, maybe starting over somewhere far away was just what he needed.

"I've been offered a job with a fashion house there," he said. "I'm seriously considering it. I have to move forward."

And put her behind him. He didn't have to say the words; Jade read the truth in his eyes.

He turned then, walked away from her. When he was at the stairs leading to the upper level of his loft, she called out to him. "Terrell, don't walk away from me."

"Why not?" He didn't even turn to face her.

As she stared at his back, she couldn't think of a single thing to say. All things considered, maybe this was for the best. She wasn't ready to take their relationship to the next level, and if Terrell had had enough of waiting for her, then so be it. She would just have to deal with it.

"That's what I thought." Terrell's voice was low as he spoke the words and a pain gripped Jade's heart unlike anything she'd ever felt before.

"Leave your key on the coffee table before you go."

So that was it…he was kicking her out, sending her out of his life, and that was it. Quietly Terrell began his ascent.

And Jade knew there was nothing else she could do. Before sex had been able to bring them closer together when they'd had a disagreement, but she knew that this time was totally different. Even if she begged him for another chance, for more time, she knew that he wouldn't give her the chance.

It was over.

Jade collected her purse, then mechanically dressed in her winter wear. As she placed the key on the coffee table, she felt eyes on her and looked to one corner of the room. Terrell wasn't there but her picture was. A picture where she'd been captured in a carefree, happy moment. A moment when she hadn't worried about her career, about what was wrong with her life, about why she and Terrell couldn't have a future.

She whimpered softly, and then quickly deposited the key on the coffee table. It made a soft *ping* sound against the glass. Hurrying to the door, she opened it and stepped into the hallway. *This is for the best,* she told herself.

But as she walked down the hallway to the stairwell, Jade was very aware that she had left a piece of her heart in Terrell's apartment.

Chapter 24

MISERABLE WASN'T AN ADEQUATE enough word to describe how Jade felt, and for the life of her, she couldn't understand the funky mood she'd been in since she'd seen Terrell five days ago. Their relationship was over, and Jade knew it was for the best. She couldn't give Terrell what he wanted, much less what he needed. And he certainly deserved better than a confused, screwed-up woman who didn't have time for love.

So why then did she feel a pain much more intense than when her marriage to Nelson had failed?

It was all Jade had been able to think of, though she'd made a concerted effort to not let her emotions affect her at work.

Knowing how important family was to Terrell, she wondered if he would indeed accept the job in Milan he'd mentioned. She wondered if he really wanted to get away from her that badly. And she wondered why the thought of him leaving made her heart sink to her knees.

From her corner on the sofa, Jade glanced at the watch-shaped wall clock. Didn't she have anything better to do on a Saturday night than sit around on her sofa and wish the hours away?

Obviously not, she thought, then frowned—and wondered why she felt like crying.

Terrell was drunk enough this Saturday night to believe that Jade was the one knocking on the door, drunk enough to jump up from his living room sofa and run to answer it. In his drunken haze, he believed it was actually possible she'd come to her senses and had come to tell him that she loved him.

But he sobered almost instantly when he saw Keisha, not Jade standing before him.

If he hadn't been drinking, he might have told Keisha to go away. Instead, he invited her in.

Silently Keisha removed her coat, then folded it over her arm. Learning forward, she took a whiff of his drink. "Whew, Scotch? It must be bad."

"Worse."

Keisha pinned him with a long look, then walked into the living room. Terrell walked behind her, finishing his drink as he did so. He continued on to the kitchen while Keisha sat on the sofa.

"What a drink?" he asked.

"I'll have a Scotch—straight."

"Must be bad," he called.

"Worse."

Less than a minute later, he sauntered into the living room with two glasses full of the potent liquor. He handed one to Keisha, then carefully sat beside her.

"You're in love with her, aren't you?"

Though drunk, Terrell had enough of his wits to wonder

how on earth Keisha would know he was seeing anyone, much less in love with someone.

"I've seen her," she said, as if she could secretly read his thoughts. Could she? "I've seen you two together. She's pretty."

"She's beautiful."

"But she doesn't love you."

That she was right hurt him, and Terrell sought the comfort of his drink. He gulped, then winced as the liquid burned a path to his stomach.

"I know how you feel," Keisha said, then took a sip of her drink. "I know how it feels to love someone who doesn't love you back."

"I suppose you do," Terrell replied, knowing she was talking about him. And he suddenly wondered if he was to Jade what Keisha was to him—a nuisance most of the time. He downed a liberal gulp of the Scotch, hoping it would burn away his pain.

They were silent for a long while, then Keisha said, "I know I'm crazy, but I still want you." Shifting on the sofa, she faced him dead-on. "I still want you."

Terrell didn't respond. What could he say?

She put down her glass, then edged closer to him. "Forget what I said about the baby. I don't need one. But I do want you, Terrell. Just once, if not forever."

Terrell looked at her face, into her hopeful eyes, and wondered why Jade didn't want him. He sipped the scotch.

She placed a hand on his chest, and Terrell didn't push it away. "What do you say, Terrell? Just once. Let's see how good we can be together."

"And if I said I could never promise you a tomorrow?" That had to be the booze talking. A sober Terrell would never even go there.

"Then I'd say at least we tried, gave it a fair shot. That's all I'm asking, Terrell. For a fair shot." Slowly she undid the top buttons on his shirt.

Terrell took another gulp of the Scotch, savored the feel and taste of it as it burned a path to his stomach, then closed his eyes.

Much later Terrell lay on his sofa, his mind in a drunken haze, pondering the mess that was his life. In Keisha, he had a woman who wanted him, no ifs ands or buts. But in Jade, he had a woman who liked him, and certainly enjoyed the sexual part of their relationship, but in the end didn't want him the way he wanted her.

If he hadn't been drunk, he would have kicked Keisha out the moment she'd started hitting on him. But he had been drunk and he'd allowed her to stay…and he was glad. Because now they at least had reached an understanding. She knew without a doubt that Terrell would never love her, but that that didn't mean they couldn't be friends. When, after she had failed in her attempt to seduce him, and Terrell had explained that he still cared for her as a person even if he didn't want to make love to her, she'd seemed to finally relax and they'd spent a good hour simply talking and laughing.

But Terrell hadn't forgotten. Jade had been on his mind the entire time. Though drunk, he'd known that sleeping with Keisha would be a Band-Aid solution to a much deeper gash than any Band-Aid could heal.

This was why, when Keisha had given him a chaste kiss good-bye and left for the night, he'd known that if he and Jade had just been in the same situation with Jade telling him she didn't want a serious relationship with him, he wouldn't have been able to stay and laugh and talk and drink with her, then leave as simply friends. His love for her went too deep, and the feeling of betrayal at the fact that she had slept with him on more than one occasion without really giving him her heart hurt too much.

Maybe one day he and Jade could reach a point in their relationship where they could be friends. Maybe, but that day was a long way away.

The intense soul-gripping reaction snuck up on Jade like a cheetah stalking its prey and pounced on her without warning. Nothing had ever affected her as profoundly as seeing little Nicholas in his baby stroller with a salon full of women surrounding the tiny thing.

She wanted one.

Instinctively she placed a hand on her stomach. Good Lord, what had happened to her? After her experience with Nelson, she'd more or less resigned herself to the fact that she couldn't get pregnant and that was fine with her. Not everyone was meant to have children, and clearly she was one of them. But as she heard little Nicholas's soft gurgling sounds, as she saw the small smile that curled on those tiny lips, she knew she wanted a baby for herself.

"He's adorable!" Sherry said, crouching beside the stroller. She gave him a finger, and though his eyes were closed, he gripped it.

Everyone in the salon, workers and patrons alike, crowded Gwen and the stroller that housed baby Nicholas. The coos and ooohs made the salon sound more like a nursery than a hair salon.

Leaning over Cassandra's shoulder, Jade stared down at the pale baby as he quietly slept. When he yawned, all the women oohed and aahed with delight.

Jade smiled at the sight, at the little bundle that was surely a gift from God. And then it hit her—the feeling of emptiness, the pang in her heart. She would never have children, never experience the joy of motherhood.

"When I see babies, I always want one," Cassandra said, her face alight as she turned to face Jade. "They're just so sweet, so precious."

"I know what you mean," Jade said softly, the words striking a chord more than ever before.

"Not that I'm ready, mind you. Not with my stage career finally happening. But I definitely want a family. Kenny and I both do."

At Cassandra's words, Jade had a very real and jarring vision of life as an old maid, sitting in a big house alone, rocking back and forth as she looked out the window at the happy people on the street. But she didn't have a piece of that happiness. She was old and alone and lonely.

Her mind drowning out the sounds of the women's de-lighted sounds, Jade remembered a biblical verse she'd heard so often as a child. *For what shall it profit a man, if he shall gain the whole world, but lose his soul?* She adapted the verse for her situation: What would it profit her to have a success-ful career and lose out on love?

Just because she hadn't found true love with Nelson didn't mean she never would. How many years would it take to reopen her salon, and after she'd achieved that, how many more before she established a loyal clientele? She would be thirty-five this year and by the time she achieved her goal, she could be well over forty. Did she want to start looking for Mr. Right then?

Especially when she knew in her heart that no matter how afraid she was of taking another risk, she had already found Mr. Right in Terrell.

She'd found him over six years ago and had pushed him

away then out of a sense of loyalty to Nelson. How could she push him away again? If she went crawling to him in a few months or even a few years, she knew it would be too late. He wouldn't allow her to hurt him again.

Maybe he wouldn't care that she couldn't give him children. And there were always other options, like adoption.

Oh, God. She loved him.

The realization actually startled her because she'd been fighting it for so long. Well over six years. And she suddenly knew how ridiculous it was to continue to fight her feelings, to let her fears get the better of her. Why couldn't she have both her dreams—a career *and* love? She trusted Terrell in a way she'd never trusted Nelson. She knew he wouldn't stand in the way of her dreams. Couldn't she have it all with Terrell?

She certainly didn't want to be like Whitney Houston, singing about "Didn't we almost have it all?"

When Sherry took the lead and headed back to her station, most others followed, going back to their tasks at hand. Folding her arms over her chest, Jade moved slowly back to the station where she'd been styling Cassandra's hair. And with the dissipating crowd her hopes dimmed, replaced once again by doubts. Desperately she wished she could have it all, but women like her weren't so lucky. Nelson hadn't thought her important enough to stay faithful to her. What if Terrell married her, then ultimately felt the same way? She didn't want to be like her parents, always on rocky ground, or like her brother, always losing the woman he loved because he was so afraid to lose the woman he loved that he smothered her. Maybe the Alexanders just weren't lucky in the love department and Jade had to accept that.

"Jade?"

Cassandra's voice pulled her from her thoughts. "Oh, I'm sorry. What did you say?"

"I said I've got to run. I'm meeting Kenny for an early dinner before I have to head for work." Smiling, Cassandra placed a hand on her forehead in a dramatic gesture. "Ah, the life of an actress. Oh, so stressful!"

Jade grinned, though her body didn't feel it. "I'm sure whatever stress you're feeling Kenny can make it better."

Cassandra winked. "You better believe it." Giggling, she gave Jade a hug, then kissed her on the cheek. "Take care, hon, and keep in touch. Oh, and say hi to Terrell for me."

Jade watched Cassandra head to the receptionist to settle her bill, wondering why people like Cassandra could find what seemed to be true love and she couldn't.

Because people like Cassandra and Kathy are willing to take risks for love.

That, Jade had to agree with her inner voice, was the bottom line. What good would it do to spend the rest of her life afraid, always running from commitment, always trying to protect her heart?

At that moment, Nicholas must have done something extraordinary because the few women around him erupted in laughter. But the loud sound apparently scared the poor thing because he started crying. For such a tiny creature, he sure did have an impressive voice.

"Terrell would make a wonderful father." Jade's soft-spoken words so startled her she at first wondered if someone else had said them. But everyone else was either getting their hair taken care of or standing around Gwen as she held her baby and gently comforted him.

She turned, walked to the shampoo area, the sudden thought of Terrell as a father making her think of his mother. And Jade knew then what she had to do.

Mrs. Edmonds was in a small, private room decorated in pale pinks and yellows. It was pleasant—about as pleasant as a hospital room could be, considering the presence of IV poles and monitors that made it impossible to forget one was sick.

Jade entered the room slowly, a potted poinsettia in hand. She was thankful that the room was empty.

"Hello, child," Mrs. Edmonds said cheerfully as Jade neared her bed. A robust woman in her sixties with salt-and-pepper hair, she instantly made Jade feel welcome. "You don't look like a nurse."

"I'm not." Jade made room for the plant along the window-sill. "I'm a friend of Terrell's."

"Jade."

Mrs. Edmonds said the word as a statement, without even a hint of doubt, surprising Jade. "Yes—how did you—"

"My son talks about you all the time."

A smile touched Jade's lips, quickly followed by heaviness in her chest. "He does?"

"Oh, yes. And now I can see why. You're beautiful."

In less than five minutes of spending time with her, Jade felt more comfortable than she'd felt during her several years' relationship with her mother-in-law. "Thank you."

Mrs. Edmonds patted a spot beside her leg, and Jade sat. "It's a pleasure to finally meet you."

"It's a pleasure to meet you, too, Mrs. Edmonds." Jade looked to the door, as if expecting someone to walk in. Or was she hoping? "I'm surprised you're alone. From what I know of your family, it seems like you're very...loved."

"I am. I thank the Lord each day for my family. But they'd been spending so much time here, I sent them home. I needed a little peace. Ya know?"

"If you'd rather be alone now…" Jade made a move to stand, but Mrs. Edmonds grabbed her arm.

"Stay. I want to get to know the woman my son's in love with."

When Terrell visited his mother later, he was surprised to learn Jade had been there.

"Jade? Are you sure?"

"I may be sick, but I'm not losing my mind."

"Sorry, Ma, I didn't mean to imply that you are. It's just that…" What did he feel? Besides shock, a sense of hope, maybe? Which was totally crazy, considering he knew Jade didn't return his feelings so there was nothing to feel even the faintest hope about. "I'm just surprised she'd come to see you."

"Because you two are having problems?"

Terrell was momentarily rendered speechless. Either his mother was psychic or she'd had a heart-to-heart with Jade. He didn't know which of the two options sounded more plausible.

As if in answer to his silent question, his mother said, "I don't know the details, Terrell, but she did tell me that she'd done something she wasn't sure you could forgive. Now knowing you the way I do, I told her that there's nothing I can't see you forgiving, not if you love her."

"It's not that simple, Ma."

"Love never is."

"Well, some things are unforgivable."

Reaching out, Mrs. Edmonds took her son's hand and pulled him close. "Don't ever say that, Terrell. I raised you to always look deeper, to understand that different people make different choices, that we all react differently to any given situation. I've known for a few days that you and Jade were having problems. You weren't talking about her, you were generally in a foul mood. But seeing her, chatting with her, I can't see how she'd do anything that you couldn't forgive."

Maybe his mother was right. Maybe Jade coming to see her was her way of trying to make amends. "I don't know."

"What's to know? You love her. She loves you."

Terrell almost laughed out loud. "Yeah, right."

His mother eyed him quizzically. "Is that it? You don't think she loves you?"

Terrell couldn't believe he was having this conversation with his mother. Sighing, he leaned his hip against the mattress. "Ma, I have loved Jade for over six years. But all she's ever done is push me away."

"She's afraid. One look in her eyes and I could see that."

Terrell shrugged. "Well, if she is, then I don't know what to do. And believe me, I've tried."

"You have to be patient, my son. She'll come around when she's ready."

"But it may be too late then." Frustrated, Terrell ran a hand over his face. "Ma, I have been patient. She knows how I feel, that I want her and only her. But she's got too many issues with her ex-husband and her family. Maybe she'll never be ready. Jade's only focus is her career, Ma. Her ex took everything away from her and I think that deep down she feels I'll do the same thing. And if that's the case, isn't it better that I forget her now and go on with my life, instead of wasting years hoping and praying for something that will never be?"

"I have never known you to give up on anything until you got what you wanted."

"Well, maybe Jade is the one thing I can't have."

Mrs. Edmonds squeezed Terrell's hand. "I hope that isn't

the case. I think she'd be a great daughter-in-law." She paused. "Now I don't know the details of your problems, but maybe what you need to do is show Jade that you love her, instead of telling her."

"Why do I feel like I'm having a conversation with a shrink?"

"Well, this is one shrink you should listen to. I was young once, too, ya know."

Playfully Terrell rolled his eyes. "Not the older and wiser speech?"

"You hush." But she smiled. "And take my word for it, if you show that woman you love her, if you let her know you always will, she'll be yours, Terrell. And you won't have to wait too long."

Chapter 25

TERRELL CERTAINLY HOPED his mother knew what she was talking about, because her words had given him an idea. What Jade needed to know was that she could have her career *and* him—in essence, that she could have it all. And Terrell wanted it all with her and no one else, so if he was taking a big risk now in the name of love, then so be it. Life was too short to sit and watch it pass you by without going for what you wanted.

He'd called Jade a few times over the last week, letting her know by his presence in her life that he still cared for her and at the very least wanted to be her friend. He wouldn't push her, but if she had any deep feelings for him at all, she would be thinking hard about him. Ultimately no matter how he felt about her, they didn't have a future if she didn't want one.

And he thought that things were starting to look up, though he didn't want to get his hopes up like when he'd seen Jade on New Year's Eve and learned she was divorced. But still his heart hadn't been able to ignore the hope that speaking to her gave him. It was her idea to get together for dinner, but Terrell had put her off, not wanting to see her until his plan was finalized. It was like a magician preparing for the grand finale— Terrell wanted to make sure everything was in motion.

It all came down to this, to the final act. Tonight would either be an ending or a new beginning.

He prayed it would be a new beginning.

Jade was nothing if not stubborn and determined, two qualities about her he loved, but two qualities he fully expected to challenge him later. Well, whatever the outcome, Jade would be sure of one thing—he loved her and he was willing to do anything to make her happy. If, after tonight, she rejected him, then Terrell knew there was no hope.

That thought scared him, but he knew it was time to see where they really stood. Tonight he would give Jade a gift of love, and hopefully she would give him her heart in return.

Jade was more anxious than she'd expected this Sunday night when she prepared for her date with Terrell. Tonight she felt deep in her heart would be a turning point. And she knew which direction she wanted to go, and could only pray that things still worked out that way.

She loved Terrell. She knew that in her heart. But love wasn't the only thing that made a marriage work. She'd learned that with Nelson.

So tonight she wanted to lay everything on the table, see if their life's goals could actually find a common ground. See if they could actually have a future.

The thought scared her to death. Taking another chance on love after what she'd gone through with Nelson was a bigger step for her than Terrell probably realized. But there was one difference this time: she knew that Terrell loved her much more deeply than Nelson ever had.

So what's the problem? her mind asked.

"I don't want to give up all my dreams for love," she replied softly.

Terrell won't make you do that.

"I don't want to disappoint him."

You won't. He loves you.

"We'll see."

And tonight she would.

"Hi," Jade said softly as she opened the door.

"Hi." Terrell's gaze swept over her leisurely, from her head to her toes, and Jade instantly felt her body come alive. What was it about this man that he could always do that to her?

"Uh, come in." Swinging the door, she held it open in invitation. "I'm almost ready."

Terrell stepped into the foyer, and Jade allowed herself to peruse his body. He'd said to dress upscale, and his loose-fitting olive-colored jacket with matching pants and beige silk shirt made him look like he'd stepped off the cover of *GQ* magazine.

She wanted him. Now and always.

"Have a seat in the living room."

"Okay."

She watched his lean frame stroll into the living room, and her heart quickened. Just the sight of him was enough to make her crazy with longing, but it was so much more than the physical, she realized. Her heart felt a longing for him that she didn't think would ever die.

Turning, she walked to the small bathroom and closed the door behind her. Her makeup was pretty much done, but she wanted to add some color to her cheeks and fix the curls around her face. Truly she wanted Terrell to be alone when he realized that the gift-wrapped package on the coffee table was for him.

Jade pulled at a few curls, giving her face a soft yet sexy look. She had to admit, she was impressed. She'd added height at the top of her hair but had finger-styled the curls, giving her a much bolder coif than she normally wore. A special do for a special occasion.

When she'd applied enough mascara and eye shadow to make her eyes look much brighter, she finally exited the bathroom. And saw Terrell standing outside the door.

"Thanks." A small smile pulled at the corners of his lips, and Jade had the feeling that he was holding back.

"That's not a Valentine's gift."

"I know. I saw the card." Pause. "I didn't think you'd remember."

"Did you open it?" she asked.

"My birthday's not till Wednesday."

"I know…but…well, I know you're busy, I'm busy."

In other words, she wasn't planning on seeing him for his birthday. Was she planning on seeing him ever again, or was this her send-off gift?

"Go ahead. Open it."

"All right." Her smile was contagious, and Terrell found himself grinning like a little boy at Christmas as he tore at the packaging, opening it to reveal a shoebox. He lifted the lid and saw that there was another wrapped box inside, a much smaller one. He lifted it out and passed the shoebox to Jade.

Within seconds, the small, blue velvet box was free of its gold foil wrap. Looking down at it, Terrell held his breath. If this was a send-off gift, judging by the box, it was an elaborate one.

He flipped open the lid. A linked gold bracelet sparkled

beneath the hallway lights. He simply stared at the gift but didn't say anything.

"You don't like it?"

Glancing at Jade, he said, "No. I do. I'm just…surprised. This must be expensive."

"You're a special man."

Terrell didn't question what she meant by that. He wasn't ready to cope until he'd shown her his surprise. Instead, he put an arm around her and hugged her. "Thanks."

"You're welcome."

Jade pulled back, wanting Terrell to kiss her, and feeling a niggling of disappointment when he merely brushed his lips against her cheek. Her heart raced and she longed to have the heart-to-heart with Terrell to see where their relationship was heading, but she knew it was too soon. They were going for a late dinner, at Terrell's request. After that, she hoped they could discuss everything.

"You ready?"

Jade nodded, then quickly checked herself out in the mirror. Her flowing black pantsuit accentuated her figure, and she acknowledged that she couldn't make herself look much better than she did now.

"I'm ready," she finally said.

"All right. After you."

Over dinner Terrell had been tempted to come right out and start the serious where-is-our-relationship-going discussion, but the truth was he didn't want to have that discussion here. If their relationship in fact wasn't going further than tonight, then Terrell wanted their last dinner together to be a pleasant one.

And it had been. Though there was definitely some tension between them, they'd been able to share pleasant conversation and even some laughs over a seafood dinner at an upscale Manhattan restaurant.

He'd specifically asked for a late dinner date with Jade, because he wanted to plan his surprise for midnight. Call him a sentimental fool, but they'd met again just after midnight on New Year's Eve, a time that had seemed to be magical for them both. Now he hoped to recapture that magic tonight as the clock struck twelve.

At about twenty minutes to midnight, Terrell asked for the bill. Jade insisted on paying since it was his birthday dinner. By the time the bill was settled and they headed to his Jeep, Terrell noted with anticipation that it was ten minutes till the clock struck twelve.

Ten minutes to a new beginning, or an ending.

They would get there in time. He had only to drive from the Upper East Side to Midtown Manhattan, and along Third Avenue. At this time of night, he didn't expect any delays. Turning right at West Fiftieth, Terrell drove west a few blocks then pulled the car to a stop at the curb and killed the engine.

"Terrell," Jade began softly. "I was hoping we could go somewhere and talk…"

"Me, too."

"Then why are we here?" She gestured to the dark street.

"I have something to show you." He opened his car door. "Come on."

Jade followed his example, wondering when she and Terrell could be alone in the comfort of his home or hers to have that heart-to-heart she so wanted.

Stepping out onto the snow-covered sidewalk, she rounded the front of the Jeep to meet Terrell. "Where are we going?"

He draped a hand across her shoulder—and Jade's pulse

quickened. She couldn't be sure if it was meant as an intimate gesture, or just a protective one. Still she savored it.

"It's not a far walk."

"What's not a far walk?" Jade asked as he led her to the opposite side of the street.

He pulled her tighter to him. "A place where we can talk."

"Oh." She looked up at him with wide eyes. "Out here? Why not at my place or your place?"

"You'll see."

With that, Jade quieted. The curiosity was killing her, but she figured she'd know soon enough. Seconds later Terrell came to a stop outside a nondescript storefront. Taking his arms off her shoulder, Terrell reached into his pocket and removed a key, which he proceeded to insert into the lock.

"Terrell," Jade began, unable to disguise her wary tone. "What are you doing?"

"Opening the door."

"I can see that." She paused as he pushed the glass door open. "But what—when—?"

"We can talk here."

"But what is this?" And why did he have a key?

"My new…studio." He reached for the light switch on the wall and flicked it on. The lights in the back flamed to life.

Jade flashed him a quizzical stare. "You bought this place?" She looked around the large, vacant, dusty space. "I thought you liked working in your loft."

"I've been wanting to get another spot for a while."

"Really? Y-you never said anything." Which for some reason hurt her. But why should she expect him to share every detail of his business with her?

Terrell's wide shoulders rose and fell in a shrug. "What do you think?"

"It's big. But not very studiolike, I don't think. Not that I'm any expert, but...I don't know."

He took her hand in his, the first real intimate contact they'd shared all night. "That's good. Because," he began slowly, "this isn't for me."

"But you said—"

"I know what I said. But I lied."

Jade looked into his eyes, searching for answers, but found none. "So you didn't buy this."

"I did." At her confused look, he linked fingers with hers and added, "I bought it for you."

"For me?" Jade nearly choked on the words. "Come again?"

Bringing her hand to his mouth, he kissed a finger. "This is for you, Jade. For another salon."

All her breath left her body in a rush. She continued to stare at Terrell, finally drawing in a slow, calming breath. "Terrell, I don't understand."

"Jade, if there's one thing you should know about me, it's that I like to take care of the people I love. You are no exception."

Though he'd said the words to her before, hearing them now was like the first time. He loved her. He'd bought a store where she could open another salon.

He stared at her for what seemed like ages, at her wide eyes, at her dumbfounded expression. And all the while, his heart beat erratically, wondering, waiting.

Finally Jade spoke. "Terrell, I appreciate this, but I can't...I can't accept this. It's too much."

"I didn't buy it outright. I put down a hefty down payment, and you can make the monthly mortgage if you're able. But if not, I can help you out."

"It's still too much."

He couldn't help it—he framed the side of her face with a

hand, enjoying the smoothness of her flesh against his palm. "Would you say that if we were married?"

"But we're not."

"And if we were?"

There was that feeling again, like some powerful force was stealing her breath. "Well, if we were married, of course I wouldn't think this was too much. But we're not married, Terrell—"

"Then marry me." He'd had more visions of this moment that he cared to count, and in none of them did he propose to Jade in a dusky store.

"Terrell…" She sounded breathless.

"I want you to be happy. I know that doing hair makes you happy, that you wanted to reopen your salon this year. Jade, if you're happy, then I'm happy."

"But…"

"Shh." He placed a finger on her luscious lips. "Jade, I know your first marriage failed, that you're afraid to take another chance. But I'm not Nelson. I will never hurt you. That's a promise, Jade, and I don't have to say it before God to prove that I'll keep it."

Instinctively in her heart, Jade knew he was telling the truth. Terrell wasn't Nelson, would never be a Nelson. Her eyes misted at the love she felt between them at that moment, and weakly she smiled. "You did this for me?"

He nodded. "Because I love you, Jade, and if it's the last thing I do, I'm going to make you happy."

"Oh, Terrell." Her fingers snaked around his waist, linking behind his back. "Nobody has ever done anything like this for me before."

"That's because nobody loves you like I love you."

"You really do, don't you?" she asked, though she'd always

known he did. But the fact that he loved her enough to give her this incredible gift, a gift she'd prayed for but didn't think she'd ever receive this year, was so overwhelming.

"Don't you know that by now?"

"I guess I did," she said softly, looking into his dark eyes, feeling light-headed just being in his arms. "But I didn't know…"

Her voice trailed off and she looked away. Terrell placed a finger under her chin, forcing her to meet his eyes. "You didn't know what?"

Looking up at him, a hot tear fell onto her cheek. "I didn't know that on New Year's Eve when I prayed for my dream to come true this year, that that dream would include you."

Terrell stilled. "And now…?"

"Now," Jade said, a second tear streaming down her cheek, "I know that you are a dream come true. I didn't know it before…I was too afraid. But now I do, Terrell. And I don't ever want to lose you."

Letting out a relieved breath, Terrell placed a hand on the back of her head, cradling her against his chest. "Sweetheart, you won't lose me."

"You might not say that when you hear what I have to tell you." He looked into her eyes, and she said a quick prayer for strength, that it wouldn't matter, that he'd still love her, that he'd still want to be with her.

"What?"

She swallowed, then spoke. "I…I can't make you a father, Terrell. I can't have children."

He took a moment to digest the information, and she continued. "I always wondered if that's what pushed Nelson away, what led him to drink, what led him to gamble and eventually cheat on me." Her voice cracked. "And I couldn't bear it if I pushed you away, too. I don't want to be a disappointment to you."

"Sweetheart." He framed her face with both hands. "Don't you know that you could never be a disappointment to me?" He flashed her the warmest of smiles. "I love you. You alone are enough to make me happy. Sure, I wouldn't mind being a father, but I can't have that but can still have you, that'll be the best gift God has ever given me."

She whimpered, and he brushed her tears away. "You mean that?"

"Jade, my love for you isn't conditional."

"It isn't, is it?" She barely managed the words through her tears.

"No." He wrapped her in a hug. "Believe me, Jade. For years I have loved you and only you. I'm not about to stop now."

And Jade knew then that her life was complete. She was in love with the most incredible man in the world. "Thank you for not giving up on me."

"I did get a bit frustrated," he admitted, then smiled at the thought that they had gotten past those dark days. "But I love you, Jade. And no matter what I try, I can't get you out of my heart."

"Stubborn." Pulling back to look at him, Jade smiled through misty eyes.

"Or crazy," he offered. "Crazy for you."

Jade brought a hand to his face, ran her fingers over the angles and grooves, then met his eyes. "I love you."

His eyes closed for a moment, then opened. "Say it again."

"I love you." And as she spoke the words for a second time, she knew without a doubt that they were true, that Terrell was her soul mate. That they were meant to be forever. That she had denied the truth for so long gave her a sense of sadness, but the sadness was washed away by the look of love she saw in his eyes.

Framing her face with both hands, Terrell slowly edged his face toward hers in what seemed like slow motion. His mouth stopped a fraction of an inch from her lips, his warm breath mingling with hers. Jade's body had never been so taut with desire in all her life.

"So you'll marry me?"

"That's the only way I'll get this salon, isn't it?" Smiling, she marveled at how far she'd come. She'd have never felt comfortable saying anything like that to Nelson, but she knew that Terrell would appreciate the humor.

"Very funny." He ran a thumb over her lips.

Jade's eyes fluttered shut. "Oh, Terrell. Yes. I'll marry you, and not because you bought this for me, but because nobody has ever made me feel as wonderful as you do."

"Is that so?" Slipping a hand beneath her coat, he cupped a breast.

She whimpered. "Nobody, Terrell. Only you."

"That's what I like to hear."

"Then take me home. End this torture."

He kissed her cheek, then suckled her earlobe, feeling his groin roar to life when Jade all but melted in his arms.

"You're evil," she managed between ragged breaths.

"I can stop."

"Don't you dare." She arched into him, pressing her breasts to his chest.

"Woman, I don't know if I can make it home—not with you driving me crazy the way you are." His tongue trailed to her neck, creating a path of fire where it touched.

"Then why go home?" Reaching for him, she stroked his arousal, and Terrell growled.

He brushed his lips over her cheek, sending shivers of delight all over her body. "There's always my Jeep."

"Then what are you waiting for?"

"Nothing. I finally have all that I've ever wanted."

"Me, too, sweetheart," Jade whispered, holding on to the lapels of Terrell's wool coat, edging her face upward to meet his.

He lowered his face to hers, covering her lips with his, devouring her mouth in a hungry kiss. His tongue delved into her hot, sweet mouth, their tongues mingling, dancing together to a rhythm of love all their own, while their arms held each other in a tight embrace, neither one of them wanting to let go of the love they had found.

They never made it to the Jeep.

Epilogue

Twelve months later...

THE BUZZ OF CHATTER carried easily over the sound of whirring dryers, the soft R&B that played on the stereo, and the sound of water splashing in the sinks at the back of the shop. Jade could barely hear herself talk, let alone think. But it was all music to her ears.

After all, business was booming at Dreamstyles, and this Saturday was no exception. What could make her happier?

Seeing her husband again. He'd been out of town for a week and was due back today, and Jade could hardly wait to see him.

As if in answer to her wish, she heard the chimes over the front door sing and instantly she looked over her shoulder in the direction of the door.

The sight of him stole her breath. Dressed in a long, black leather coat and all black beneath, Jade smiled at the thought that he was truly hers. Though they'd been married six months now, every time she saw him, she felt like pinching herself to see if she was actually dreaming. But she wasn't. The dream was a reality.

"Terrell!" Ignoring the client at her station, Jade ran to him and threw herself in his arms. Her regular clients knew the story of how Dreamstyles came to be and were used to Jade and Terrell's public display of affection. "You're home!"

"Hey, sweetheart. Did you miss me?"

"You know it."

"I missed you, too." He kissed her briefly but passionately.

Jade took his hand. "I'm so glad you're here. I've got some news."

"What kind of news? Did something happen while I was away?"

Leading him to the back of the salon, she replied, "Yes, but it wasn't something I could tell you over the phone."

"This is serious," Terrell, said, his smile fading as he stepped into the office with her.

"Afraid so." Jade leaned against the oak desk.

He stepped toward her. "How bad is it?"

"I guess that depends on your point of view."

"You've lost me."

"Well, whether or not you still want to be a father. If you don't then this is bad news. But if you do—" a smile spread over her face "—then this is the best news in the world."

Terrell's expression was guarded. "Are you saying what I think you're saying?"

"Yes!" Jade exclaimed, once again throwing herself into his arms. "We're pregnant!"

Excitement washing over him, he whirled her around. Then he deposited her on the desk and stared at her. "You're sure?"

Jade's head bobbed up and down.

"But I thought… You're sure?"

When her doctor had told her the news, she'd been dumbfounded. She'd had him repeat the test twice, which he did, and each had had the same result. She was indeed pregnant. "Yes, Terrell. My doctor confirmed it yesterday."

"I can't believe it."

"God has answered our prayers." She'd come to accept that having a family wasn't right for her and Nelson, and that that's why it didn't happen. But she and Terrell were meant to be and God was proving that by blessing them with a child.

"And everything's gonna be okay?"

"Yes. The doctor said he doesn't anticipate any problems."

"How far along are you?"

She touched her belly. "Three months."

He wrapped his arms around her. "Sweetheart, you have made me the happiest man on this earth."

"You deserve to be happy. You've given me so much, Terrell. I'm so glad I can give you the gift of fatherhood in return."

"You were always enough."

"I know." She beamed at him. "But now because of our love for each other, we're gonna have a little Terrell or a little Jade in six months."

"I didn't think I could be happier than the day I married you, but I was wrong."

Jade framed his face, the love flowing between them strong and tangible. "I love you."

"God, do I ever love you."

She leaned forward to kiss him, but he placed a hand on

her shoulder, holding her at bay. He placed the other hand on her flat belly, letting it rest there.

Their eyes met, held. Then Terrell spoke. "A baby."

"It's incredible, isn't it?"

"You're incredible. You're beautiful."

"Just remember that when I'm as big as a cow and need to be pampered."

His fingers tangled in her hair. "How could I ever forget?"

"Oh, I'm going to enjoy this."

The corners of her lips curled wryly. But Terrell wiped the silly smile off her mouth with a mind-numbing kiss. A kiss that proved to Jade once again that with Terrell in her life, all her dreams for a wonderful future had indeed come true.

About the Author

Kayla Perrin lives in Toronto, Canada, with her husband of six years. She attended the University of Toronto and York University, where she obtained a Bachelor of Arts in English and Sociology and a Bachelor of Education, respectively. As well as being a certified teacher, Kayla works in the Toronto film industry as an actress, appearing in many television shows, commercials, and movies.

Kayla is most happy when writing. As well as novels, she has had romantic short stories published by the Sterling/Mac-Fadden Group.

She would love to hear from her readers. E-mail her at: kaywriter1@aol.com. Mail letters to:

Kayla Perrin
c/o Toronto Romance Writers
Box 69035, 12 St. Clair Avenue East
Toronto, ON Canada
M4T 3A1

Please enclose a SASE if you would like a reply.

The stunning sequel to *The Beautiful Ones...*

feel THE *fire*

NATIONAL BESTSELLING AUTHOR
ADRIANNE BYRD

Business mogul Jonas Hinton has learned to stay clear of gorgeous women and the heartbreak they bring. But when his younger brother starts dating sexy attorney Toni Wright, Jonas discovers a sizzling attraction he's never felt before. Torn between family loyalty and overwhelming desire, can he find a way to win the woman who could be his real-life Ms. Wright?

"Byrd proves once again that she's a wonderful storyteller."
—*Romantic Times BOOKreviews* on *The Beautiful Ones*

*Available the first week of November
wherever books are sold.*

ARABESQUE®

www.kimanipress.com

KPAB0221107

DON'T MISS THIS SEXY NEW SERIES FROM

KIMANI ROMANCE!

THE LOCKHARTS
THREE WEDDINGS & A REUNION

*For four sassy sisters,
romance changes everything!*

IN BED WITH HER BOSS by Brenda Jackson
August 2007

THE PASTOR'S WOMAN by Jacquelin Thomas
September 2007

HIS HOLIDAY BRIDE by Elaine Overton
October 2007

FORBIDDEN TEMPTATION by Gwynne Forster
November 2007

KIMANI™
ROMANCE

www.kimanipress.com

KPBJ0280807A

Sex changed everything...

Forbidden Temptation

ESSENCE BESTSELLING AUTHOR

Gwynne FORSTER

The morning after her sister's wedding, Ruby Lockhart finds
herself in bed with her best friend, sexy ex-SEAL Luther
Biggens. Luther's always been Ruby's rock...now he's her
problem! She can't look at him without remembering the
ways he pleasured her...or that she wants him to do it again.

THE LOCKHARTS

THREE WEDDINGS AND A REUNION
FOR FOUR SASSY SISTERS, ROMANCE CHANGES EVERYTHING!

*Available the first week of November
wherever books are sold.*

KIMANI
ROMANCE

www.kimanipress.com

KPGF0401107

Business takes on a new flavor...

SEX ON FLAMINGO *Beach*

Part of the Flamingo Beach series

Bestselling author
MARCIA KING-GAMBLE

Rowan James's plans to open a casino next door may cost resort manager Emilie Woodward her job. So when he asks her out, suspicion competes with sizzling attraction. What's he after—a no-strings fling or a competitive advantage?

"Down and Out in Flamingo Beach showcases
Marcia King-Gamble's talent for accurately
portraying life in a small town."
—*Romantic Times BOOKreviews*

*Available the first week of November
wherever books are sold.*

KIMANI™
ROMANCE

www.kimanipress.com

KPMKG0411107

Could they have a new beginning?

Pride
AND
Consequence

Favorite author

ALTONYA
WASHINGTON

When devastating illness strikes him, Malik's pride causes
him to walk out on his passionate life with Zakira.
She is devastated but dedicates herself to their business.
But when Malik returns fully recovered, Zakira is stunned...
and still angry. Now Malik will need more than soul-searing
kisses to win her trust again. He will have to make her
believe in them...again.

**Available the first week of November
wherever books are sold.**

KIMANI
ROMANCE™

www.kimanipress.com

KPAW0421107

The Knight family trilogy continues...

to love a
KNIGHT

WAYNE JORDAN

As Dr. Tamara Knight cares for gravely injured
Jared St. Clair, she's drawn to his rugged sensuality and
commanding strength. Despite his gruff exterior, she can't
stop herself from indulging in a passionate love affair with
him. But unbeknownst to Tamara, Jared was sent to save
her. Now protecting Tamara isn't just another mission for
Jared—it's all that matters!

"Mr. Jordan's writing simply captures his audience."
—*The Road to Romance*

*Available the first week of November
wherever books are sold.*

KIMANI™
ROMANCE

www.kimanipress.com

KPWJ0431107

A volume of heartwarming devotionals
that will nourish your soul...

NORMA DeSHIELDS BROWN

Joy

COMES THIS MORNING

Norma DeShields Brown's life suddenly changed
when her only son was tragically taken from her
by a senseless act. Consumed by grief, she began
an intimate journey that became
Joy Comes This Morning.

Filled with thoughtful devotions, Scripture readings
and words of encouragement, this powerful book
will guide you on a spiritual journey that will sustain
you throughout the years.

*Available the first week of November
wherever books are sold.*

www.kimanipress.com   KPNDB0351107

GET THE GENUINE LOVE
YOU DESERVE...

NATIONAL BESTSELLING AUTHOR
Vikki Johnson

Addicted to COUNTERFEIT LOVE

Many people in today's world are unable to recognize what a genuine loving partnership should be and often sabotage one when it does come along. In this moving volume, Vikki Johnson offers memorable words that will help readers identify destructive love patterns and encourage them to demand the love that they are entitled to.

Available the first week of October wherever books are sold.

www.kimanipress.com

KPVJ0381007